BLACK creek

GREGORY LAMBERSON

MEDALLION

Medallion Press, Inc.

Printed in USA

This novel is dedicated, with concern and good thoughts, to the past and current residents of Black Creek Village, formerly known as Love Canal.

Published 2016 by Medallion Press, Inc., 4222 Meridian Pkwy., Suite 110, Aurora, IL 60504
The MEDALLION PRESS LOGO
is a registered trademark of Medallion Press, Inc.

Copyright © 2016 by Gregory Lamberson
Cover design by Arturo Delgado

Names, characters, places, and incidents are the products of the author's imagination or are used fictionally. Any resemblance to actual events, locales, or persons, living or dead, is entirely coincidental.

Typeset in Adobe Garamond Pro
Printed in the United States of America

ISBN 978-1-60542-599-3
10 9 8 7 6 5 4 3 2 1

First Edition

ACKNOWLEDGMENTS

I now live about a twenty-minute drive from the real Black Creek Village, once known as Love Canal. I wish to thank Matthew Patterson for taking me on my first tour of the containment zone where Hooker Chemical notoriously disposed of its toxic waste, and nearby Cayuga Island, also known as Teacher's Island; and Chris Cosgrave for driving me around those same areas during the writing of this book. Thanks, as always, to my editors and everyone else at Medallion for their efforts on my behalf.

"The profound and devastating effects of the Love Canal tragedy, in terms of human health and suffering and environmental damage, cannot and probably will never be fully measured. . . . [W]e cannot undo the damage that has been wrought at Love Canal but we can take appropriate preventive measures so that we are better able to anticipate and hopefully prevent future events of this kind."

> Dr. Robert P. Whalen
> New York Health Commissioner
> 1978 investigative report

ONE

Paul Goodman did not see the winged insect until after he had said good morning to his twelve-year-old son, Evan, who stood staring at the window at the opposite end of the dining room table. Outside, a lawnmower droned: Saturday chores.

When the boy failed to respond, Paul circled the rectangular table. At first he thought the silhouette on the glass was a smudge of mud applied by a human thumb or maybe a small feather. But as he drew closer to his son, he saw the translucent wings spread open. At least the insect, whatever it was, acknowledged his presence. "What have we got here?"

"I'm not sure," Evan said.

Paul leaned closer. The body of the insect stretched two full inches in length. In shape, it resembled a wasp; in size, a dragonfly. Black-and-yellow stripes ringed its fur coat, like those of a yellow jacket. The window was raised, the metal screen admitting a warm breeze, and the insect had become trapped between the two overlapping panes of glass. It clung to the inner pane, its antennae moving in a steady rhythm, its legs motionless. Paul felt as if he were being sized up by the accidental prisoner. The wings closed and he shuddered.

1

He had never cared for bees, particularly the bloated queens that populated Helen's flower garden in the side yard. This seemed different, somehow: alien.

Evan's eyes did not leave the visitor. "Do you think it's a yellow jacket?"

"Not like any I've ever seen. It's too big. Too . . . thick." He imagined the size of the insect's stinger. "Maybe your mother knows." Paul called for Helen, and the insect's antennae straightened.

"What?" Helen called from the den they shared on the first floor.

"Could you come out here, please?"

The French doors separating the den from the living room swung open and Helen entered the dining room, her dark hair spilling over the shoulders of her sweater.

"I'm trying to finish grading papers before I start lunch," Helen said. She taught social studies at Niagara Falls High School, where their daughter, Piper, was a junior, while Paul taught English at Niagara Falls City District School, where Evan attended.

"I already started lunch," Paul said.

"You're kidding."

"I peeled the potatoes, stringed the green beans, washed the meat, and preheated the oven."

"That was nice of you," she said.

"My mama raised me right." He gestured at the window. "Look what your son's captured."

Helen moved close to the window, and the insect moved in a circle like a centipede. Its sudden movement caused her to jump back with a startled cry. Paul and Evan stifled their

2

giggles, but Paul experienced a deep, unexplainable feeling of revulsion that gave way to territorial hatred. The urge to kill the insect clenched his fists.

"What the hell is *that*?" Helen said in a shrill voice.

"We were hoping you could tell us," Paul said.

"How should I know what that is? You've lived here two years longer than me."

"Only because I'm two years older," Paul said.

They had both been born and raised in Niagara Falls and had been high school sweethearts.

"You said you were more experienced than me," Helen said. "That should include entomology."

Evan turned to his father for the first time. "What's that?"

"The study of insects," Paul said.

Helen narrowed her eyes at the visitor. "It looks . . . prehistoric."

"Dinohornet?"

"Maybe Mr. Johnson knows," Evan said.

"Good idea," Paul said, taking his phone from the pocket of his jeans. Ken Johnson taught science at NFCDS. Like the Goodmans, he lived on Cayuga Island, known as Teacher's Island to the locals.

"Is this really necessary?" Helen said.

Paul selected Ken's number from the menu on his phone and pressed it. "I'm trying to educate our son."

"Can't you just use Google?"

Paul clucked his tongue. "Google's no substitute for a teacher–pupil dynamic." The phone on the other end of the signal rang.

"The living room's a mess," Helen said. "Tell him to

meet us outside. He can see it just as well from the other side of the window."

"Hello?" Ken said in a cheerful voice.

"It's Paul."

"Good morning. What can I do for you this fine Saturday?"

"It's afternoon."

"The hours blur with a new baby in the house."

"I remember those days well." He found it hard to believe a dozen years had passed since he and Helen had brought Evan home. "Just keep telling yourself—"

"'It gets better in six months.' I've heard it many times. Only three months to go . . ."

"I know you're busy, but can you stop by? Evan thinks he's made the scientific discovery of the century."

"As luck would have it, I was just on my way out to get Pampers. I can swing by on my way."

"Great."

Outside, Helen mouthed.

"I'll meet you in the driveway," Paul said.

As soon as he saw the mail truck pass his house, Dan Bartkowitz pulled on his Windbreaker and opened the front door, which brought Trapper, his bloodhound, circling his ankles. He had lived alone for four years, since his ex-wife, Marie, had left him and the state. He had brought Trapper home from the pound soon after.

"Out," he said to the dog, who wagged his tail and obeyed.

4

BLACKcreek

As Dan stepped outside, damp air clung to his cheeks. Even though the temperature felt unseasonably warm, his bones told him winter would come early this year. Closing the door, he strode across the porch and descended the steps while Trapper raised one hind leg and squirted a bush on the lawn. Dan made his way along the paved driveway to the mailbox, which rested on a post at the edge of the sidewalk. The mailbox resembled a classic 1950s convertible with a red body and a white top. Across the street, Henri Metzger pushed his mower across his lawn in neat rows, his hair and beard snow white. Henri waved to Dan with one hand, offering a crooked smile. Dan returned the wave to the Gulf War veteran to be polite. Henri's wife, a math teacher, had left him, too.

"Hey, you Polack!"

Trapper wagged his tail and Dan turned to see his next-door neighbor, Jim Makowski, lumbering toward his own mailbox, posted on the far side of Dan's front yard. "What do you want, you Polack?" Dan said.

A retired police officer and widower from Arizona, Jim had moved to Cayuga Island two years earlier and had become Dan's closest friend. Jim wore his hair in a crew cut, and thick glasses rested on the edge of his nose. He was ten years older than Dan and attended church every Sunday. The two men rendezvoused midway between their mailboxes every day, at least until winter set in.

"I'm getting my mail, you Polack," Jim said. Despite his height, he had a slow gait due to arthritis.

"Why don't I get it for you? I could read it all out loud before you reach that damned box."

"The worst kind of Polack is a blaspheming Polack."

They opened their mailboxes at the same time. Dan used his left hand, keeping the stump where his right hand had been in his jacket. He had lost the hand in a machine shop accident six years earlier and refused to wear any kind of prosthetic device. Holding the mail, he closed the box and used his fingers to examine the return addresses on the envelopes: bills and ads, the usual junk.

Jim stood reading something beside his mailbox. Trapper took a few steps toward Jim, then looked back at Dan.

"Go on," Dan said, and Trapper trotted along the sidewalk toward Jim. "What do you got there, you Polack? You need some help reading it?"

Without looking up, Jim said, "No, I've got this. It's a postcard from my daughter, Faith. She uses big letters and small words so I can read it. Hello, Trapper." Jim reached into his pocket with his free hand and produced a Milk-Bone. Trapper sat on the sidewalk, and Jim tossed the treat into the air above the dog's head. Trapper leapt off the sidewalk and snapped his jaws, then landed on all fours and crunched it.

Dan moved closer. "What's it say?"

"She and her husband can't make it up for Thanksgiving this year. They want me to come to Florida instead."

"So go."

"Maybe I will."

"It gets cold here by Thanksgiving. The bees built their hives high in the trees over the summer. That means it's going to be a bad winter."

Jim fixed him with a flat stare. "Every winter's a bad winter."

"So why didn't you stay in Phoenix?"

"I got tired of the heat and the scorpions."

"The ducks and geese migrated early. That means winter's coming early, and it's going to be cold. You should go."

Jim looked at him with mock impatience. "I said, 'Maybe I will.' What part of that didn't you understand, you stupid Polack?"

Dan slid his mail into his jacket pocket and took out his pack of Seneca cigarettes. "Florida's nice."

"I know that."

Dan shook loose a cigarette and stuck it between his lips. "The fishing's great down there."

"I don't like to fish."

Dan lit his cigarette. "What kind of a Polack don't like to fish?"

"You like it so much, why don't you go to Florida?"

Exhaling, Dan smiled. "I've thought about it."

"Somehow I doubt that."

"I like it down there."

"So move down there and fish, and stop your useless yapping."

Dan removed his stump from his pocket. "I can't fish with one hand."

"Then stay here and freeze. What kind of a Polack loses his hand in a machine shop, anyway?"

A Subaru passed and slowed down to turn in to the driveway on the far side of the Goodmans', his other next-door neighbors. Francine Kaminski got out of the Subaru, her expression as grim as every other time she visited her mother. Those visits had become more frequent since

Joanne's diagnosis. Joanne and her late husband, Bill, had lived in that house since before Dan and Marie moved into the neighborhood twenty years ago. She had been an English teacher until she had Fran, who had grown up in the house. Fran lived in Tonawanda now, with her husband and two sons. She did not bring the boys to see their grand-mother. Dan hadn't seen Joanne outside the house in over a month.

"She doesn't look very happy, does she?" Jim said behind Dan.

"She's having a tough time."

"Why don't you mow Joanne's lawn?"

"I have a hard enough time mowing mine with one hand. Why don't you mow it?"

"She's not my next-door neighbor."

Dan smirked at Jim. "It would be the Christian thing to do."

"All right."

The front door of the brick house across the street, next to Henri's, opened and Ken Johnson exited. He made straight for the street and crossed it, avoiding Henri. A black man with a short beard, Ken wore khaki slacks and a leather jacket over a burgundy shirt. Dan could not remember having ever seen the science teacher in jeans. Behind him, Henri stuck out his tongue like a wild man and shook his head, then laughed. Dan and Jim ignored him.

"Good morning, gentlemen," Ken said as he approached them.

"It's afternoon," Jim said.

"So it is. Hey, Trapper Dog."

Trapper offered a tentative wag of his tail.

"Where are you off to in such a hurry?" Jim said.

"To see the scientific find of the century, apparently," Ken said as he passed them.

"Come on," Dan said to Jim.

The two men and the dog followed Ken to the property bordering the opposite side of Dan's yard. Paul Goodman and his son Evan exited their colonial house and greeted Ken. Paul had a slight build and wore his reddish-brown hair parted at the side, his mouth surrounded by trimmed whiskers. Evan wore his sandy-colored hair in bangs, his T-shirt emblazoned with superheroes poised for action.

"It's in the side window," Paul said.

"Hi, Mr. Berkowitz. Hi, Mr. Makowski. Hi, Trapper," Evan said rapid-fire.

"Hello, young man," Jim said.

"Hey, kid," Dan said.

Helen Goodman exited the house and closed the door. Paul and Evan hurried alongside the house, and Helen joined Ken behind them.

"I see you brought backup," Helen said, nodding at Dan and Jim.

Ken looked over his shoulder. "Why not? The more witnesses to this moment in history, the better."

Dan flicked ash from his cigarette onto the concrete driveway. "Let's get on with the show."

Helen and Ken followed Paul and Evan, and Dan and Jim brought up the rear.

"How's Jenny?" Helen said as they passed her minivan.

"Still fat," Ken said in a tired voice.

Helen's expression registered shock, and Ken raised his hands.

"Her words, not mine."

"Maybe you shouldn't repeat them."

"Maybe you're right."

The entourage joined Paul and Evan, who stood with their backs to Paul's black Jeep. Paul pointed at one window of the house.

"There," the English teacher said.

Ken's eyes followed Paul's finger to the glass. He moved closer. "What the hell?"

"Not you too," Helen said.

Dan and Jim stood behind Ken, gazing over his shoulders. The insect clung to the glass, offering a view of its underside, its antennae moving.

"Jesus," Dan said.

Jim's features contorted with disapproval.

"Do you know what it is, Mr. Johnson?" Evan said.

Ken peered at the window. "I have no idea. I've never seen anything like it. I mean, I've never seen anything so big."

"Do you think Evan's made a discovery?" Paul said.

"That's unlikely. There are enormous insects in the tropics and South America, even Florida. But how on earth did it get this far north, at this time of the year?"

Evan's features sagged.

"I blame Hooker Chemical," Dan said.

"You blame everything on Hooker," Jim said.

"I blame Hooker for the VD I got in the war."

"You weren't in any war."

"I still blame Hooker."

"Polack."

Ken took out his smartphone and recorded the insect.

Helen crossed her arms. "If it's not a candidate for cataloguing at the Smithsonian, no one will object if one of you kills it."

"I'll go get my rifle," Dan said.

"You can't shoot it with one hand," Jim said.

"You want to bet?"

"Quiet, Polack."

"I think we should just put it in something," Paul said. "Wouldn't you like to show it to your classes, Ken?"

"And drive to work with it? Just the two of us, in my little car? No, thanks. And where would I keep it all weekend? Jenny would never stand for it. She'd toss it out the front door, and me with it."

Paul looked at Dan and Jim.

"How would I protect myself?" Dan said. "I've got only one hand."

Jim frowned. "You can keep it in my garage, but I'm not feeding it."

Paul set his hand on Evan's back. "Go into the basement and get one of those mason jars. Make sure it has a lid."

Evan started forward, but he stopped when Helen yelped. All eyes turned to the window as the insect crawled to the bottom of the wooden frame. It disappeared for a moment, then emerged upside down along the bottom of the frame, freed from the glass panes.

"Oh my God," Helen said.

The insect peered at the group. All of them backed up.

"It's big and it's ugly, but it's still just a bug," Jim said.

"Says the man who keeps a loaded revolver on top of the Bible beside his bed," Dan said.

"Hold still," Ken said. "No sudden movements."

Trapper barked at the insect, which launched itself into the air, spreading its wings and circling the spectators at Dan's eye level. Helen turned her head away and Paul jerked Evan close to him.

"Whoa!" Ken said, raising his hands.

The insect flew straight at Jim, who stood tallest. His mouth and eyes widened, and he turned sideways, allowing the insect to soar through the space where his head had been.

Dan picked up a thick branch from the ground and brandished it like a club.

"Dad!" Evan threw his arms around Paul, and Helen joined them.

The insect darted between Ken and Jim, and Dan swung his weapon, missing his target and Jim.

"Watch it, you Polack!"

The insect rose to the sky and disappeared. Everyone gazed upward, searching.

"I'm going inside," Helen said. She took Evan by the hand and pulled him toward the house.

"Thanks for coming over," Paul said to Ken. "Did you get good footage of that thing?"

Staring at the screen of his phone, Ken shook his head. "I wasn't close enough to get much of an image."

"Next time."

Ken's expression turned serious. "Unless it was one of a kind."

"A mutation?"

Ken pocketed his phone. "I don't know."

"It's going to be one hell of a winter," Dan said.

TWO

Helen came downstairs dressed for work and shivering. She always got up first, followed by Paul. The kids showered before bed. She made her way through the living room to the dining room, where she raised the thermostat, then entered the kitchen and switched on the lights. She opened the blinds on the window over the sink, which overlooked the apple tree beside the house, then the blinds over the back door, which led to the wraparound deck. Rather than a fence, shrubs surrounded the yard, and a shed occupied the far right corner of the property. She looked forward to seeing the rabbits that lived beneath the shed, which rested upon cinder blocks, two at each corner, with a ramp leading from the padlocked door to the ground.

Rabbits weren't the only occupants under the shed: a wiggly trench, five inches wide, stretched from the shed to the deck, earth-black. Upon investigation, the trench bore no tracks, leaving her to speculate that whatever had divided the yard in two had done so with a bloated belly. A possum, maybe, or a raccoon. Paul had set out some nonlethal traps, but the cages had captured only squirrels, which he had freed. Whatever species the uninvited visitor belonged to, Helen hoped it had left the rabbits alone. Rats and rabbits would cohabitate a single nesting area, but she did not know if such social amenity applied to other critters as well.

Brewing a pot of coffee, Helen became aware of a low clicking emanating from somewhere behind the stove. The sound had a persistent, echoing rhythm so precise she had originally mistaken it for the furnace downstairs. Gazing at the stove, she frowned. The kitchen and dining room had not been part of the original house; they had been added by a previous homeowner. The added rooms had been built over a crawl space, and the deck had been built next to that. Whatever vermin lived beneath the deck must have tunneled their way into the crawl space, and each fall they were attracted to the heat from the stove's pilot lights. Two years earlier, Paul had pulled the stove out and discovered rice-sized rat droppings along the sides of cabinets. He had called an exterminator, who had baited the yard and stuffed steel wool into the visible crevices and around the circumference of the hole that fed the gas line to the stove. But the sound returned, and when Paul pulled out the stove again, he found no more droppings. Nor had the steel wool been displaced. As long as the rodents were under the house and not inside it, Helen was content, but now she gave the stove a kick, and the sharp echo silenced the intruder.

"And stay down there," she said.

Paul entered the kitchen, knotting his tie. "Company?"

"They must follow a calendar."

"I'll pull the oven out tonight and see what's what."

"Maybe you should call the exterminator again."

"He won't do anything I haven't learned to do, and we can use the two hundred dollars for something else, like food and heat."

Paul set the table in the dining room while Helen scrambled eggs. By the time breakfast had been laid out on the table, Evan joined them and sat down.

"Where's your sister?" Paul said.

Evan shrugged. "Getting ready still. Makeup and stuff."

Helen smiled. Paul asked Evan some variation of the same question every morning, and Evan gave him some variation of the same answer. She sat and sipped her coffee. "Paul, why don't you clean up some of that debris in Joanne's backyard?"

"Maybe she doesn't want me picking it up."

"Either she doesn't know it's there, or she just doesn't care. She hasn't been outside in months. Fran will end up picking it up, and she's got enough on her plate."

"All right, I'll take care of it when I get home today."

"Could you see if she needs anything from the store, too?"

Paul fastened his gaze on hers. "If I'm going to pick up all the branches and rake the leaves, I want to just do the work and get out."

"You mean you don't want to talk to her?"

"Bingo."

"I'll help, Dad," Evan said.

"Thanks, sport."

"I guess I'll just pop in to see her while you're in the back then," Helen said.

"That sounds fair to me."

Piper entered wearing a barrette in her hair and a sweater that accentuated her growing curves. She reminded Helen of herself at the same age.

"Good morning," Paul said with exaggerated cheer.

Piper slumped into her chair. "It's Monday—what's so good about it?"

"It's only a three-day week. You've got Thursday and Friday off for Thanksgiving."

"Big deal."

"You're such a cynic." Paul smiled at Evan, who grinned.

"Brian Darcy is going away for Thanksgiving," Evan said.

"Ohhhhh," Paul said.

"Quiet, you little geek," Piper said.

"Hey," Helen said.

"I am a geek," Evan said. "A proud geek. At least I don't let *girls* ruin my vacation."

"Good thing," Piper said.

"What's gotten into you?" Helen said.

"If you must know, I'm having my period."

"Ew," Evan said.

"Take some aspirin," Helen said.

"Like that really helps."

"I'm just glad Brian Darcy isn't really the source of all this frustration," Paul said.

"Dad, *please*."

Paul sipped his coffee to keep from getting into trouble.

"Mom doesn't turn into a bitch when she has her period," Evan said.

"Oh, how would you know?" Piper said.

Helen held back her laughter.

"Does she, Dad?" Evan said.

Helen and Piper stared at Paul.

"Your mother is a model of decorum at all times," Paul said.

"Good answer," Helen said.

"Sure she is," Piper said.

Holding her tongue, Helen felt her temples start to throb.

The four of them filed outside and Paul locked the door. Across the street, Henri used a blower to clear his lawn, guiding leaves to the curb, a cigarette dangling from his lips.

"He's at it early," Helen said.

"He's obsessed with that lawn," Paul said.

"He's obsessed with his tools."

Piper and Evan marched down the porch steps to the driveway.

"Have a good day," Paul said. When neither of his offspring responded, he waved his arm. "'See you later, Dad!'"

Helen giggled and swatted his arm. Although Paul could have taken Evan with him to the middle school and Helen could have taken Piper with her to the high school, their children insisted on taking their respective buses.

"Did you treat your parents like this?" Paul said.

"I was worse."

"Payback is a bitch. I feel sorry for Brian Darcy."

Helen laughed. "So do I."

They trotted down the steps hand in hand, each carrying a bag slung over one shoulder. Helen used her remote control to unlock the door to the minivan, and Paul opened the door.

"Have a good day at school," he said.

"You too." She turned her cheek and he kissed it.

"Maybe we can make out later."

"Okay, but that's as far as it can go—I'm having my period too."

"Ew," Paul said.

Helen swatted his arm and got in, and he closed the door. As she keyed the ignition, he walked to his truck. Unlocking the door, he watched Helen back out of the driveway, then pass their kids up the street. She tapped her horn and they gave her a dutiful wave.

Paul got into the Jeep and started the engine. He allowed the vehicle to warm up, then switched on the radio and listened to Shredd and Ragan, a couple of morning jocks broadcasting from Buffalo. He backed out of the driveway and pulled onto the street, catching up to his kids before they reached the bus stop. Slowing to a stop, he lowered his window. "Hey, Piper Goodman!"

Piper and Evan turned to him.

"Have a nice day, sweetheart."

Rolling her eyes, Piper relented and smiled. Paul winked at Evan and resumed driving. He followed one winding street to another, each block populated by attractive homes separated by enough land to avoid the clustered feeling of the city. To his right, he glimpsed the Niagara

BLACKcreek

River through the spaces between houses. Cayuga Island was barely an island: surrounded on three sides by the river, it fell on Cayuga Creek to separate the neighborhood from Niagara Falls proper. As he drove over the small bridge leading to the city, the morning jocks ran down the Niagara Falls police blotter, ticking off the antics of drug addicts, drug dealers, and other reprobates apprehended by the police in comical situations. A mile and a half later, his morning commute took him past Black Creek Village.

Helen stood facing her class of juniors, her back to the blackboard. Outside the second-floor window, the gray sky darkened. She had become as anxious for Thanksgiving break as the restless kids. She had twenty-two students in her junior social studies class, including Piper, who sat in the third row of four, neither hiding nor sitting up front. Helen knew from speaking to other teachers that Piper sat in the front row in her other classes. Since her daughter scored straight As, she had no intention of pushing her in the class she taught.

"I hope you all had a good weekend," Helen said. "I know I assigned some interesting reading. Let's talk about Jim Love, Elon Hooker, and Lois Gibbs."

En masse, the students opened their textbooks. Helen knew Piper had done her reading, but she respected her daughter's wish to remain in the background, at least for the first round of questions.

"Mr. Darcy, tell me about William T. Love."

Piper's eyes turned to Brian Darcy, seated at the desk beside her. They had been dating since school had started in September. Brian smiled, then met Helen's gaze.

"Love bought up all the land around here so he could create a big industrial city called Model City," Brian said. "It was supposed to be powered by hydroelectricity from dams. But Nikola Tesla invented AC power, which was more practical, so Love's plans didn't make sense. His investors pulled out after the panic of 1893, and then Congress made things worse by passing a law preventing the removal of water from the Niagara River, to preserve Niagara Falls."

"Very good. How far did he get with his plan? Someone else." Helen looked at Piper, then settled on the blonde girl on her other side. "Mandy."

"Love's workers dug only a mile of the canal before his money dried up," Mandy said.

"And what happened to the canal?"

"It filled with water?"

"That's right." Helen paced before the class. "This was wonderful for the local children, whose parents wanted them to avoid the river. Now they had a place to swim in the summer and skate in the winter. So what did Love do with his useless pit?"

"He sold it to the City of Niagara Falls in the 1920s, and the city turned it into a dump."

"A dump for what?"

"Chemical waste."

Helen nodded. "For more than twenty years, the City of Niagara Falls and the US Army dumped chemicals into the canal. Then who bought it?"

"Hooker Chemical."

"Elon Hooker bought the land so his company, Hooker Chemical and Plastics, could use it for *their* chemical waste. And what did Hooker do with the land?"

"Hooker removed the water and put clay all over the bottom."

Helen made eye contact with each student in the class. "Then Hooker began dumping fifty-five gallon metal barrels of waste into the canal. The company dumped twenty-two thousand tons of chemicals twenty-five feet beneath the clay, and by 1953, the dump was full. So what did Hooker do next?"

Mandy bit her lip. "Um . . ."

"They covered the canal with soil, and grass and plants started to grow out of it," Piper volunteered without looking at Helen. "The city bought the land from Hooker to build a new school on. Hooker thought this was a bad idea, but he sold all the land to the city anyway—for one dollar."

Helen suppressed a smile. She liked that Piper had stepped up to the plate to spare Mandy embarrassment. "There's nothing suspicious about that, is there? Hooker advised the city against building a school on that land, and he made the city sign an agreement freeing Hooker Chemical of any liability. When excavation began for the Ninety-ninth Street School, construction workers found two additional dump sites filled with metal drums. So what did the school board do?"

Now Piper looked at her. "They moved the site."

"How far away?"

"Less than one hundred feet."

"Eighty-five feet," Helen said for effect. "Four hundred children attended that school when it opened its doors." The students sat in rapt attention, and Helen walked behind her desk. "More toxic chemical barrels were discovered when a twenty-five-foot piece of land collapsed, creating a giant hole. Rainwater filled that hole, bringing whatever contamination might be down there to the surface. In 1955, just two years after Hooker stopped dumping chemicals in the canal, the city opened a second school, the Ninety-third Street School, six blocks away. Two years after that, it built sewer lines for low-income housing to be built on the remaining landfill. The workers actually created openings in the clay base of the canal for the new sewer lines, freeing the toxic chemicals buried in the clay all those years. Then the construction of the LaSalle Expressway near the dump site prevented rainwater and chemicals from emptying into the river, causing the canal to overflow. What else happened?"

"Residents reported finding pools of black oil in their basements," Brian said.

"For twenty years, no government agency tested the canal, the surrounding land, or the sewers for toxicity. Kyle, what happened in 1976?"

Kyle Walsh, an overweight boy with curly hair, sat up. "There was a lot of extra snow on the ground because of the blizzard of '76. When the snow melted, it caused flooding, and the flooding spread the chemical waste."

Helen nodded. "What else?"

"Two reporters tested sump pumps near the canal and found toxic chemicals."

"What was done about it?"

Kyle scrunched up his face. "Nothing?"

"In 1978, another local reporter conducted a survey on health issues and birth defects in the area. What were those birth defects? Calvin."

Calvin Ritter, a member of the basketball team, clicked his pen. "Oversized feet, heads, and hands."

"This reporter's name was Michael Brown, and he urged residents to take action. The New York State Health Department conducted an investigation and reported an unusually high number of miscarriages. Then Brown discovered the dump site was actually three times larger than anyone had believed and loaded with dioxins. The Agency for Toxic Substances and Disease Registry found more than four hundred different chemicals in the air, water, and soil, some of them carcinogenic. Which brings us to Lois Gibbs . . . Piper Goodman."

Piper did not hesitate. "Gibbs had a son who suffered from asthma and epilepsy. He had urinary tract infections and a low white blood cell count. She did research on the canal and learned her neighborhood was built on top of chemical waste. Because her son had gotten sick after starting school, she tried to get him transferred. The school said no, so she started a petition and learned a lot of her neighbors were sick. They complained about bad smells and chemicals rising from the ground."

"How were they affected? Josh."

Josh Cantor cleared his throat. "There were a lot of different illnesses and cases of mental retardation."

"Niagara Falls Mayor Michael O'Laughlin assured his

constituents there was nothing wrong with Love Canal, but in 1979, the Environmental Protection Agency classified the area an environmental disaster. What did Lois Gibbs do?"

"She spent two years trying to prove that the waste dumped by Hooker Chemical caused all the problems in Love Canal," Piper said. "Some people thought she was a hero. Others thought she was a pain in the ass."

Helen leaned against the edge of her desk. "By then, Hooker Chemical had become a subsidiary of Occidental Petroleum. Did the residents of Love Canal sue Occidental Petroleum?"

"They tried, but they couldn't prove the toxic chemicals came from the canal," Mandy said.

"Because of the controversy, the residents couldn't even sell their homes and move away," Helen said.

"They should have moved anyway," Piper said.

Helen sensed Piper was readying for an argument. "Sherry, what happened in 1978?"

Sherry Kovac, a bright girl with curly hair and wide glasses, was one of Helen's best pupils.

"President Carter declared a federal health emergency in Love Canal and ordered the Federal Disaster Agency—"

"Federal Disaster *Assistance* Agency . . ."

"—to help the city deal with the problem."

Helen clasped her hands. "It was the first time in US history that emergency funds were used for a crisis other than a national disaster. Scientists descended on Love Canal. What did they learn?"

"One-third of the residents suffered chromosomal damage," Piper said.

"How did the government help these people?"

"They relocated eight hundred families."

Helen tapped the back of one hand on the palm of the other. "The US government *evacuated* Love Canal because it wasn't safe for human habitation. The State of New York had to purchase seven hundred eighty-nine houses as part of the settlement. Mandy, what happened to all those empty houses?"

Mandy sat up, surprised to have been called on again. "Most of them were torn down?"

"Why not all of them?"

"Some people stayed behind."

"Ninety out of about nine hundred families in Love Canal decided to remain in their homes. Approximately 10 percent of the population. For years, it was possible to drive past vacated houses on deserted streets in a ghost town. What about now, Brian? Is Love Canal a forbidden zone?"

"Um, no."

Helen raised both arms. "*No?*"

"They covered the most toxic area with plastic and reburied it. Then they fixed up three hundred houses and tore down most of the rest."

"That's right. They reburied almost twenty-two thousand tons of toxic waste, planted new grass, and 'rehabilitated' three hundred homes. The Love Canal Containment Area is a grassy field eighty feet wide and three thousand feet long, surrounded by an eight-foot-high cyclone fence. What about the rest of the neighborhood?"

"They renamed it Black Creek Village."

Helen cocked her head. "Hm. *That's* a pretty name."

Scattered snickers.

"How many of you have been to Black Creek Village?"

Every student in the class raised a hand.

"How many of you have walked around that fence?"

The hands remained in the air.

"How many of you played at that fancy million-dollar playground when you were kids?"

Every hand remained in the air.

"Then it must be safe, right?"

"No," several students said as the hands came down.

"So why did people move there?"

"Cheap housing," Mandy said.

"Nearby family," Sherry said.

"These are perfectly logical reasons," Helen said. "But people moved there because the federal and city governments say it's safe to live there now."

"Jeez, your mother was on fire today," Mandy said as she and Piper joined the tide of students in winter coats.

"She gets like that sometimes," Piper said.

They headed toward the parking lot, where Brian stood leaning against a red Chevy Malibu with rust around the wheel wells, a grin on his face.

"You got it!" Piper said.

"My father added me to his insurance yesterday."

"Not bad," Mandy said.

"All these months flipping burgers paid off," Brian said.

Piper jumped up and down. "Oh, my God, take me for a ride!"

"I guess I don't have to be your chauffeur anymore," Mandy said.

Brian opened the passenger door for Piper, who slid into the Malibu.

"Take good care of her," Mandy said.

Brian winked at her, then hurried around the car and got in. Piper watched him key the ignition, then she switched on the radio and searched the stations.

"This is so exciting," she said, settling on a college radio station that played alternative music.

"Where do you want to go?" Brian said as they circled the lot.

Piper thought about it. "Love Canal."

Even driving with caution, it took Brian just seven minutes to reach Black Creek Village. Tapping her foot to the beat of the music as they followed Colvin Boulevard, Piper watched Love Canal come into view: small working-class ranch houses bunched together on the right, grassy fields on the left. As children, Piper and her friends had explored the woods to the right of the containment field, where paths opened up onto asphalt squares where houses had once stood, driveways led nowhere, and fire hydrants no longer served a purpose.

Brian turned left onto 102nd Street. Long stretches of

grass and trees, lots where many houses once stood, separated the houses that remained. Piper counted four occupied homes and two with For Sale signs at the edge of their deep front yards. Turning right onto Frontier Avenue, parallel to the LaSalle Expressway above, they drove to 101st Street. A pile of concrete rubble took up the corner on their left, and a fenced-in depot populated by construction equipment and trucks had taken over the corner on their right.

"Can you believe they're actually building something here?" Piper said.

"Maybe it's a hotel," Brian said.

They followed the cratered street past Wheatfield Avenue, which dead-ended, and continued on to the next block.

"Oh, my God, stop here," Piper said.

Brian slowed to a stop at the edge of a weedy yard occupied by a squat one-story house constructed from cement blocks and surrounded by a crooked four-foot-high chain-link fence. The gate was missing, and plywood backed broken windows. There was no porch, and a metal sign nailed to the front door read, THIS PROPERTY HAS BEEN CONDEMNED. A detached garage behind the house was also made of cement blocks.

"It looks like a bunker," Brian said.

"A haunted bunker."

"Can we keep moving?"

"Please."

They passed only two more houses on the street, both on the left and both occupied. Turning left on Colvin, they passed 100th Street, which had three cement barriers to prevent people from driving along the street that flanked the containment field. The grass before the eight-foot fence had no sidewalk. Through the fence, which had been posted with NO TRESPASSING signs, Piper observed one square mile of green grass peppered with occasional trees. In the center stood two brick maintenance buildings, and two cars were parked near the buildings. The entire site might have been a park, and Piper knew that on the opposite side of the field, a rusty metal sign and unimpressive keypad provided the only security at locked gates.

"Can you imagine working in there? Every time they mow that grass they could be releasing toxins into the air," Piper said.

"You're overthinking. Besides, it's probably no worse than living across the street."

Clearing the containment area at 95th Street, Brian turned left. Piper eyed the woods on the right, and then they passed two different assisted living communities. When they reached Frontier again, Brian pulled over to the side of the road. A small ambulance approached them from the opposite direction, and he left the engine running for heat. The ambulance passed.

"Do you want to get out and walk around?"

"No," Piper said.

He slid his arm around her shoulders. "Good."

Piper pulled away. "I feel like we're being watched."

"Like the government has secret cameras all over? Look around. No one would bother with this place. It's a dump in more ways than one."

Piper looked out her window at the strip of trees ahead, below the expressway. "No, like someone's watching us, not a camera. Let's just get out of here."

Brian moved his arm. "I wish you'd make up your mind."

"I'm sorry. I was just curious after class today. Blame my mother."

"No, thanks, I don't want to get on her bad side." He shifted the car into gear and pulled away. They passed three more cement barriers at this end of 100th Street, identical to those on the other side. Brian turned around and drove back toward 95th Street. The winding road took them past a modern-looking one-story office building and the playground where children played during warm weather.

Wearing work gloves, Paul and Evan picked up branches from the ground in Joanne's backyard and stuck them into one of her garbage totes. Trees surrounded Joanne's property, unlike theirs, and debris covered most of the yard. Paul had told Evan to stay away from the shed because he had seen rats crawling around it in the past, and he reserved the task of gathering tools from the shed for himself.

"Dad, look at that," Evan said in an awed voice.

Paul turned to where his son stood facing their house, a low corral fence separating their property from Joanne's. "What am I looking at?"

"*There*." Evan pointed at the second floor of their house.

Paul's eyes moved along the second floor. A large black shape clung to the siding of the house, from the flat roof over the kitchen addition to the edge of angled roof above the original structure, at least seven feet tall. He moved closer for a better look. The shape was tubular and yet bulbous, like globes stacked on top of each other, the connecting points filled in with mud. On closer inspection, he saw the thing was dark gray, not black.

"It's a giant cocoon," Evan said.

"I'd hate to see the butterfly that comes out if it is," Paul said. "No, that's a hornets' nest. I've never seen one so big. They must have spent a long time working on it, right under, or over, our noses."

Evan turned toward Paul. "That insect I found in the window!"

"Maybe." Paul lowered his eyes to the kitchen window. Inside, Helen stood over the sink, washing dishes. "Let's not tell your mother about this. She'll just panic."

"What are we going to do?"

"I need to buy some wasp spray. A lot of it. We ran out, and I didn't think we'd need any more this year. Obviously, I was wrong. When Mom isn't home, you'll hold the ladder so I can go up there with a rake or a shovel. Whatever's in there is probably dead or hibernating. I'll knock it down and spray whatever's inside, just to be safe."

"How long do you think it's been up there?"

"Maybe all summer, but it must have started small. I'm surprised the wind hasn't blown it down. Let's finish up out here and go inside."

As the wind picked up, he felt a chill.

THREE

Jenny Johnson awoke to the sound of baby Marcus wailing in the next room. Hadn't she just gotten up to change his diaper? Rolling over, she hoped to tell her husband, Ken, to take care of their son, but his spot on the bed was empty and she heard the shower running. She looked at the clock. It was after seven o'clock already. Somehow she had slept for two hours straight, but it sure didn't feel that way. Forcing herself to rise, she stepped into her slippers and pulled on her robe. Ken always raised the thermostat before taking his shower, but Jenny never felt the change until later in the day. She went into the baby's room, turned on the light, and smiled at her infant son.

"Hi, Marcus," she said, smiling as she lifted him into her arms. "Good morning."

Marcus stopped crying and cooed, thank heaven. She made baby talk as she carried the five-month-old into the hallway and turned on the stairway light. She still had excess weight from her pregnancy, and her ankles ached with each step down.

In the living room, she set Marcus down on the plush

sofa. Leaning over him, she pulled the cord for the drapes, admitting pale morning light. She drew in a breath: a layer of fresh snow covered the yard, the street, and the yards of the houses across the street. The first snow that had stuck. No one on the street had started parking their cars in their garages yet, and the dusting had left the vehicles looking powdery. Ken was not going to be thrilled to scrape the windshield of his car, but Jenny loved snow, at least this early in the year, before Christmas. The multicolored holiday lights in the Goodmans' front window glowed.

Jenny lifted Marcus into her arms once more and showed him the view. "Look, sweetie. Snow."

Marcus gurgled. Jenny carried him past the plastic Christmas tree, leaving the lights for Ken to turn on. She still hated bending down. In the kitchen, she put Marcus in his high chair and prepared his formula. While the bottle warmed, she raised the blinds over the sink. This was their first winter in the house, and she had never seen snow in the backyard before. The bottle warmer beeped, and she withdrew the plastic bottle and tested it on her arm. Satisfied, she picked up Marcus again. Her entire day seemed to consist of picking the baby up and putting him down, but she did not complain. She stuck the bottle into his mouth, and he sucked it like one of her nipples, his brown eyes shiny.

"You like that, don't you?"

Jenny heard the upstairs bathroom door open. Glancing outside, she froze. A stag stood fifteen feet away, in front of the gray apple tree, motionless and staring at her, its large antlers curved toward each other high over its head. The creature had not been there a minute ago. For a moment

36

she thought snow covered its body, but then she realized its entire coat was white except for a few gray splotches. She had never seen a deer in the neighborhood before, let alone one with white fur. Its eyes were pink.

"Ken?" she called. "Kenneth!"

The stag bounded away, disappearing in a heartbeat.

Five minutes later, she heard Ken on the stairs. Marcus had finished his bottle, and she patted his back, waiting for him to burp.

"Snow," Ken said in the living room. His voice carried a tone of defeat. He entered the kitchen tying a knot in his tie. "Did you call me?"

"Five minutes ago. It's a good thing we weren't being robbed."

"We moved here so we wouldn't have to worry about getting robbed."

She told him what she had seen as he poured himself a cup of coffee.

"Are you sure? The only white deer I've ever heard of around here live at the old army depot in Seneca County."

"This one was an albino."

"Well, that settles that. The white deer at the base aren't albinos. They have recessive genes: their fur is white, but their eyes are a normal brown. I've talked about them to the kids at school."

She nodded at the window. The light outside had grown brighter. "Look outside. Its tracks are still there."

Ken leaned over the sink, peering outside. "Those look like deer tracks, all right. And they are white—because they're in the snow. Speaking of which, I have to go clear the snow off the car. I'm not sure I'm ready for this winter."

"Your lunch is on the counter."

"Thanks." He kissed her, then Marcus. "You two have a good day."

When he left, Jenny glanced out the window again.

Standing inside his garage, Henri pressed the button on the wall and the door rumbled open, allowing morning sunlight to seep inside. Panzer, Henri's Siberian husky, wagged his tail.

"Go get it, boy."

The unleashed dog ran outside and turned in circles, flinging snow in all directions with his nose. Laughing, Henri drew his snow shovel from the wall. He would change the oil in his snowblower later; he didn't need the orange-and-black machine for the inch of snow out there now. Panzer urinated in the front yard and Henri shoveled the snow in his driveway, scraping the concrete and tossing the snow aside. He had been shoveling snow every winter for most of his six decades, and he accepted the chore as part and parcel of living in Niagara Falls. It wasn't so bad: the TV newscasters made it sound worse than the reality. Most winters were relatively mild, if long lasting. The bozos on TV only ever reported the occasional major storm, which added to the general misperception that western New Yorkers were on the receiving end of the heaviest snowfall in the country. New England got worse; Minnesota got worse; hell, even Syracuse got worse.

BLACKcreek

Next door, Ken Johnson scraped ice off the windshield of his Japanese car. Fucking jigaboo. The street hadn't looked the same since that black and his wife moved in. He didn't really mind them; they seemed friendly enough, and it wasn't like they drove down the street blasting rap music or anything. But once you opened that door, there was no telling what might walk through it. Cayuga Island was home to plenty of minorities, but none had ever lived on Henri's street before. He had always viewed York Avenue as the last bastion of civilization on the tiny island, and now that was gone. Herbert Sikes, who had lived in that house until cancer got him, would have shit his pants if he had known who would end up living there.

Ken saw him but didn't bother to wave. That was fine with Henri. They understood each other just fine. He felt winded by the time he had finished shoveling, and he lit a cigarette. Ken backed out of his driveway and drove off.

"Come on, Panzer."

The dog, which had one pink eye and one blue eye, followed him back into the garage, where Henri lowered the door. He hung the shovel and went inside, trailing smoke. On the landing of the basement stairway, he stomped snow from his boots and was about to climb the two steps to the hallway that led to his dining room when a loud sucking sound came from the basement.

"What the hell is it now? Come on, boy."

He went downstairs, followed by Panzer. If his garage was cluttered, Henri's basement was a downright mess. Thirty years' worth of junk had been stored down there, including items once belonging to his ex-wife and two kids, none of whom spoke to him anymore. He intended to get rid of it one of these days, which meant one of these years, which meant the kids would have to worry about it whenever he died, which he expected would be sooner rather than later. He had been smoking two packs a day for over twenty years, and the number of his neighbors who'd died or were suffering from cancer had not escaped his notice. He hoped a heart attack would claim him instead, as he preferred the idea of a quick death to protracted suffering alone in a hospital. Turning on the lights so he wouldn't trip over any of the bulky objects gathering dust, he heard another sucking sound.

Henri moved into the back area, home to the washer, dryer, furnace, and water heater. A dark pool inched across the cement floor from the pit for the sump pump, which must have clogged.

"Goddamn it," he said.

Moving to the pit, he gazed down and frowned. When the pump had broken down in the past, he had been able to see his reflection in the water. Now he saw only blackness. The pit coughed black goo in his direction and he recoiled. None of it touched his face. The sump pump kicked in, and the water level receded, the pump issuing another sucking sound. Mystery solved.

Then the liquid stopped receding and the pit refilled.

"Son of a *bitch*."

He'd be damned if he was going to call a plumber. He would just have to get his hands dirty. Intending to step back, he almost toppled. His boot had become stuck to the floor. He pulled his leg up, and translucent black goo stretched from the floor to his sole until it snapped. Panzer sniffed the substance on the floor.

"Get the hell away from there!"

Panzer retreated.

Henri inhaled on his cigarette and contemplated the oily substance on the floor. He was about to toss his cigarette on the floor but thought better of it. The last thing he wanted was to start a fire. Goddamn Niagara Falls.

After speaking to her mother's oncologist, Fran Kaminski entered Joanne's private room at Roswell Park Cancer Institute in Buffalo with her shoulders slumped. Roswell was one of the top cancer facilities in the nation. Joanne lay in bed, gazing at a game show but not seeming to pay attention, her hair unkempt and an intravenous needle in her arm. They had been waiting for results from the barrage of tests conducted over the last few days, and after receiving the news from one of the many doctors who had spoken to them since Joanne's arrival, Fran had called her brother Terry in New York City. Terry had insisted that Fran give Joanne the news in person.

Joanne turned to Fran and, perhaps reading her body language, fumbled with the remote control on the bed and turned off the television. She did not appear frightened. Fran stood beside her mother and clasped her shoulder.

"Well?" Joanne said.

Fran felt numb. "Four to six weeks."

Joanne looked down for a moment, then straight ahead. Her hand settled over Fran's. "Can I go home?"

"That isn't possible, Mom."

"Why not?"

"You need someone to watch after you."

"Hospice . . ."

"Hospice will send a nurse for only a few hours a day. You need around-the-clock care. I'm sorry, but I can't do that. I've got the boys, and Frank—"

"Frank." Joanne made no attempt to hide her disapproval. "I don't mind dying—that's part of the deal—but I don't want to die here or in any other hospital. I want to do it in my own home."

"I'm sorry, Mom. I wish I could do what you wanted." If Terry had been willing to take time off from work, it might have been possible; they could split the responsibilities. But he had his own life, and it wasn't easy for him to get away. "You know I'll come see you every day, and Terry will come out when he can."

The simple act of sighing left Joanne looking exhausted. "Bring the boys to see me soon, before I start to look any worse."

"I will. I promise."

"Tell Frank to stay home. We'll both be happier that way."

Fran knew her mother was right, but she didn't say so.

"I never smoked. I guess we both know what put me here."

Fran's parents had lived in Love Canal, and they had moved to Cayuga Island only because the government had paid their relocation expenses. Terry and Fran had both been born on the island. "Did I ever tell you I knew Lois Gibbs?"

"Yes, Mom."

"Someone's got to look after my house."

"Helen and Paul Goodman already said they'll take care of it."

"I hope they come to see me."

"I'm sure they will."

"That reporter spoke to me, back then. The one who wrote all those articles. I should have saved them, but we didn't take anything with us."

It took Fran a moment to realize her mother was still talking about Love Canal. Joanne's pain medication made her groggy. Fran caressed her mother's forehead. "I know, Mom."

Joanne looked out the window. "It's snowing. Did I ever tell you about the blizzard of '76?"

"Many times." The blizzard was legendary.

"We thought that was bad—the one that flooded the canal—but the one in '77 was even worse. The area was paralyzed for four days. Cars were buried and impossible to find. People were stranded in office buildings, in restaurants, and at strangers' homes. The National Guard came to help. Can you imagine that? Twenty-nine people died. President Carter declared New York and Pennsylvania federal disasters. A snow drift covered one entire end of our house. Your father just walked right up that slope to get on the roof, and our dog Chester followed." The rhythm of her speech slowed. "You should have seen all those Canadians who came to help. They came across the lake on snowmobiles."

Her voice trailed off, her mouth hanging open, and her eyes closed.

Evan got off the school bus alone and walked the two blocks home. Dan Bartkowitz was shoveling the snow in his driveway with one hand, leaning the shaft of the shovel over his stump, while Jim Makowski stood watching.

"Hi, Dan. Hi, Jim."

The two men waved.

"Hi, Evan," Dan said.

"Hello," Jim said.

"Do you need some help?" Evan said.

"No, no."

"Leave him to his own devices," Jim said. "He doesn't deserve your help."

"Okay."

As Evan continued to his driveway, he heard Dan call Jim a Polack. He took out his key and unlocked the front door. The house was empty: Evan's parents were still at school, and Piper was driving around with her boyfriend, Brian. Evan liked Brian, who never spoke to him like he was just a kid.

Evan went into the kitchen and made himself a bowl of cereal, which he carried into the living room. He wasn't supposed to eat in there, but no one would know. Switching on the TV, he sat down and surfed the channels until the doorbell rang. Setting aside his cereal, he stood and answered the door. Tommy Burgess and Grant Byrd stood on the porch. They lived halfway across the island and must have walked to the Goodmans' home as soon as they got off the bus.

"You know I'm not supposed to let anyone in when I'm alone," Evan said.

"We don't want to come in," Grant said. "Let's go hang out."

"I have to do my homework. So do you."

Tommy peered inside. "You're watching TV."

"I have to eat first, don't I?"

"'I have to eat first,'" Grant said. "Come on, let's go hang out. It's the first day of snow."

Evan hesitated. "I have to wait for my mom or dad to get home first. Or my sister."

"That's so lame," Grant said. "It will be dark by then, and they won't let you out. Come on, let's just go do stuff for a little while. You'll be back before they will."

Evan knew Grant was trying to manipulate him, but he considered his logic. He did want to go out and play. The temperature had been cold ever since Halloween, and he was beginning to feel housebound. "Let me get my coat." He held out one hand. "Stay out here."

As he closed the door, he glimpsed a shared smile between Tommy and Grant. He took his bowl of cereal into the kitchen and put it in the refrigerator. Then he wrote a note for his parents on the refrigerator message board just in case they beat him home.

When Evan stepped outside onto the porch, clad in his winter coat, hat, and gloves, Tommy and Grant hurled handfuls of loose snow at him.

"Ambush!" Grant said.

Evan scooped snow from the railing to make a snow-ball, but the powder would not pack. "We can't even make snowballs."

Tommy and Grant ran laughing to the sidewalk, and Evan ran after them. The boys slid through the snow on the sidewalk. They followed Rivershore Drive downhill to where it became South 86th Street. The bridge that crossed Cayuga Creek rose above them.

"It's colder than a witch's tit," Tommy said as they walked.

"Speaking of tits," Grant said, "did you guys see Beth in that sweater today? She's got buds."

"I think she's just wearing an empty training bra," Tommy said.

"No way. Those were real."

"Who cares?" Evan said.

"All you care about is comic books," Grant said.

"Tommy reads comics too."

"Spider-Woman has *tits*," Tommy said, grabbing the air.

"Evan likes Spider-*Man*," Grant said.

They walked to the bridge and Evan stopped. "This is as far as I'm going. I'm not allowed to cross the bridge."

Tommy and Grant ran to the middle of the railing and gazed at the water below.

"Come on," Tommy said. "This isn't crossing the bridge. It's standing on it."

Evan didn't budge.

Rolling his eyes, Grant returned to where the bridge

began. "You are such a pussy."

Evan shrugged.

"Do you always do what your parents tell you?"

"I'm out here with you guys now, aren't I?"

Tommy joined them. "Hey, I've got an idea: let's play hide-and-seek."

Evan expected Grant to scoff at the idea, but instead the boy faced the park below and turned back to them with a devilish glint in his eyes.

"Okay." Grant pushed Evan. "You're it! Turn around and count to one hundred."

Tommy and Grant took off in unison, hopping the safety railing and running down the grassy hill, freckled with snow, toward the playground in the distance. Frowning, Evan turned to face the street and counted out loud. Cars crossed the bridge and Evan glanced at the sky to hide his embarrassment. The wet sound of a car slowing to a stop caused his Spidey sense to tingle: he hoped it didn't belong to either of his parents. Bracing for trouble, he lowered his gaze to the Chevy Malibu idling across the street. Brian looked at him from behind the wheel, and Piper got out on the far side of the car.

"What are you doing out here?" she said.

"I'm hanging out with Tommy and Grant."

"Where are they?"

He nodded at the woods. "Hiding."

Piper shook her head. "If you get in trouble, I didn't see you. Understand?"

Evan nodded, Piper got back into the car, and Brian drove off. Realizing he had lost count, Evan turned. He climbed over the railing and slid down the hill. When he reached the playground, he saw no sign of his friends. Turning to his left, he faced the chain-link fence that flanked the narrow woods along the creek. Bare trees with gray bark reached to the sky. He cupped his hands around his mouth.

"Ready or not, here I come!" His voice echoed, and he climbed over the fence.

Evan entered the woods, making his way between trees and descending the slope leading toward the embankment. He did not get far before he slipped, arms flailing, and landed on snow. In the process of pulling himself up, he muddied his gloves and the knees of his jeans. So much for keeping his act of disobedience a secret.

He looked left to right as he penetrated the woods, the sounds of traffic fading behind him. None of the tree trunks were wide enough to hide both of his friends, so they must have split up. Standing still, he concentrated on the woods around him. Silence blanketed the terrain. He narrowed his eyes at dense bushes, barren of leaves. Something darted through the brush to his right, and he turned to see a squirrel run up a tree. Whirling back, he caught his breath. The woods seemed darker—emptier. One of his targets had probably veered to the left, the other to the right. He resumed walking, his sneakers dislodging branches beneath the snow. He knew Tommy and Grant could hear him, so there was no sneaking up on their hiding places.

Evan jumped behind a tree, grasping its trunk, and peered behind it. Neither boy crouched there, and he could see behind several other trees from this vantage point. He saw no sign of his quarry. Turning, he eyed the creek below, through the trees. It ran deeper in the winter, the current stronger. He wondered if they had gone all the way down the embankment. Nothing would surprise him. "Hey, guys?"

Neither boy answered.

The woods grew silent except for the sounds of the creek and his breathing, and he felt grateful darkness hadn't settled. He took a step backward. A twig snapped beneath him, causing him to suck in his breath.

"*Rargh!*"

Evan cried out, his entire body constricting even as he recognized the voice. Grant staggered before him, doubled over with laughter. Evan inhaled, trying to calm his nerves. Grant steadied himself against a tree.

"Oh, man, you should have seen yourself jump!"

Evan clenched his fists.

"Oh, boy, I really scared the hell out of you." Red from laughing, Grant stood erect and looked at Evan's fists. "What are you going to do—hit me? I don't think so."

Evan contemplated striking Grant, but he had not been in a fight since second grade, and he knew the trouble he was going to get into for going outside would pale in comparison to what would happen if he tangled with Grant. He took another deep breath, exhaled, and relaxed.

Then he heard it: a high-pitched scream like a girl would make. He faced the direction from which it had come and supposed it was Tommy's turn to tease him.

But when Tommy burst from the brush between two trees in the distance and sprinted toward them, the expression on his face told Evan something terrible had happened. He had only seen looks like that in the movies, the R-rated ones he wasn't supposed to watch. Tommy's eyes bulged and his mouth was frozen open. He ran so fast his face turned crimson. "Run," he shrieked.

Evan steeled his muscles, poised to run. "What happened?"

"*Run*!"

Grant broke into a sprint.

"What happened?" Evan said again.

Tommy rocketed past him. In the distance, the brush from which Tommy had emerged shook, and Evan saw the vague silhouette of a shape on the other side, something huge in his mind. He turned and fled.

Tommy ran ahead of him, Grant ahead of Tommy. They wove between trees and charged up the slope. Evan imagined footsteps behind him, getting closer. Heart pounding, he pumped his arms the way Mr. Haas had taught them in gym, which made his legs move faster. Grant staggered ahead and disappeared from view. Tommy continued running without breaking stride. Evan thought he would have to help Grant up, but Grant clambered to his feet and he and Evan ran side by side. Tommy jumped onto the fence and clawed his way up it. He threw himself over the top and landed on the other side.

The cold air hurt Evan's throat and he wanted to slow down, but panic drove him forward. He and Grant reached the fence and scaled it, dropping onto the ground where Tommy laid curled up. Only when Tommy rolled over did Evan see the tears streaking the boy's face and the snot dripping from his nostrils.

"What is it? What's wrong?"

Tommy's wild eyes returned to the woods. "It was *horrible*."

"What was?" Grant said.

"I don't know!" Tommy's quivering lips hid his teeth. "We have to get out of here." Without waiting for them, he jumped to his feet and ran toward the street.

Evan and Tommy exchanged confused looks, then got up and followed their friend. Evan glanced back at the woods, which had grown darker.

FOUR

Paul's snowblower rocked from side to side, blasting a steady stream of snow and ice out the chute and into the side yard. On either side of his driveway, the white walls chiseled by the blower reached above his knees. The heavy snowfall had started Christmas Eve and had continued almost nonstop for three weeks. All around him, snow covered the trees, bushes, and cars, making the entire landscape resemble melted marshmallows.

And still the snow fell, the fluffy flakes descending at a straight angle. He had awakened early to tackle the snow so he and his family could make it out of the driveway. The muscles in his arms and lower back ached, and the bitter cold stung his nostrils. This was Saturday afternoon, and all the men in the neighborhood attacked their driveways while the sun offered some measure of warmth.

Across the street, Henri operated his own machine. The white-haired man, who wore a fur hat with ear flaps, proved an almost constant presence during winter, stopping only to smoke a cigarette and never to warm his hands. One yard over, Ken pushed his machine. To Paul's left, Dan pushed his own blower, and in the next yard, Jim tackled his driveway. During the warmer months the neighbors spoke to each other, but during the long winter they did little more than nod and wave as they battled the elements.

The roar of an engine and the sound of a heavy blade scraping frozen asphalt announced the arrival of the snowplow. Paul had been about to turn onto the sidewalk, but he waited for the bulky metal monster to blast snow at the mouth of his driveway and fill it once more with packed snow. He turned away, tensing his muscles as a white cloud raced in his direction. The snow enveloped him, striking the backs of his legs and licking at the exposed skin on his face. He resisted the urge to curse and steered the blower onto the sidewalk, dismissing the enormous plow as it sped down the street.

Over the past few weeks, he had maintained a carved passage through the snow along the walk, creating sharp ridges on either side. The blower's chute blasted snow in a high arc that landed on his front yard. He reached Joanne's driveway next door, which he cleared for Francine's periodic visits. Part of him wanted to clear a path just from the street to the front door, but Helen expected him to do the entire driveway. When he reached Joanne's garage, he saw Dan struggling to remove the fresh ice pack at the lip of his own driveway; Jim and Henri had already returned to the shelter of their homes. Shivering, he burrowed through the snow, stopping only to warm his fingers when they ached from the cold.

BLACKcreek

Brian turned off the LaSalle Expressway onto the Robert Moses Parkway with Piper beside him. Evan sat alone in the backseat. On their right, they passed one jagged industrial structure after another, most of the buildings comprising Occidental Petroleum, the company that had bought Hooker Chemical. Snow blanketed the terrain separating the parkway from the factories, and white steam billowed from the smokestacks that rose into the gray sky. Power lines ran from skeletal towers that looked black against the sky.

"It's so ugly," Piper said.

"It doesn't last long," Brian said. "But long enough."

"I like this song," Evan said. "Turn it up."

Piper turned up the radio, and the driving vocals of the Foo Fighters filled the car. The factories receded from view, and before long the Niagara River appeared beside them on the left, covered with ice, and the skyline of Niagara Falls, Canada, came into view in the far distance: sleek towers and hotel casinos that outclassed those on the American side.

"Welcome to Niagara Falls, USA," Brian said, "where you have a great view of Niagara Falls, Canada."

"My dad says corruption is what keeps the American side from being developed," Piper said.

Mist rose from behind the trees ahead as they entered the state park. Naked trees and snow covered the ground that sloped down to the walkway that followed the river to the falls ahead. Brian drove to the far end of the park and entered the parking lot, which was occupied by scores of cars, the Rainbow Bridge looming beyond it.

"Anyone want to walk to Canada?" Brian said.

"Not in this weather," Piper said.

Brian pulled up to the booth and paid the parking attendant, then searched for a parking space. "I guess we're not the only tourists today."

"You mean we're not the only ones who are crazy."

He pulled into a spot, and they tugged on their hats and gloves and wrapped their scarves around their necks.

"I can't believe we're doing this," Piper said.

Brian got out first and cursed. Piper shushed him, then got out too, and Evan followed. The sounds of the doors shutting echoed. Wind assailed them, knifing through the fabric of their clothes.

"Oh, my God." Piper latched onto Brian's arm. "Let's get this over with."

They hurried into Prospect Point Park. Although the pathways had been cleared, a fresh layer of snow now covered them. The Goodmans had made trips to the falls every summer for as long as Piper could remember, and she still enjoyed the Maid of the Mist boat ride. Anytime friends or family from out of town visited, a trip to the park was mandatory. The family hadn't been there at wintertime for several years. Evan turned in circles, gazing at the trees.

"What are you doing?" Brian said.

"I'm looking for black squirrels."

"Black squirrels hibernate too, you goof," Piper said. "Especially this winter."

Making their way through the gates, they passed people heading in the other direction. The elevators that took people down to the dock for the Maid of the Mist were closed, but the doors to the building were open to allow access to the observation deck. Piper hugged Brian for warmth, and Evan ran for the door leading to the deck.

"No running!" Piper said, but Evan had already reached the outside. Stepping onto the deck, which arched partway across the Niagara Gorge like an incomplete bridge, Piper squinted as wind chopped at her face. Perhaps three dozen people crowded the deck, a lot for wintertime. Evan darted from vantage point to vantage point, working his way around the deck. Piper looked over the metal railing at the base of the gorge two hundred eighty-two feet below. The boat dock was empty. She locked arms with Brian and led him to the end of the deck, and they looked at the frozen water below. Massive slabs of ice pushed against each other, and snow covered the entire gorge.

"Wow," Evan said from somewhere behind them.

Piper turned in his direction, but Brian pulled her back toward him.

"Hey."

She raised her eyebrows.

"My mom got moved to the day shift."

"So?"

"So I've got the house to myself every day until about six."

"You do?"

"*We* do."

Piper knew what he was getting at. They had been dating for almost six months, and Brian had started dropping hints about them becoming more intimate with each other.

"Do you really think I'm going to discuss this here?"

Piper crossed the deck and joined Evan at the railing that provided the only view of the American falls and Canada's horseshoe falls in the distance. Through the mist rising from the base, the American falls gleamed in the gray sunlight, the water's surface encased in ice from top to bottom. Water rushed beneath the ice and through portals that had opened. At the top, the water continued to cascade and fall; there was simply too much for all of it to freeze. Great formations of ice rose from the base, bulky and angular.

"That's so beautiful," Piper said.

Standing behind her, Brian wrapped his arms around her, and she held his forearm and laid her head against his chest.

"That is so cool," Evan said.

Darkness pressed down on the neighborhood as Paul returned his snowblower to the garage. A fresh layer of snow already covered his tracks. He set the blower aside and allowed it to wind down, then entered the garage and warmed his hands, which ached. Outside, the wind gusted snow along the street. Snow had also crept into the garage, and he grabbed a shovel suspended from the wall and used it to force the snow back out. He hung the shovel on its designated nail, killed the engine on the blower, and brought it inside. Then he pressed the wall-mounted button and the garage door lowered, cutting the sight of the snow swirling outside. The pickup truck he had owned for twelve years took up most of the garage, his snowmobile parked in the back. He had held onto the truck just for recreational purposes.

Pulling off his gloves and unwrapping his scarf, he opened the side door and entered the stairwell. He sat at the top of the stairs, facing the basement below, and unlaced his boots, which he deposited on the landing. The furnace hummed as he stood and went into the house.

"Coffee or cocoa?" Helen said in the kitchen.

"Cocoa, please." He crossed the dining room.

Helen filled a mug with steaming cocoa as he entered the kitchen, tore a paper towel from a roll, and blew his noise. Vegetables cooked on the stove and there was a roast in the oven. Right now, the kitchen was the warmest room in the house.

"Thanks for doing Joanne's driveway," she said.

Paul tossed the paper towel into the wastebasket, then cupped his hands around the mug to warm his fingers, and blew on the cocoa. "Hers is worse than ours."

"It won't be long now. Fran says she's getting worse."

"I'm sorry to hear that. I suppose I'll still have to do it, so Fran can get in and out when she starts clearing out the house."

She rubbed his back. "You're a good guy."

He sipped the cocoa. "I try."

A sharp metallic echo rose from behind the refrigerator, and Paul and Helen turned in its direction, then looked at each other.

"It was doing that the whole time you were outside," Helen said.

"So why didn't you kill it?"

Helen affected a southern accent and batted her eyelashes. "Who, little old me? I might faint at the sight of vermin."

Sighing, Paul returned to the stairwell, sat on the step, and pulled his boots back on. The laces were wet now. He opened the door and entered the garage, where he located a garden shovel with a long handle from behind the snowblower. He carried the shovel inside, closed the door, and tromped into the kitchen, where he handed the shovel to Helen.

"Here, hold this."

Helen held the shovel before her like a weapon.

Paul opened the lower freezer of the refrigerator and reached inside with one hand, using the other to grab the top edge of the freezer.

"Stand back," he said.

Helen backed up, her fingers gripping the shovel's handle.

"One . . . two . . . three!"

Paul pulled the refrigerator out of its niche, and Helen pushed the shovel into his hands. No critters darted out at them. Paul relaxed his muscles and peered at the floor behind the refrigerator.

"There are no droppings on the floor."

"Maybe it's 'dropping' inside the refrigerator."

Paul handed the shovel back to her and seized the edges of the oven.

"Careful," Helen said.

He tried freeing the oven, but his position proved too awkward, so he turned the dials on the stove's front, shutting off the gas. Then he dropped the oven door and felt a welcome blast of heat. He pulled on an oven mitt, seized the door handle, and pulled the oven forward three feet. He held out his left hand, and Helen returned the shovel to it. Then he looked behind the stove. Shadows covered the space between the stove and the wall, but one patch was darker than the rest. Paul jerked the shovel's blade closer to his face.

"What is it?" Helen said.

"Get a flashlight."

Helen thumped to the far cupboards so hard the stove shook. She jerked open Paul's tool drawer, and the objects inside the drawer bumped against each other. "*What is it?*"

Paul pulled the stove out another foot, which yanked the plug out of the wall. Helen slapped the flashlight into his open palm and he squeezed behind the stove and aimed the flashlight at the floor. Half the steel wool he had used to plug the hole for the gas line had been pushed out, and a dark shape lay a foot away from it. The circle of light from the flashlight settled on the shape, and he recognized the stiff pink feet of a dead rodent. The rat was maybe eight inches from the tip of its nose to the start of its tail. From its midsection to its hindquarters, its fur and flesh had been peeled off, revealing decomposing muscles. Setting the flashlight atop the stove, Paul brought the shovel behind the stove.

"Oh, my God," Helen said in a rigid tone. "What is back there?"

Paul pushed the tip of the shovel against the dead rat's head, but it held tight to the floor. He gave the handle a harder push, and the shovel's blade slid beneath the rat, separating its putrid body from the wood with a sound like adhesive tape being pulled from a rough surface. Backing up, he raised the blade of the shovel into the air, careful not to bump it against the stove.

"What is that?" Helen blurted.

Paul lowered the rat, giving her a good look. "That's a rat, or what's left of one." He rotated the shovel so he had a good view of the rat's rear end. Not only had its fur and flesh been shredded, but a jagged stump marked where one rear leg had once been.

"What happened to it?"

He crossed the kitchen and dumped the rodent into the garbage, then returned to the stove. "Something got its ass." He picked up the flashlight, pushed the stove farther out, and leaned forward, shining the light on the two-inch hole for the gas line. Blackness greeted his gaze.

"Something what?"

"I don't know." Standing, he opened the cupboards over the stove and removed a brown paper bag, from which he removed a plastic bag of rat poison. He shook three green blocks of poison out onto the floor near the hole, each one two inches long. Holding the gas line out of the way, he kicked each block down the hole and into the darkness. "Hand me some steel wool from under the sink."

Helen opened the cabinet, rummaged through the cleaning supplies there, then handed him a clump of steel wool. "That didn't stop this one from getting inside."

Paul pulled the steel wool, elongating it. "That rat was running for its life. It chewed through what was there because it knew it would die otherwise. It wasn't fast enough." He bent down and stuck the steel wool into the hole, sealing it. "Bleach."

Helen handed him a gallon of bleach, which he splashed along the wall and on the floor.

"Brillo pad."

She looked under the sink, then handed him a Brillo pad. Crouching on one knee, he scrubbed the splotches where the rat had stuck to the floor. Helen moved to the back door, and he knew she was looking for the long trench dug by whatever used their lawn as an expressway from the shed to the deck. He had looked for it several times too, but deep snow covered the entire backyard.

Brian drove home from Niagara Falls along Buffalo Avenue, which afforded a view of the front of Occidental Petroleum. The plant occupied over one hundred acres of land, employed two hundred workers, and operated twenty-four hours per day, seven days a week.

"What do they actually make here?" Piper said.

Brian shrugged. "Beats me. Poison?"

Piper took out her phone and searched Occidental's website. "Chlorine, caustic soda, and Dechlorane Plus, a chlorinated fire retardant. Get this: 'Hazardous wastes are generated as a result of some production activities.'"

Brian snorted. "Meet the new boss."

"'As a result of the Resource Conservation and Recovery Act facility investigation, Occidental has concluded that hazardous waste constituents have been released to the soil and groundwater beneath the facility.'"

"But two hundred people work there."

"It goes on to describe all the steps they're taking to protect workers, and how the state monitors them."

"I still wouldn't work there."

"Neither would I." She bit her lip. "I want to write an article for the school paper."

"Like people around here aren't sick of reading about it already."

"Kids at school don't know."

"Of course they know. Your mom spent a whole week on it a couple months ago! They just don't care."

"Lois Gibbs deserves a statue right in the middle of Love Canal. Instead, we all pretend the canal never existed. Black Creek Village, my ass."

In the backseat, Evan played a video game.

Brian sighed. "Can we change the subject? We came out here to see Mother Nature."

"That was great," Piper said. "But now all I see are these factories."

"Not anymore."

They passed the end of the factory land, but when Piper looked into the side mirror, she still saw the industrial park.

Paul carried the snow shovel for the roof and a regular garden shovel into the upstairs bathroom. Standing behind him, Helen closed the bathroom door. Paul leaned the shovels against the wall, then raised the blinds over the window and threw the window locks. He forced the window up.

"You're crazy," Helen said.

"It isn't crazy to make sure our roof doesn't collapse from all this snow."

"No, it's crazy to climb out the window like this."

"It's easier than climbing a ladder from the yard. Just stand by to call 911 if I fall."

Paul climbed face-forward through the window, setting his hands into two feet of snow. At least the wind had blown some of it away. He wiggled his hips through the window, then his legs, and stood, moving toward the house so he had the greatest support beneath him.

"Okay, let's have them," he said.

Helen fed the shovels through the window and Paul leaned them against the side of the house. Synapses fired in his brain and his body turned rigid. Slowly he turned his head to where he and Evan had seen the giant hornets' nest two months earlier. He had forgotten all about it, and apparently so had Evan.

"What is it?" Helen said inside the bathroom.

"Nothing," Paul said.

The nest had disappeared, leaving only a few shreds of darkness clinging to the siding and to the soffit beneath the angled roof's edge, like gum smeared on a sidewalk. The stronger winds must have torn it away. He poked at the snow with the shovel, but it turned up no evidence of the nest.

"What are you doing?" Helen said. "It's cold in here."

"It's colder in my shoes."

As Paul shoveled snow to the edge of the flat roof, over the ice that rose from the gutter, and onto the deck and yard below, he wondered what had happened to the occupants of the nest.

Dan sat in his overstuffed chair, watching a History Channel documentary on World War II while a cigarette burned in the ashtray beside him and the electric heater focused a current of warm air in his direction. Trapper lay on the floor at his feet. The house was drafty, and Dan didn't even use half the rooms, so he relied on space heaters as much as possible.

On the TV, a long-dead movie star narrated the events surrounding the Battle of the Bulge. Resistance had just broken out along the Elsonborn Ridge when a loud sloshing sound caused Dan to jerk his head in the direction of the kitchen. Using the remote control, he paused the documentary and rose to his feet, a task made difficult by his girth.

"What the hell is it now?"

Trapper's ears perked up. Dan turned on lights as he moved toward the kitchen, the dog at his heels. He stood on the linoleum in the kitchen, watching and listening. The sloshing sound resumed a great liquid belch coming from the sink. At least there was no water on the floor. Dan moved to the sink, which he had cluttered with dirty dishes. He moved the plates, bowls, and cups from one sink to the other, revealing a syrupy green liquid clinging to the stainless steel. Using a dirty spoon, he scooped up some of the substance, then raised the spoon to his nose. A burning sensation filled his nostrils, and a foul odor like sewage made him gag. Dropping the spoon, he reached for the hot-water knob, but before he could turn on the water, the sink belched again and the fluorescent-green liquid gushed upward from the drain, splashing his forearm.

"Goddamn it!" Dan jerked his hand back and examined his right arm. His long shirt sleeve smoldered, and he unbuttoned the shirt with one hand and pulled it off. He stared at his forearm, which glistened with a green hue. His nostrils weren't the only thing that burned. Tossing the shirt into the sink, he ran cold water over his arm. Satisfied none of the substance remained on his flesh, he squirted dish detergent on the sink and directed the water over it, then wiped the surface with a paper towel, which he tossed into the overflowing waste can.

"Son of a bitch," he said as he turned off the water. He wanted to move to Florida.

At 9:30 p.m., in her one-bedroom, ground-floor apartment located in the Vincenzo Senior Homes off 95th Street in Black Creek Village, Denise Hornsby turned off the bathroom light and went to bed, as per her regular routine. The assisted living community consisted of forty units spread out among ten identical two-story apartment homes, five on each side of the drive. She had chosen the location because

the rent was so inexpensive. It didn't bother her that 95th Street faced the fenced-in containment area; at eighty-one, she did not expect to live long enough for any contaminants to do her harm. She had made dozens of friends here, and the staff were friendly. She had lived in the complex for over two years but had only been in this newer building since fall.

Pulling back the comforter, she climbed into bed and picked up her large-print book, an Agatha Christie mystery novel. She had read it before, but that didn't bother her. Her younger son, Maurice, had bought her an e-book reader that allowed her to increase the font size of any book she wished to read, but she hated the damned thing. Outside her window, the wind howled and snow spattered the glass. The weather caused her arthritis to flare up, and her bones told her winter would stretch into April instead of March. She read a chapter and a half before drowsiness set in. Miss Marple would have to wait. Setting the book and her glasses on the bedside table, she switched off the lamp.

Streetlights shining through the blinds projected long shadows across the popcorn ceiling. Branches from the bushes out front waved taunting fingers. Denise pulled the comforter up to her neck and closed her eyes. Tomorrow would bring another dull day.

Her muscles relaxed and her breathing slowed. Then a strange chill traveled through her body, and she had the distinct feeling she was being watched, a sensation she had never experienced here before. Opening her eyes, she tried to focus on the ceiling, which seemed darker than usual, its pattern of late-night shadows reconfigured. Reaching to her side, she fumbled in the darkness for her glasses, which she slid over her nose and ears. The shadows on the ceiling came into focus: in the center of the window frame and within the branches of the bush loomed a larger shape, thick and massy. With her heart pounding in her chest, Denise turned her head toward the window. She identified the shapes as the head and shoulders of a large man watching her, his features inscrutable in the light.

Denise sucked in her breath, then groped for the cordless phone, which she took from its cradle. Setting the phone beside her, hidden from her Peeping Tom, she moved her hand along the surface of the cradle until her fingers located the large square button at the bottom. She pressed the button, then grabbed the phone and raised it to her ear. Her eyes returned to the window, where her unwanted visitor continued to stare at her.

"Yes, Mrs. Hornsby?" a woman answered from the management office at the assisted living community. Denise recognized Adele Principe's voice.

Her heart pounded louder. She had good reason to be afraid: the other three units in the house were still vacant, leaving her alone.

"Mrs. Hornsby?"

"There's someone outside my apartment," Denise said in a strangled whisper.

"Where?" At least Adele sounded concerned.

"He's right outside my bedroom window."

"Is he trying to get inside?"

"No, he's *watching* me."

"Don't move, Mrs. Hornsby. I'll send someone right over."

"Don't hang up. I'm scared."

"All right, just stay calm." Adele spoke to someone else. "Will, pick up."

A male voice squawked over a walkie-talkie on the other end.

"Denise Hornsby, unit twelve F, says someone's outside her window."

The male voice squawked again.

"I'm calling the police." Adele returned to the phone. "Mrs. Hornsby, Will Chance is on his way."

Denise closed her eyes.

"Mrs. Hornsby?"

"Yes?"

"Is this person still there?"

Denise squeezed her eyes tighter. "I don't want to look."

"Please, Mrs. Hornsby . . ."

Denise opened her eyes. The shadows on the ceiling had returned to normal. Her eyes darted to the window. The shapes had vanished.

Denise wasn't going to tell Adele the shape had disappeared. That would just lead her to cancel the security check. For all she knew, the pervert was still outside her window. "I—I don't know. It's dark . . . my glasses . . ."

"It's okay. You're not in any danger. Will will be there in one minute. I'm going to get off the phone and call the police just to be safe."

"Thank you." Denise's voice croaked. Staring at the window, she half expected the shape to jump back into view, but it didn't. She glanced at the clock, which showed 10:45 p.m. She knew she would not be able to fall asleep, but at least Carol Burnett would be on in fifteen minutes. Being old alone sucked.

Will zipped his coat, pulled on his cap and gloves, and exited the unit he had been working in when Adele had called. Falling snow sliced the darkness at a forty-five-degree angle. Bitter cold wind knifed through his pants and thighs, and he jammed his fists into his pockets. Adele was a cute chick, but it irritated him that she always called him for the shit assignments. He crossed the side road to the parking lot, where he used his remote to unlock his Sentra and start its engine. Sitting askew across the front seat, he twisted the control to defrost, grabbed the scraper brush, and tackled the snow and ice covering the little car. By the time he had finished, he knew he could have walked to Denise Hornsby's unit, but damn it was cold outside.

Sitting inside the car with the brush on the seat beside him, he slammed the door, secured his seat belt, and shifted the car into gear. The windshield wipers cleared falling snow as he drove to the other end of the community. Of course the snow-removal contractor had not been through yet, so he had to go slow to avoid losing control of his vehicle. Turning up the volume on the radio, he leaned over the steering wheel to see better. Clean white snow covered the drive. As he proceeded to the third house from 95th Street, a figure lumbered into the road ahead of him. The headlights illuminated the falling snow but not the figure, which he took to be a deer. He stomped the brake pedal and the car slid.

"Damn!" He tried pumping the brakes instead.

The car veered left, toward the units, and as he passed the animal it turned in his direction. He thought he glimpsed a human face surrounded by fur, but then darkness swallowed the figure and the car skidded to a stop. Looking over his shoulder, he saw nothing, so he opened the door and got out. Through the snow, he saw no living being. Darkness cascaded around him, and he listened to snowflakes striking his ski jacket. Where the hell had the animal gone? In his mind, he constructed the image of a man-sized bear.

Will got back into his car, closed the door, and pulled into a parking spot. Getting out again, he took a long flashlight from his pocket and powered it on. He hated security calls, even though they usually proved to be nothing. He was a caregiver, not a guard. He understood the clients needed to feel safe, but the housing company should have sprung for twenty-four-hour guard service. He did not intend to get killed by a burglar or robbed by a rapist. Black Creek Village was known for its contaminated past, not for its crime rate, but it was close enough to the City of Niagara Falls that paid security would not be out of line. He aimed the flashlight where he thought the wild animal had been, but the snow reflected the light into his eyes.

Sighing, he proceeded to the apartment house, taking care not to slip on the icy sidewalk. Hornsby's unit was on the left, so he cut across the snow-filled yard. Adele had said the old woman was in bed, so he started on the side with the bedroom windows. No pervert stood outside her windows, so he trudged through the snow, which reached his knees, to the back of the property. The exertion winded him, and he told himself once again that he had to stop smoking. The few lights behind the houses offered little illumination, and he swept the beam from the flashlight back and forth from the houses to the trees. Someone could have been back there, but he saw no footprints.

Will trudged back along the side of the house, careful not to shine the flashlight on Mrs. Hornsby's window. So far she had been a model resident, and he could not remember her needing a security check before. The flashlight's beam settled below the window, illuminating dislodged snow. Moving closer, he shone the light into the two deep holes where someone had been standing. Two sets of footprints gaped at him: one leading to the window from the sidewalk and the other leading back, some of them overlapping. Mrs. Hornsby had been telling the truth. Who the hell would spy on a retired old lady?

Moving parallel to the prints, he followed them, the flashlight making the snow around them glow stark white. The prints were wide apart: whoever had made them was either tall or had been running or both. When he reached the sidewalk, he aimed the flashlight at the middle of the drive: whoever had made the prints had run into the access road. He followed them, stopping where he had seen the animal. It had been a man after all. The prints continued into the empty land across the street from Mrs. Hornsby's unit. The space beyond the land was black. Will moved forward, aiming the flashlight at the darkness, but the falling snow deflected the beam. He knew what lay within that darkness: the fence that protected the Love Canal Containment Area. Headlights struck him from the mouth of the drive, and he faced an oncoming vehicle.

"What have we got here?" Gigi Brown said as she steered the patrol car along the drive of the assisted living community.

The headlights caused the snowflakes falling before them to glow and cast faint illumination on a short man standing at the curb on the left.

"Maybe that's our peeper," her partner, Lou Bescaglia, said.

The short man stood sweeping a flashlight over the darkness beyond the grounds. He turned in their direction but made no move to run.

"He doesn't look suspicious to me," Gigi said.

"Standing outside in this weather isn't suspicious?"

"He must work here." Gigi slowed to a stop beside the man and lowered her window. He appeared to be in his midtwenties and in good shape. He wore a red ski cap and needed a shave. "What are you doing out here?"

The man lowered his flashlight and switched it off. "I work here. My name's Will Chance. The same person who called you called me."

She knew he was telling the truth. "Do you have ID?"

"Oh, sure." Will raised the bottom of his ski jacket, revealing a laminated photo ID clipped to his belt. He removed the card and handed it to Gigi, who studied its image and compared it to the man standing before her. Without the cap, he had wavy blond hair. She thought he was cute for a white boy. She handed the ID back to him. "What's going on?"

"One of our residents complained about a Peeping Tom," Will said, pointing at a house across the street. "Mrs. Hornsby lives on the ground floor, over there. I checked it out, and there are footprints leading to her side window and back into the street." He looked at the ground. "The tracks are filling in, but they go through this little field."

"You mean toward the containment area?"

"Yeah."

"Is the resident okay?"

"I guess so."

"Well, you go check on her. We'll take a look over there and circle back to take a statement from her."

"Okay." Will crossed before the car and headed toward the house.

Gigi turned the car around and drove out of the complex. Lou looked out his window as she drove along 95th Street, the fenced-in containment site on their left and the field on their right. The patrol car crept on, its headlights casting a glare on the fence. The darkness beyond the fence made her shiver.

"You see anything?" she said.

"Of course not," Lou said. "There's nobody out here in this."

"Let's circle around and head back."

Lou fidgeted. "We better not get stuck out here."

"You scared?"

"No, I just don't want to have to walk back to civilization."

Gigi turned left, parallel to the LaSalle Expressway above. The darkness became oppressive and the windshield wipers maintained a steady rhythm.

"It's creepy out here at night," Lou said.

"It's creepy in the daytime."

"Yeah."

They stopped talking and listened to the sound of the wipers. The headlights highlighted trees as they passed them. Gigi could only see fifteen feet ahead of them as the car moved through the snow.

"How often do you think the plow comes through *here*?" she said.

"Not oft—"

A soft explosion made Gigi flinch, and the windshield turned white.

"Son of a bitch!" Lou said.

For a moment, Gigi thought she had plowed into a snowbank. Then the wipers parted the snow and she realized someone had lobbed a snowball at the windshield with precision. It took the wipers a few passes to clear the snow, and she decelerated. Beside her, Lou drew his Glock.

"Don't slow down," he said in a high-pitched voice. "That's what they want."

Gigi gripped the steering wheel, her brown knuckles turning white. "Who wants that?" She narrowed her panicked eyes on the road ahead.

"Whoever threw that. I don't know. They want us to

stop so they can pick us off."

"With what, more snowballs?"

"Just drive, damn it!"

Gigi pressed down on the gas pedal. Lou reached over and activated the strobes and the siren. Gigi's heart beat faster. She made a left-hand turn and they raced toward Colvin. When the streetlights appeared in the distance, Lou lowered his weapon, but he did not holster it.

"You want to tell me what's got you all fired up?" Gigi said.

"You're young. You don't know."

"Know what?"

"I've lived here fifty years. I've heard things."

"What kind of things?"

"Stories that would turn your skin white."

They reached Colvin, leaving the darkness behind them.

"You want me to call this in?" Gigi said. "Get some more units out here because someone threw a snowball at us?"

"Of course not. People will just make fun of us." At last he holstered his Glock. "Let's just go get the old lady's statement."

FIVE

February 12

Korbel Sloan awoke before sunrise even though he did not have to get up for work. He had been laid off from his job at the tire factory eight months earlier and had exhausted his unemployment insurance benefits. The only jobs in the area he had been able to find paid minimum wage, and at his age, he wasn't willing to stoop that low. At only thirty-nine, he was living on his retirement savings, and that money would be gone soon too. The bills had begun to pile up and collection agencies had started bugging him. Just getting up each day had become a challenge.

He lay in bed, staring at the grimy ceiling and buried in a heap of blankets and comforters because he had to keep the heat turned low: fifty degrees at night, sixty during the day. He could not wait for winter to end. February was always the worst, even when he'd had a job. Skipper stirred at his side, then jumped to the floor. The dog's nails clattered and his tags jingled. Korbel had taken to allowing the dog to sleep with him for body heat, and now Skipper was letting him know he had to urinate. Sighing, Korbel threw back the covers and sat up. He had worn his clothes to bed—

another attempt at warmth. Skipper whined and wagged his tail, gazing at his master. The dog was a mutt, like him.

"Okay, okay," Korbel said, sliding his feet into his worn slippers.

Light crept through the translucent bathroom window. Korbel closed the door to keep Skipper out, then relieved himself. When he turned the faucet knob to wash his hands, nothing happened. He had paid the water bill, so the pipes must have frozen. He couldn't afford a plumber. Tears welled in his eyes, obscuring his vision. What the hell would go wrong next? He stood motionless, tears running down his cheeks. When the water cleared from his eyes, he twisted the faucet knobs to their off positions and left the bathroom. He didn't bother wiping the tears from his cheeks.

Entering the living room of the ranch house, he opened the drapes so he wouldn't have to turn on any lights, ignored the glaring white view outside his bay window, and went into the kitchen, where he tried the sink, hoping for running water there even though he knew that was impossible. Raising the blinds over the sink, he gazed at his neighbors' house. Faint sunlight from the rising sun glinted off the long icicles descending from the gutters and windows. He wondered if the Blachs had water or if his pipes had frozen because he kept the temperature so low.

Skipper stood at the front door, which Korbel opened, letting in cold air. Skipper ran down the steps and into the path Korbel had shoveled to the driveway. A fresh layer of snow covered the driveway, maybe two inches high. Skipper stood parallel to the snowbank on one side of the driveway, raised a leg, and squirted a stream of urine at the snow. Steam rose from the snow, and the dog ran back to the house.

"No number two?" Korbel said. "I don't blame you." Skipper ran inside and Korbel closed the door without even glancing at the fenced-in containment area across the street. Back in the living room, he stood with his back to the door and weighed his options.

"It's okay," he said to himself. "Everything's going to be okay. You survived Iraq; you can survive this. It's just winter."

Skipper stared at him.

"Don't look at me like that—I'm not crazy. I'd talk to you if you talked back. When you do is when I need to worry."

He carried the two space heaters stationed in the living room into the kitchen, where he opened the cabinet under the sink and studied the pipes.

"Fuckers."

He pulled a metal bucket and a toilet plunger from the cabinet and plugged in the space heaters, which he set inside the cupboard facing the pipes and switched on. He did not own a hair dryer. He considered closing the cabinet doors but decided against it. His knees cracked as he rose and moved to the thermostat, which taunted him with its low setting. He raised the temperature to sixty-eight, then turned to Skipper, who sat next to his food dish. "Enjoy it while you can."

Korbel filled the empty dish with dry food. The dog looked at the dry nuggets, then at him. The furnace rumbled to life in the basement.

"No water means no gravy. You'll have to eat it like that."

Skipper lowered his head and closed his jaws over the food, crunching it.

Korbel went into the living room and dressed in his boots, coat, hat, and gloves. He retrieved the metal bucket from the kitchen and a plastic pail from the downstairs bathroom and carried them outside. Cold air stung his nostrils. Standing at the bottom of the steps, he filled one with snow, then the other, and carried them inside to the bathroom, where he dumped the snow into the bathtub. After closing the drain, he went outside for more snow. At least there was plenty of it.

Half an hour later, when snow filled the entire tub, he set the bucket and pail down, fetched the space heater from the bedroom, and set it between the tub and the sink. After plugging it in and switching it on, he closed the door. With nothing else to do but wait, he went back downstairs and fixed a bowl of cereal.

Exiting Ken Johnson's science classroom, Evan carried his books into the second-floor hallway of Niagara Falls City District School. He spotted Tommy walking alone ahead of him and ran to catch up. Over the last two months, he had seen his friend only in school. Tommy had gone into self-imposed exile, never leaving his house except for school unless in the company of his parents.

"Tommy!"

Tommy turned at the sound of Evan's voice. "Hey."

Evan stopped before him in the middle of the corridor. "What's going on?"

Shrugging, Tommy resumed walking. "Not much."

Evan fell into step with him. "Hey, do you want to hang out after school?"

"No, thanks."

"Why not?"

"I just don't feel like it."

Evan did not plan to give up that easy. He and Tommy had been best friends for as long as he could remember. "Do you want to sleep over at my house on Friday?"

"I don't think so."

Evan stopped and turned to his friend. "What's wrong with you?"

Tommy faced him. "Nothing. Why?"

"Because you're acting like we're not friends anymore. You don't want to do anything."

"That's my business."

Evan felt himself turning red. "You know it's my birthday next month."

"So?"

"So my mom and dad say I'm not having a party this year. They just want to take me and a few friends to a movie and out to eat. I hope you're coming."

Tommy frowned. "I don't know. We'll see."

"It's only a month away."

"I'll think about it, okay?" Tommy turned away.

"Hey, crybaby!"

Tommy froze. Evan turned to his right. Grant stood near the lockers with Roy Hawks and Randy Shatt. The one good thing about Tommy's strange behavior was that Evan hadn't seen much of Grant, either.

"Crybaby, I'm talking to you," Grant said.

Tommy turned to the other boys.

"See? He knows what I'm talking about." Grant glanced at his companions. "You should have seen him out in the woods, crying like a little girl."

Tommy shook his head, then walked away.

Grant bounded forward and shoved him from behind. "Hey, don't turn your back on me when I'm talking to you."

Tommy spun back, his eyes wild. Excited voices rose around Evan.

Grant raised his fists. "Come on, you little pussy. I'll make you cry again."

Evan ran between the two former friends and tossed his books to the floor. He extended his arms, holding them both back. "Cut it out."

Grant lunged forward and Evan used both hands to hold him back.

"I said, cut it out."

Grant leaned close to Evan, his lips quivering with anger. "Who are you to tell me what to do?"

Evan felt dozens of pairs of eyes on him, waiting to see how he would react. He knew Grant only wanted to scare him. Evan lowered his hands so they no longer touched Grant's chest. He closed them into fists. "Just leave him alone, okay? He didn't do anything to you."

Grant glared at Evan. His eyes moved to where Tommy stood and he snorted. Then he stepped back and kicked out. Evan flinched and jumped out of the way, but Grant's kick had not been aimed at him. Instead, Evan's schoolbooks flew across the hall.

"You're both pussies," Grant said.

Frowning, Evan went to retrieve his books, which meant turning his back on Grant as Tommy had done. Bending down on one knee, he gathered one book and one folder, which had torn at the seam, and collected scattered papers. The crowd parted and he stared at a familiar pair of worn leather shoes. Raising his eyes, he met the disapproving gaze of his father.

"What are you doing?" Paul said.

Evan lowered his eyes and returned to picking up his books. "I dropped my books."

"Is that so? Grant, what happened to Evan's books?"

Evan glanced at Grant, who shrugged.

"If he says he dropped them, then I guess he dropped them."

Paul turned to Tommy. "What about you, Tommy? Did you see what happened to Evan's books?"

Tommy shook his head. Evan stood, and Kathy Schindler, a girl from his class, handed his math book to him.

"Thanks," he said in a quiet voice. He hoped his father would not make a scene. It was hard enough having his parent for a teacher.

"If nothing happened, then everyone had better get to class," Paul said.

The students in the corridor went into motion.

Happy to escape his father, Evan caught up to Tommy again. "What the hell did you see in those woods that day?"

Tommy did not answer.

Korbel sat at his desk next to the TV in the living room, scanning local employment sites for jobs. The results of his search further lowered his morale, and he saw a minimum-wage food-service job in his future. Not for the first time, he thought about the pistol in the desk drawer. It would be so easy to slide that metal barrel into his mouth and squeeze the trigger. But what would happen to Skipper?

In the rear of the house, a loud, almost mechanical thumping sound preceded the sudden sputtering of water. Korbel jumped out of his seat and ran to the kitchen, followed by Skipper. Water flowed in a white gush from the faucet.

"All right," Korbel said. He looked at the digital clock display on the stove. "And it only took four hours."

He shut off the water, then adjusted the pressure so a steady drip would prevent the pipes from freezing again. He remembered the pipes in the entire area freezing for a whole week one year. Skipper stared at him, panting.

"Out?"

The dog wagged his tail.

"Come on, then."

After he had dressed, Korbel fastened a leash to Skipper's collar, then opened the door. Fluffy snow fell outside. "Let's go."

Cold air swept inside and Skipper led Korbel outside. Korbel closed the door and locked it, not that he believed anyone would ever break into his ramshackle house across the street from Love Canal. They crossed the driveway, careful to avoid the deep ridges of ice that made it uneven. The traffic on Colvin was heavy at this time of day, and Korbel watched a school bus pass him, the faces of children peering out at him. He and Skipper walked parallel to the containment area across the street. After they had passed the Muslim community center, the Black Creek Community Park, and the Masonic Lodge, they crossed the boulevard at 95th Street. When the traffic had cleared, he crossed the street, Skipper trotting beside him.

Cold wind clawed at Korbel's thighs, encouraging him to walk faster. Passing the retirement communities in the distance, they drew as close to the woods as they could from the sidewalk. Korbel unleashed Skipper, and the dog leapt into the snow beside the sidewalk and jumped in a circle, using his muzzle to fling snow in Korbel's direction.

"Cut it out," Korbel said, laughing.

Skipper bolted toward the woods, leaping like a horse over obstacles on a racetrack. The dog shrank as he bore down on the naked gray trees and disappeared within the brush. Korbel smiled. The dog loved to run through the woods, chasing squirrels and rabbits. He tried not to think about what diseases or contamination the critters carried. After all, he had lived in the neighborhood for eight years, and his own body probably bore chromosomal damage, no matter what the doctors at the VA hospital in Buffalo told him. He had bought the house because the price had been so low, believing he would marry his girlfriend at the time.

He removed his gloves, slid a pack of Newports out of his pocket, turned his back to the wind, and after several attempts managed to light a cigarette. He permitted himself one smoke a day, never inside the house. He stood on the sidewalk, smoking and listening to the passing cars, and waited for Skipper to return. The snowfall grew heavier. He finished his cigarette and tossed the butt away. He pulled on his gloves, then cupped his hands around his mouth. "Skipper!"

He did not see the dog.

"Skipper!"

Nothing. He waited a few minutes, then called again.

"Don't make me come after you," he said under his breath.

Several minutes passed, and his teeth chattered. He called the dog again, then set off for the woods, trudging through the snow. Halfway to his destination, he promised himself he would quit smoking altogether. No one bothered to shovel the asphalt paths that had once been streets, and by the time he reached the woods his jeans were wet from his knees down. Now when he called the dog, his voice tightened with anger. He made his way between the trees into one of Skipper's favorite spots, a clearing that had been a cul-de-sac before the houses there were torn down. A set of recent dog tracks crossed the clearing and disappeared into the trees.

"*Skipper*!"

Silence greeted his ears. This far from the road, he barely heard the traffic. Turning in a circle, he wondered how many homes had stood here before the evacuation. The surrounding woods had closed in on the space, shrinking it. His toes turned cold and he grew flush with anger.

"Skipper, get over here!"

The dog did not respond.

Korbel entered the woods, searching for signs of the dog. He moved in circles, calling the dog's name, but saw no sign of his pet. Debris snapped beneath his boots and branches slashed at him. Emerging from the woods, he realized he had stumbled into another abandoned cul-de-sac. Where the hell was his damned dog?

He crossed another section of woods. At least the snow was shallower around the trees. Facing a frozen pond, he stopped, his eyes widening. Steam rose from the ice near the pond's center, and through it he glimpsed a bright green liquid burbling. He stood mesmerized by the sight. God only knew what kind of chemical had risen from the former toxic waste site. Fucking Niagara Falls.

Helen parked the minivan in the massive lot at Roswell Park Cancer Institute. She had only visited Joanne twice, and the decline of her neighbor's health between those visits had been staggering. Fran had texted her that morning to let her know Joanne had taken a turn for the worse, and as she walked through the lobby to the elevator she felt guilty for not making more time for the dying woman.

She exited the elevator on the fifth floor and made her way beyond the nurse's station to a small hallway with a closed door. She knocked on the door and opened it. Fran sat near the bed, holding Joanne's hand, her expression tired. Helen didn't even recognize the emaciated bald woman on the bed. Cold packs had been placed on her forehead, arms, and shins, and a tube fed oxygen into her nostrils.

"Today's the day," Fran said. "She's stopped fighting, and she isn't responsive."

Helen stood beside Fran and set a hand on her shoulder. "I'm sorry."

Joanne's eyes were closed and her mouth open.

"After all these weeks, I don't know how to feel. She's suffered so much. We're trying to bring her fever down, but it isn't working."

Helen's eyes followed a tube that ran from beneath Joanne's gown to a plastic urine bag hanging from the bed frame. The liquid in the bag was brown. "Why don't you go get something to eat? I'll stay here with her."

Fran appeared unable to move. "I'm not hungry."

"Go on, stretch your legs. Go to the cafeteria and grab a bite to eat or a coffee. I'll get you if anything changes. I went through this with my mother."

Fran stood. "I could use a break . . ."

"Of course you could."

Fran leaned close to Joanne and kissed her cheek. "Mom? Helen Goodman is here. She's going to sit with you while I get something to eat. I'll be back fast; I promise."

Fran left the room and Helen moved to the bed's safety guard and took Joanne's hand. "Joanne? I don't know if you can hear me, but I'm here. You're not alone. Fran will be back soon. You should be proud of the way she's looked after you."

Joanne's breathing continued at the same rhythm. Helen sat in the chair and turned on the television. The five o'clock news had been on for half an hour.

A middle-aged woman in a nurse's uniform entered and checked Joanne's vital signs. Her expression turned grave. She recorded the vitals on Joanne's chart, then repositioned the cold packs. "We have to make sure she doesn't get bedsores."

The nurse left and Helen watched the news, which always depressed her. One robbery, one fatal car accident, and one local political scandal inspired her to surf the channels. After seeing what else was on, she returned to the news. Now the weatherman discussed the impending storm. Outside, the sky had turned dark.

"Make sure you have gas in your snowblower and plenty of food in your pantry, because we have a major storm warning for this weekend," the silver-haired weatherman said. "Three different storms are forming in the north, the west, and the east, and get this: they're threatening to *converge* on Saturday. Expect plenty of lake-effect snow, freezing temperatures, and the worst conditions of the season. I blame the groundhog."

Helen sighed. Would winter never end? Her school district had already used up all its snow days.

When Fran returned, the six o'clock news had started. "Thank you, Helen. I hope I wasn't too long."

Helen rose from the chair. "Not at all."

"I called my brother."

"Is he coming?"

"He can't." She lowered her voice. "Maybe this weekend." She looked at Joanne. "It looks like it will just be me and Mom at the end. Thank God for these nurses."

"I'll be right back. I'm going to call Paul. I'll stay and

keep you company tonight."

"Oh, you don't have to do that. You and Paul have already done so much."

"I want to," Helen said. "I'll stay as long as it takes."

Korbel returned home to warm up, then decided to drive around looking for Skipper. Unfortunately, his driveway had filled up with enough snow to make backing his Kia out of the garage impossible, and his snowblower hadn't worked for two years, so he had to shovel it by hand. When he finished, he tossed the shovel into the backseat. He drove around the entire Love Canal area, making periodic stops to get out and call Skipper's name, his voice carrying over the desolate landscape. No new snow fell, and the snow on the ground reflected moonlight into the gray sky, creating high visibility. On 95th Street, he stood at the edge of the woods, not far from where he had last seen the dog, his voice echoing in the night. After two hours, he drove around Niagara Falls, checking every nearby side street for signs of his lost companion. At last he returned home, where he called the police department and Animal Control. No one had turned in his dog. Sitting at his computer, he created a flyer using a photo of Skipper:

LOST DOG!!!

NAME: SKIPPER.
BREED: FRIENDLY MUTT,
MALE, SEVEN YEARS OLD.

LAST SEEN IN THE WOODS
ON 95TH STREET, IN BLACK CREEK VILLAGE,
NEAR THE CONTAINMENT AREA.

I CAN'T AFFORD TO OFFER A REWARD, BUT THIS
DOG MEANS EVERYTHING TO ME.

PLEASE CALL A

He added his name and phone number and struck the Print Screen button. On the eleven o'clock news, the television weatherman, a former used-car salesman, addressed the camera: "Forget Snowpocalypse, forget Snowmageddon, and forget Frankenstorm. A monster of a storm of epic proportions is heading in our direction. Two of them, in fact. Fasten your seat belts. You haven't seen anything yet. Enjoy your Friday the thirteenth, because Valentine's Day could be one for the history books."

Korbel stood, entered the enclosed porch, and opened the front door. Standing in the doorway, he gazed across the street at the containment area. Skipper knew the way home. What the hell had happened to his dog?

SIX

February 12

The first thing Brian Darcy noticed after he switched off his alarm clock was the silence in the house. On a normal weekday morning, he heard his mother making noise in the kitchen as she prepared breakfast, or his father asking where she had put a certain tie he wanted to wear to work. Today, nothing. He sat up and clambered out of bed, clad in flannel pajamas. Thick socks protected his feet, so he didn't bother stepping into his slippers. He opened his bedroom door and hurried through the ranch house's hall. Even as he reached the kitchen, he knew he had been left alone in the house. His parents had made plans to spend Valentine's Day weekend at a bed and breakfast in Pennsylvania, so he thought maybe they had gone out for something they needed for their trip. The kitchen light, suspended over the round table on a chain, shone down on a note. Three twenty-dollar bills lay on top of it. He folded the bills in one hand and picked up the note. His mother's neat handwriting covered the lilac stationery.

Honey,

We decided to get a head start to beat the storm. There's leftovers in the refrigerator and plenty of canned and frozen food. Here's some spending money. Make sure you're home by 10:00 p.m. every night. No sleepovers and no parties. We'll be home Sunday evening. Your father says the snowblower is all gassed up.

We love you.

Mom

Setting the note down, Brian smiled. Only his mother would call having a friend stay over at his age a sleepover. He looked at the stove and saw she had left him scrambled eggs. He had no intention of throwing a party or having one of his friends stay over, but he did hope Piper would agree to spend some quality alone time in the house on Saturday. He hadn't lost his virginity and neither had she, and after five months, the time and circumstance seemed ideal. Taking a plate from the cupboard, he served himself breakfast and sat at the table. He had never had the house to himself for an entire weekend before, and he planned to make the most of the opportunity.

In the shower, it occurred to him he could skip school and his parents wouldn't find out for a while and probably wouldn't care if he told them the truth. But that would mean waiting until after school to see Piper, and she counted on him for rides to and from school. Dressing in his bedroom, he checked under his dresser to make sure the condoms he had purchased remained where he had hidden them. His fingers touched the box, and he gathered his books, went into the living room, and took his coat from the front closet.

Bundled for the weather, he opened the side door that led into the attached garage, which was as deep as it was wide. His father's pickup truck faded in the shadowy rear of the garage, the Polaris snowmobile secured to its trailer. Brian's breath materialized before him as he glanced past his car at the double-wide garage door. Ice covered the windowpanes in the door, causing them to glow while preventing sunlight from entering the frigid space. Pressing the wall button near the door with a gloved hand, he listened to the door opener rumble to life. The door lifted with a rattling sound that echoed, and his driveway and the street before it came into view: layers upon layers of whiteness, broken up by occasional splashes of frozen gray slush, curved drifts pressing against carved ridges. Even colder air swept into the garage, and Brian climbed into his car to escape it. The cold seat numbed his buttocks as he keyed the ignition, his breath lingering before his eyes.

Once he had freed the car from the garage, he opened the car door, which struck the wall of snow piled high on his side of the driveway. The encroaching snow had reduced the driveway over the course of the winter, and he had to turn his body sideways to get out, then take sidesteps to pass the front of the vehicle. His parents had the only remote controls for the door opener, so he had to sprint to the inside door, disengage it from the track above, and pull it shut.

All around his Niagara Falls neighborhood snowblowers chugged. Clouds covered the sky and the air felt dense. Returning to his car, Brian watched a snowplow speed in his direction. He slid sideways along the snowbank, jumped behind the wheel, and slammed the door just as the plow hurled snow in his direction, dousing the car.

"Get ready for a wild weekend," the morning radio jock said. "We're looking at *apocalypse snow*."

"No kidding." Brian backed out of the driveway, his wheels spinning when they encountered the packed ice left by the plow at the lip of the driveway. He rocked the car back and forth, braking and accelerating, and managed to free himself. His wheels spun again in the street, and the first car behind him slowed in case he got stuck, but the tires achieved traction. Taking his place in the slow-moving traffic, he headed toward Cayuga Island, five minutes away.

The JetBlue aircraft shook with such violence that Terry Wyler dropped the John Grisham paperback he had been reading. His stomach lurched as the book fell to the floor, and he dug his fingers into the armrests. The plane continued to shake, and panic rippled through the cabin. Terry pressed his back into his seat and squeezed his eyes shut to avoid the terrified expression of the woman sitting beside him. He tried not to think of the Colgan Air Flight 3407 disaster outside Buffalo Niagara International Airport back in 2009. That accident had occurred in February too, and all forty-nine passengers had been killed. He had still lived with his family on Cayuga Island then.

The wind tossed the plane and tilted it from side to side. Terry thought of his one-bedroom apartment in Queens and the lobby of the movie theater he managed in Manhattan, and he wished he was at either location at that moment. He wished he was anywhere but aboard this plane, bound for his hometown where he and his sister planned to bury their mother. Until his brief visit to see his mother six weeks earlier, he hadn't been to the homestead in over two years. His job required him to work weekends, and company policy prohibited him from taking off two consecutive days, which left only vacations for travel, and he chose not to spend that time in Niagara Falls.

"This is the captain," a voice said over the loudspeaker as the plane stabilized.

Terry opened his eyes as his heartbeat slowed.

"We've obviously encountered turbulence, which we expect to continue for the ten minutes remaining until our arrival in Buffalo. Please remain seated with your seat belts fastened until we land."

Terry ignored the book at his feet. He had not been enjoying it anyway, because the story differed in too many ways from the movie. Leaning forward, he switched on the small television screen set in the back of the seat ahead of him. He had not requested headphones, so he zipped through the channels, searching for something mindless he could follow without audio. He stopped on a weather channel, which showed massive animated white clouds bearing down on western New York from all directions. The magnitude of the graphics took his breath away. The news-man standing before the image wore a grave expression.

"Please turn that off," the woman beside him said.

Terry considered arguing, but he had seen enough. He resumed channel surfing and stopped on a travel channel that showed vacationers wind surfing on a body of blue water bathed in sunshine.

"I'm sorry," the woman said. She wore her gray hair in a ponytail. "I hate flying."

"It's okay." Terry did not enjoy flying either, especially today, and he wished he had taken Amtrak instead. Glancing out the window, he glimpsed snowy rural landscapes through the cloud cover. Settling back in his seat, he tapped one foot on the floor. The plane had been in the air for an hour, and he wanted it to land already. Several minutes later the plane dipped to one side.

"This is the captain again. We are now beginning our final approach to Buffalo Niagara International. Please remain in your seats with your seat belts fastened. The time is 11:55 a.m., and the temperature in Buffalo is currently seven degrees below zero."

Moans rose from the seats around Terry, followed by some laughter. Terry raised one finger to switch off the television, but before he could press the button the plane shook again and he returned his hand to the armrest. This time, the shaking did not stop.

"Please let this end," the woman beside him said.

Houses and strip malls came into view as the plane descended. The shaking increased, and the descent felt too fast.

"Oh, God," the woman said.

BLACKcreek

The pressure on Terry's chest increased and he took a deep breath as he watched the runway come up fast. Bile climbed his throat and he swallowed burning acid. The plane touched down and a whine filled his ears. It shook again, and the other side came down harder. The plane raced forward and Terry's fingers ached from how hard he pressed them against the armrests. He thought the plane traveled too fast, and he imagined it crashing into the airport and exploding. Then the speed decreased and his muscles relaxed. The whine faded, replaced by the nervous laughter of the passengers around him. Someone clapped.

The plane taxied to the airport, and a few minutes later a bell chimed and passengers stood and opened the overhead baggage compartments. Terry retrieved his book, knowing he would want it again sometime over the weekend and when he came back to the airport for his return flight. While the passengers waited to deplane, he studied the crews working on the tarmac outside. Even bundled, they appeared cold. The line of passengers waiting to get off shrank, and he stood and pulled his travel bag out of the upper compartment.

He carried the rolling suitcase to the front of the plane, where the flight attendant wished him a good day. Walking the gangway, he zipped his coat. He saw three dozen people sitting inside the gate waiting for the next flight as he entered the sunlit airport. The small size and population set him at ease, a welcome relief after the chaos of JFK. He passed the food court, which consisted of only half a dozen fast-food eateries, then rounded the glass-enclosed waiting area and passed the security lines and ticketing counters.

The airport had a single escalator, which he took to baggage claim. Then he stood shivering on the sidewalk, across the street from the car rental agencies. There was no getting lost in the Buffalo Niagara airport.

A horn honked and a familiar Subaru pulled up. The trunk popped open and he tossed his luggage inside. When he closed the trunk, Fran stood beside him.

"You didn't have to get out," Terry said.

Fran stood there, her lower lip quivering. He did not want her to burst into tears, so he hugged her. She clung to him, her body shaking.

"Come on, let's get in the car." Easing her away from him, he saw tears in her eyes. "Stop, Fran, or I'll start."

Looking away, Fran dabbed at her eyes. "Yeah, let's get going."

Terry got into the passenger seat and Fran slid behind the wheel.

"How was your flight?" she said.

"Terrible. I felt like a kite in a hurricane."

Fran pulled away from the curb. "There's a big storm coming. They say some areas could get six feet of snow by the end of the weekend."

"So I hear. God bless lake-effect snow. That should kill our turnout tomorrow."

Fran drove to the airport exit. "Are you hungry?"

"Starving."

"How about some wings? There's a Duffs in the Falls now."

"That's progress."

Fran headed toward Genesee Street and Route 33

beyond it. Terry studied the mountains of snow piled around the sidewalks. The shoveled paths through them resembled alien landscapes on a science fiction television show.

"How are Frank and the kids?" he said.

"The boys are having a hard time with this. They've never had to deal with a death in the family before. They were pretty close to Mom."

"Will I see them tonight?"

"You'll see them at the funeral tomorrow. Frank, meanwhile, has been impossible."

"There's a surprise."

"He resents all the time I've spent with Mom, and all the time he's had to spend watching the boys."

"I'm sorry to hear that."

"I've decided to leave him."

"I'm not sorry to hear that." Terry hid his surprise. Even after the years of bullying she had suffered, he never thought Fran would leave her husband.

"I want to wait until the dust settles. I can't throw too much at the boys all at once."

"Just don't change your mind."

"It isn't easy, Terry. It means big changes."

"The boys will be better off."

"So how about you? How's your girlfriend?"

Terry had to think about who Fran meant. "Sheila? We broke up a long time ago. That was easy."

"Are you seeing anyone new?"

"No one steady."

"Life in the big city. What about your acting career?"

"That's going nowhere fast. This job limits when I can

go on auditions, and even if I book a gig, getting the time off is impossible. I had to fight just to get this weekend off."

"That's too bad."

"Life in the big city is expensive. I've reached the point where I know I have to quit and start waiting tables if I hope to ever have the career I want."

"That sounds like a plan."

"I hate waiting tables."

Fran shook her head. "Life sure didn't turn out the way I expected."

For the first time in years, Terry felt like they had something in common.

After lunch, Fran drove Terry to Cayuga Island. As they crossed the bridge spanning Cayuga Creek, Terry gazed at the smooth white snow covering the frozen creek, which appeared smaller to him every time he came home. The winding road led them around the island. Snow climbed up the sides of the houses, reaching toward the icicles that hung from the windows and gutters. The piles along the sidewalks and driveways had surpassed three feet. Terry shook his head. The circle took them to Joanne's house, and Fran pulled into the driveway.

"Paul Goodman's kept the driveway clear," Fran said. "We owe him and Helen thanks."

Fran popped the trunk and they got out of the car. Terry pulled his suitcase from the trunk and closed it, then followed his sister to the front door, which she unlocked. The cold numbed his face. They went inside and stomped snow off their shoes.

"It's actually warm in here," Terry said.

"I stopped by and turned the heat up before I picked you up." Fran switched on a lamp. "I'd appreciate it if you turned it back down to fifty degrees when you go to bed. I changed the sheets in your old room, and the refrigerator is stocked for the weekend. You'll have to cook yourself dinner. I bought you real food and frozen dinners."

"What time are you picking me up in the morning?"

"The viewing starts at eleven. How about if I pick you up at ten?"

"That sounds good."

"I left contractor bags and empty boxes upstairs. If you get bored, you'd be doing me a favor if you started clearing stuff out. I haven't spoken to a Realtor yet, but I'm sure we'll sell the place faster if it's empty."

"Sure."

She hugged him again. "I'm glad you're here."

He did not answer and she left, closing the front door behind her. He wandered through the dining area and into the kitchen, where he checked the refrigerator and the cabinets one by one. The food items would have to go, but he imagined Fran could sell the dishes at an estate sale. He supposed she would want him to come back for that, too.

He returned to the living room and climbed the stairs, which offered comfortable squeaks beneath his steps. He inspected his mother's room. Fran had stripped the covers from the bed. The air felt denser in the room, and he sensed his mother's presence, old and fading. Boxes and contractor bags stuffed full of clothing filled Fran's old room, and he knew she had moved a lot of junk out of his room and into hers. He entered the room where he had grown up. Same bed, same dresser, same bookcase. Movie posters covered the walls, mementos of his youth. He raised the shade over one window and peered through the layer of ice at the backyard, engulfed in snow. Then he sat on the edge of his bed. He had felt ashamed of the house growing up, and part of him relished the opportunity to sell it. But another part of him realized he would no longer enjoy the warm illusion that his childhood home would always be available to him when he needed it and that his mother would no longer answer when he spoke to her.

Like the students in his class, Paul kept glancing at the clock on the wall. The gray sky had darkened, and while no snow had fallen this afternoon, the sense that the superstorm would soon descend upon them was pervasive. Everyone wanted to go home and not just to enjoy the weekend. Six more minutes to go. Mr. Durick, the principal, had already canceled after-school activities and had instructed all the teachers to leave as soon as the students had cleared out.

Evan sat in the second row next to Tommy Burgess. Grant Byrd sat in the third row on the opposite side of the classroom. The rift between the three boys, which Evan had declined to detail, had widened over the past several weeks.

Paul closed his guidebook. "Before we all leave to enjoy the weather this weekend, I've decided to revise your homework assignment."

Groans rose around him.

"I'm sure you've been getting a lot of that today, haven't you?"

Heads nodded.

"You're to read one full chapter of *Lord of the Flies* for every day you're out of school, and you're to complete the assignment for that chapter."

The groans grew louder.

He leveled his gaze at Evan. "Do yourselves a favor and read one chapter a day. Don't wait until the last minute and try to read it all—you'll have a hard time. Read the study guide!"

The students gathered their books.

"Don't look so glum. Be happy."

"It's no fair," Shelly Litz said. "First we get a snowstorm on the weekend, when we don't get to miss school, and if we do get to miss school next week, we have to spend it doing homework."

"Horrible, absolutely horrible. The Donner party wished they'd had some good reading material to take their minds off their winter troubles."

The bell chimed and the students rushed for the door.

"Evan Goodman, make sure you go straight home."

Evan slipped out the door and melted into the crowd.

Smiling, Paul packed his own items and went to the main lobby, where he joined the other teachers in watching the students board the yellow school buses, multicolored jackets blurring in the rush.

"Ready for the storm?" Ken said to him.

"The snowblower's all gassed up. You?"

"We can live on baby formula if we get snowed in."

Paul's smile widened.

"You going to do Joanne's driveway?"

"I don't know if I'm going to do my *own* driveway." Paul took out his phone.

"I hear that."

Helen had sent him a text: *Meet me at the supermarket. Copy that*, he texted back.

As Brian drove past Black Creek Village en route to his house, Piper watched a black man holding a sheaf of papers cross Colvin Boulevard ahead. She had seen him before, walking his dog.

Leaving Black Creek Village behind, Brian made a left turn onto a side street, then a right. Piper knew what Brian had in mind as his family's house came into view, and she felt nervous. The car slowed to a stop at the driveway, which had been buried in a foot of snow.

"Damn it," Brian said. "It isn't even snowing. That's just from the wind."

"It's no big deal. Do you want me to help?"

"No, you wait here."

Brian opened the door, allowing cold into the car, and jogged into the snow. He made his way to the garage and heaved the door open, and Piper watched him roll out the snowblower and start it. Her phone vibrated, and she took it out. A photo of her mother's face filled the screen. Piper read the accompanying text: *Go straight home.* Piper felt relieved: she had intended to postpone Brian's plans until the next day anyway. Watching the snow fly out of the blower's chute, she texted her response: *Okay.*

"My mom wants me home," she said when Brian got back into the car.

The eagerness in his face collapsed. "How come?"

"This storm," she said in a tone that emphasized how obvious she found the answer.

"But there's nothing happening, and your house is only five minutes away."

She set one hand on his thigh. "Not today."

"She probably won't even let you out of the house tomorrow."

"You might be right."

Brian blew air out of his cheeks. "We won't get a chance like this again."

"Yes, we will." Leaning across the seat, she kissed him on the mouth.

"Don't get me all worked up," he said.

She caressed his cheek. "Blame the weather, not my mom."

"I blame Hooker Chemical," he said.

Helen pushed her cart through the crowded aisles of the supermarket. As she turned in to the canned goods aisle, another cart crashed into hers with a rattling screech.

"Oh, hey there, I'm sorry," Dan said. He had filled his cart to the top.

"That's okay," Helen said.

"Would you look at this place? You'd think it was the end of the world. I always say the big difference between men and women in a supermarket is that women tear around the corners like there couldn't possibly be anyone on the other side, and men just leave their carts in the middle of the aisle and walk away, like no one else could be coming through. I guess I proved myself wrong."

"I promise not to tell anyone."

Dan nodded toward something behind her. "Here comes your poorer half."

Helen turned as Paul joined her with a full smile and an empty cart.

"Fancy meeting you here," Paul said to Helen.

"He found us out," Dan said.

"What took you so long?" Helen said.

"I had to snowblow the driveway," Paul said.

"You mean you had to watch Evan do it."

"I don't let him do it unsupervised. I like his little fingers too much."

"Excuse me," a woman behind Paul said. "You're blocking the entire aisle. Could you commiserate somewhere else? I'd like to get home before the storm starts tomorrow."

"Oh, sorry," Paul said, moving his cart out of the way.

Helen glared as the woman pushed her cart past them.

"Have a nice day." Dan turned to Helen and Paul. "Storms bring out the worst in people. I have to get going. Good luck tomorrow."

"You too," Paul said as Dan pushed his cart in the opposite direction.

Helen took out a sheet of paper, tore the list in half, and handed the bottom part to Paul. "Here you go. I'll see you at home."

Paul looked at the list. "Are you expecting company?"

"If we really get hit, we could be snowed in for weeks. Stop dawdling."

Paul saluted her.

"Do you mind?" a man said behind him.

Paul managed to smile as he pushed his cart away.

In the living room of Joanne's house, Terry pushed the iron back and forth over his suit while meteorologists and anchorpeople broadcast their predictions of doom on one of the local news channels. He owned three suits for work and had packed the black one, and it had gotten wrinkled on the trip. The doorbell rang. Looking up, he switched the iron off and set it down on the board, then crossed the room and opened the door. An attractive woman with long dark hair stood on the stoop, a scarf wrapped around her neck and muffs covering her ears. She held a bulging plastic bag in one hand. Gusts of wind blew snow behind her.

"Hi. I'm Helen Goodman."

"Oh, hi. Please come in."

Helen stepped inside and Terry closed the door.

"Thanks for all your help with the house."

"My husband, Paul, did most of the work. I'm so sorry about your mother. She was a nice woman and a great neighbor."

"I appreciate that."

Helen raised the bag in her hand. "I brought you dinner. Fran said you don't like to cook, and I didn't invite you to join us because I doubted you'd want to eat with total strangers."

He accepted the bag. "That's very considerate of you."

"It's just a chicken from the market, but it's cooked. The side dishes are cold."

"Thank you."

Helen glanced at the TV. "So you know about the storm."

"It's all I've heard about since I got here."

"We're going to do our best to make the funeral, but . . ."

"Don't worry about it. I'm sure Mom would understand."

"How long will you be in town?"

"I'm scheduled to fly back to New York on Sunday. We'll see."

Helen took a slip of paper from her pocket. "Here's our number. If you need anything, don't hesitate to call."

Terry made a show of looking at the number on the paper. If he needed anything, he would call his sister. "Thanks. I will."

Helen returned to the door. "This neighborhood won't

feel the same without Joanne. Good night."

Terry watched Helen leave the house and close the door behind her. He walked back to the ironing board.

"Hold onto your hats. It keeps getting better," the weatherman on TV said. "It now appears a *third* storm is bearing down on our area, this one from Canada. All three storms are expected to strike early tomorrow morning. Snowzilla is coming!"

Terry took his phone out of his pocket and auto-dialed his sister.

"Hello?" Fran said.

"The news is starting to scare me."

"That's their job."

"Why don't you pick me up an hour early, and we can have breakfast?"

"If you want to eat somewhere decent, I'd better get you at 8:30."

"See you then."

Paul served meatloaf, mashed potatoes, and green beans to his wife and offspring at the dining room table. The local news anchors droned on from the television in the living room.

"We've got enough food to last two weeks if we need it," he said.

"More," Helen said.

"You make it sound like we're going to be trapped here," Piper said.

Paul traded a knowing smile with Helen as he sat down.

"At least we won't be like the Donner party, right, Dad?" Evan said.

"Right."

Piper looked at her brother. "Everything's going to be fine. It's going to be just like every other storm: everyone's going to watch the news and nothing's going to happen. You and Dad will snowblow tomorrow, and then it will be like any other day."

Helen sampled the meatloaf. "Three storms are speeding toward us right now. If just one of them hits us, you might be right. If two hit, you're going to see a real mess outside. If all three hit at the same time like they're predicting, you'll remember the outcome for the rest of your life."

Piper issued a defiant stare. "I'm going out with Brian tomorrow."

"Ha," Paul said.

"What?"

"You're not going anywhere tomorrow," Helen said.

Evan's eyes went back and forth between his mother and sister, as if he were watching a tennis match.

"I have plans," Piper said.

"What plans are those?" Helen said.

Evan puckered his lips and made a kissing sound.

Piper looked aghast. "Stop that, you little creep!"

"I ran into Brian's father at Tim Horton's the other day," Paul said in a casual tone. "He said he and Brian's mother are going away this weekend. They probably already left."

Helen focused on Piper, who looked away before resuming her stare.

"What?" she said.

"You're not leaving this house tomorrow. Brian is welcome to come over here for a meal if he's able to get out of his house and reach us."

Piper rose. "I am not a prisoner h—"

"Sit down," Helen said in a steely voice.

Piper looked at Paul. "Dad?"

"Sit down and eat," Paul said.

Piper collapsed into her chair. "This is so not fair."

"Let's just see what happens tomorrow," Paul said.

Helen gave him a taste of the icy stare she had been giving their daughter.

"Maybe the storms won't come," he said.

Two hours after dinner, Paul went into the garage and opened the door, which revealed high winds blowing snow across the driveway, making it almost impossible for him to see the houses across the street. The light from the garage door opener cast a dingy glow over the garage, which protected Helen's minivan, the snowblower, the lawnmower, and a snowmobile. Moving along the minivan, he stepped outside, where the wind staggered him, and grabbed the garbage and recycling totes. He turned his back to the wind but snow still wrapped around him. He pulled the totes inside the garage and pressed the button on the wall. The door rattled shut and he stood listening to the wind howling outside. Then he closed his fingers around the handle of the snow shovel and went inside.

Paul emerged from the basement stairway into the short hall outside the downstairs bathroom. He leaned the snow shovel against the wall, kicked snow off his boots, and took them off. They thudded on the floor and he moved them onto the plastic mat near the coatrack. He peeled off his layers of winter wear and heaped them over the rack, then carried the shovel into the living room, passing Evan, who sat on the sofa watching television.

"What are you doing with that?" Evan said.

Paul opened the door to the foyer and leaned the shovel against the closet door, next to the front door. "Putting this where we'll need it." He closed the door. "Make sure you turn all the lights off before you come up."

"Okay."

Paul climbed the stairs and knocked on Piper's door before opening it. She sat on her bed, shoulders against the headboard, texting on her phone.

"Good night," he said.

"Good night," Piper said in a tight voice.

"Don't stay up too late."

She rolled her eyes.

Shaking his head, Paul closed the door and went into the bedroom he shared with Helen, who crossed the room and hung clean clothes in their closet. She wore a long peach-colored nightgown.

Paul closed the door behind him, pushed the button lock in the knob, and stripped. "Who is that person in the next bedroom?"

"Your daughter."

He tossed his discarded clothes into a hamper and pulled on a pair of flannel pajamas Helen had left on the bed. "Are you sure about that? I remember when we were her favorite people in the world."

Helen circled the bed and got under the covers. Paul flipped the light switch and climbed under the covers with her, the digits of the alarm clock glowing red behind her. Lying on his back, he rubbed his feet together for warmth and she snuggled against him. Light from the streetlight outside glowed through the narrow slats of the blinds.

"Do you think they've done anything yet?" Paul said in the darkness.

"Who?"

"Piper and Brian."

Helen hesitated. "Do you want to know?"

Paul sighed. "I don't if the answer's going to be yes."

"Evan will be next."

"I'm not worried about that."

"Of course not. Men."

"It will be a long time before he's a man. Piper's growing up so fast."

"That's what women do." She kissed him. "Relax. I don't think she's done anything serious."

He felt better.

"Yet."

A snowplow rumbled by outside, casting yellow strobe light into the bedroom.

SEVEN

February 13

Throughout the early morning hours, the residents of Cayuga Island, Black Creek Village, and Niagara Falls listened to the wind wailing outside their homes, rattling windows and blowing tree branches against the siding. Snow had not begun to fall, but the ferocious wind blew the existing snow across yards, sidewalks, and streets.

At 1:30 a.m., standing in the doorway of the house that served as the management offices of the Vincenzo Senior Homes, Will lit a cigarette and did his best to exhale the smoke outside. The clouds of snow blowing across the drive prevented him from seeing the houses on the other side. He did not relish the thought of making his rounds. The main office door opened behind him, causing him to flinch.

Adele emerged from the office, wearing her coat.

He moved to discard the cigarette. "Sorry."

"That's all right." She moved closer to him. "Can I have one?"

He tried to hide his surprise. "Sure." He took out his pack and withdrew a cigarette for her, which she slid between her lips. He took out his lighter and lit it.

She moved into the doorway and exhaled. "It's going to be a long night. Ramy called in sick."

He took a drag on his cigarette. "At least you get to stay inside."

"You should stay in too."

"It doesn't work like that."

She moved closer to him. "No one should be out on a night like this. Keep me company."

Will could not believe this was happening. After all these months. Knowing that if he looked away the spell would be broken, he held her gaze. "Okay."

She smiled. "I'm just kidding. I'll keep the coffee hot for you, though."

His heart sank and he changed the subject to hide his embarrassment. "I hope we can get our cars out. It would suck to be trapped here."

"Yeah."

Three apartment houses down the drive, Denise Hornsby awoke with a start. Wind whistled outside her bedroom window. Groping in the darkness, she located her eyeglasses, put them on, and turned to the window, half expecting to see the Peeping Tom gazing in at her once more. But after the previous incident, she had closed the curtains. Faint light gleamed through the pink fabric, broken up by the shadows of tree branches and nothing else. Leaving her glasses on, she laid her head back on the pillow and closed her eyes.

BLACKcreek

Officers Gigi Brown and Lou Bescaglia patrolled Black Creek Village in relative silence, listening to the calls on their car radio. The wind shook the patrol car from side to side, and Lou drove under the speed limit. As they passed 95th Street, the darkness of the containment field ahead on the right engulfing the surrounding light like a black hole, Gigi glimpsed a figure running across the street behind them.

"Hold up," she said.

Lou slowed to a stop. "What?"

"Back up."

Lou reversed the automobile to 95th. Gigi peered out her window at the long, dark road and the field that separated it from the Vincenzo Senior Homes.

"What is it?" Lou said.

"I thought I saw someone running across the street."

"Maybe it was that Peeping Tom again."

"Exactly what I was thinking."

"I'm kidding."

"I'm not."

"You really want me to go in there again so you can find out?"

Gigi narrowed her eyes at the terrain. "No. I don't see anything now. Must have been my imagination."

But as the car moved forward, she found herself searching the darkness beyond the fence surrounding the containment field.

Korbel bolted upright in the middle of the night and felt disoriented: the air in the room did not feel like that in his bedroom. As the wind roared outside and the front bushes smacked the porch windows, he remembered he had slept on the sofa in the living room on the chance Skipper would come home and he would hear him. He settled back on the sofa. He missed that damn dog. Listening to the wind, he fell asleep.

Henri Metzger sat in his chair with Panzer asleep on the floor beside him. He cleaned his Winchester hunting rifle while *Warkill*, an old Montgomery George movie he had seen many times, played on TV. A Japanese soldier had just staggered out of a cave screaming with a rat gnawing on his neck when a snowplow passed the house, splashing a yellow warning light on Henri's window. As far as he could tell, snow hadn't fallen yet; the wind just kept blowing what was already out there. He would have to get up early in the morning and start blowing. Recalling the blizzard of '77, he knew he was prepared for Snowzilla: he had enough food stocked to last him and Panzer a month.

Part of him hoped for the worst. He was retired and didn't have to travel anywhere, so what did he care? Let the storm come. He wanted to see how his neighbors fared under difficult conditions. Teachers. They didn't know the meaning of real work, and with their soft hands they sure didn't know much of anything about survival. Especially those darkies next door.

The screen turned black.

"What the hell?" The motion of Henri rising caused Panzer to look up. "Ah, Jesus Christ!"

He could survive without a lot of things, but satellite TV wasn't one of them. He reached for both of the remotes he needed to check for service, but before he had a chance to do anything with them, the picture came back on. He sat once more.

"False alarm, Panzer. Probably a Jap satellite dish."

Dan awoke to the sound of the snowplow on the street. Its first pass had stirred him, and now its return trip on his side of the street brought him fully awake. He glanced at the alarm clock, which showed 3:06 a.m., and wondered if the snow had started yet, but he didn't care enough to get out of bed and look out the window. Since he did not work, the only challenge the coming storms posed to him was snow-blowing his driveway and the sidewalks. He waited for the roar of the plow to subside and closed his eyes.

Embattled by the wind, Will ran across the drive to the office building of Vincenzo Senior Homes. He wore his scarf wrapped around the lower half of his face like a bandit, and he squinted to protect his eyes from the dusty snow. His legs turned numb and felt naked. Scrambling through the snow that had blown onto the front walk, he took out his keys, unlocked the door, and staggered inside, where he slammed the door and entered his code into the alarm keypad. He took a moment to recover, then moved toward the office door, pulling off his gloves.

Heat greeted him as he entered the office and pulled off his hat. Tossing it onto an unoccupied desk near Adele's, he unzipped his ski jacket. "It's freezing out there—below zero. Nice and warm in here, though."

"I raised the temperature to seventy-eight," Adele said, scanning a weather report on her monitor.

"Breaking the rules. I like that."

"Tonight's a special case. I made fresh coffee while you were out. Is everything okay?"

He rubbed his hands together. "Yeah, sure. Mr. Resnick just needed help finding his glasses so he could take his meds."

Adele stood and moved closer to him. "It occurred to me while you were out there—we really could get stuck here. Just like we got stiffed tonight, no one might make it in tomorrow."

Will sighed. "That would suck."

For the second time that shift, she moved close enough for him to smell her perfume. "Maybe we should find a way to make the best of it."

He tried not to swallow. "Yeah, sure. What do you have in mind?"

She moved still closer, and he felt her breath on his lips. "Nothing serious."

He knew that if he hesitated, she would just say she was joking again, but if he kissed her she could claim sexual harassment, and he needed this job.

She kissed him. Softly at first, then with greater passion. He responded, sliding one hand around her waist and his tongue inside her mouth. When she pressed her breasts against him he knew he had made the right decision. They stood there kissing until Adele stepped back.

"Why don't you take that coat off and stay awhile?" she said.

Will took off his ski jacket and tossed it onto a desk. Adele walked to a wall switch and turned off the overhead fluorescents. Only the lights from her monitor, the surge protectors, and various instruments illuminated them. When she returned to Will, she peeled off her sweater, and when she kissed him again he slid his hands up her bare back to her bra strap, which he managed to unhook without too much difficulty.

Helen's eyes opened and she stared at the shadows of tree branches on the ceiling. Paul snored beside her. The steady sound had awakened her, and now the howling wind kept her awake. She rose from bed, careful not to disturb her husband, and went to the window, where she twisted the wand control for the blinds, opening them. Below, snow had filled the driveway and drifts had moved across the front lawn like frozen waves. The wind blew steady gusts of snow along the street, obscuring her view of Henri Metzger's house. A branch from the young oak tree growing at the corner of the Goodmans' house struck the window like a clawed hand, causing her to flinch and suck in her breath. Exhaling, she smiled and closed the blinds.

She exited the bedroom and used the bathroom, then entered Evan's room. He slept with the door open and the covers half off, and Helen drew them over him and kissed him on the cheek. Then she went into Piper's room, which required her to open the door. Her daughter slept on her back, her breasts rising and falling, a reminder to Helen that she was no longer a girl but a young woman. Helen moved to the window facing the backyard and opened its blinds. Beyond the flat roof below the window, which extended over the kitchen and dining room, moonlight reflected off the snow, causing it to glow, and in turn illuminated the trees. She hoped the rabbits under the shed were okay.

Returning to her own bedroom, Helen climbed back into bed with Paul and rolled him over so he would stop snoring.

Naked, Adele lay back on her desk with her knees raised and her feet at the edge of the desk. Will stood naked as

BLACKcreek

well, and he leaned over her, continuing to kiss her. He cupped her breasts, her nipples erect in the cold. Then he straightened up and entered her. Adele squealed, biting her lower lip, and pulled him closer to her. They studied each other's eyes, difficult to see in the faint glow of the screen.

"More," she said.

He pushed harder, and she squeezed his buttocks, her fingernails digging into his cold skin.

"*More.*"

Will pushed harder and faster, trying not to get too excited. Adele turned her head from side to side, moaning as perspiration formed on her chest. She flailed one arm, and a label printer fell off the desk and clattered onto the floor.

"Wear a rubber," she said.

Grunting, Will pulled out, using the opportunity to calm down. His skin felt damp in the cold air as he searched the floor for his jeans. Adele raised herself to her elbows and giggled.

"What's so funny?" Will said as he located his jeans and picked them up.

"You're still wearing your socks."

"You're damned right I am—this floor is freezing."

He pulled his wallet from his jeans, dropped them, opened the wallet, and took out a foil-wrapped condom.

"How long has that been in there?" Adele said

"Not long," Will said with a wry smile.

"You sure?"

He grinned. "I'm sure."

By the time Will returned to the desk, his erection had wilted.

"Aw, what happened?" Sitting up, Adele closed her fingers around the shaft of his penis and tugged on it, her eyes locking on his. "Let me take care of that."

Will would have preferred a blowjob, but his penis grew stiff again. Smiling as if she had read his mind, Adele lay back again. This time, instead of raising her knees, she bent them sideways, forming a diamond with her legs as she thrust her pelvis in a playful manner. Will tore open the foil pack, pulled out the condom, and unrolled it over his penis. Adele spread her arms.

"Hurry up. It's cold."

Will reentered her and welcomed her embrace, then resumed pushing. He had just found his rhythm when the telephone rang. Adele craned her head to look at the phone.

"Don't answer it," Will said.

"I have to." Adele lifted the phone from its cradle. "Vincenzo Senior Homes. How may I help you?"

Will continued to thrust into her.

"Hi, Sharon."

Will tried to block the middle-aged supervisor's round face from his mind.

"I'm . . . on the floor, checking the connections to my monitor."

Will gritted his teeth.

"Um, the screen keeps blinking off. Right. Okay, I will."

Turning his head, Will increased his speed.

"Really? Are you sure? I guess we don't have any choice then."

Adele tried to hang up, but she fumbled the move and dropped the phone on the desk. Will snatched it up and slammed it down, then drove himself harder into Adele. She smiled, rediscovering her pleasure, when a tremor ran through Will's body and he ejaculated.

Adele's smile faded. "You're kidding, right?"

Will's chest heaved as he pulled out. "Sorry. You fell behind when you took that call."

Adele sat up. "Good thing I did. Sharon would have been pissed. It's just like her to call at 4:30 in the morning."

Will flicked the light switch and grabbed a roll of paper towels to clean himself. "What did she want?"

The fluorescents flickered to life as Adele slid off the desk. "What do you think? There might be a travel ban tomorrow. If there is, she isn't coming in. What can she do, right? So I could be stuck doing a double *and* I didn't get off."

"She ruins everything."

Adele snorted. "You got that right."

"You want to try again later?"

She picked up the fallen label maker. "No, thanks. I've got too much work to do."

"Another night, then."

She looked at him. "We're never going to have this place to ourselves like this again—I hope."

Will pulled up his briefs. "Someplace else, then. Your place. Mine. After dinner, or a movie."

She got dressed. "You mean go on a date?"

He shrugged. "Yeah."

She cocked her head. "Maybe. I'll think about it."

Will pulled on his jeans. "Great."

A great thumping sound caused Denise Hornsby to awaken with a flinch. It sounded as if a tree had fallen against the outside of the house. Staring at the window, she listened to the wind howling outside. Had the wind snapped a limb off the tree? Her heart skipped a beat and she held her breath. She turned on the light, which dispelled any shadows on the curtains, then climbed out of bed and made her way to the window.

Standing before the curtains, she listened to the wind for a good while. She did not believe her prowler had returned, but fear crept into her body nevertheless. Taking a deep breath, she reached for the curtains until she felt the fabric in her gnarled hands and tugged them apart. Through the swirling snow kicked up by the wind, she glimpsed the darkened house next door, a good fifty feet away. Had any of the residents there heard the same sound she had?

The night exploded, pieces of the darkness hurling at her and cutting her face. Only when two powerful hands seized her frail biceps did she realize enormous fists had punched through the window. Then a powerful force lifted her off her feet and jerked her through the opening, jagged pieces of glass slicing her flesh and nightgown. Freezing air gripped her. Her eyes registered a hulking figure covered in fur, and then the snow on the ground rushed toward her. Brittle snow filled her open mouth and pressed against the lenses of her glasses, and the last thing she heard was the sound of her neck snapping.

EIGHT

Paul's eyes shot open. His body usually woke at 5:45 a.m., just ahead of the alarm, but he had gone to bed intending to get up early to get a head start on snowblowing. He looked at the clock: 5:16 a.m. Outside, someone else's blower droned already. Henri, no doubt. Easing Helen's arm from his chest, he sat up, threw back the covers, and got out of bed. She rolled over, turning her back to him in an effort to escape the sudden influx of cold air beneath the covers. He opened the blinds enough to look outside. The snow had still not come, but the wind had re-formed the terrain below, and his driveway had disappeared in a sea of whiteness. The wind continued to blow, and sure enough, Henri struggled with his blower across the street. A plow drove by, blasting snow at the mouth of his driveway, and Paul suppressed a smile as the man's body stiffened with anger.

Closing the blinds, he garbed himself in layers, then went downstairs. In the living room, he drew open the drapes and gazed at the bleak world outside. Through the blowing snow, he could not see the river beyond the houses across the street. He turned on the TV and lowered the volume. As he had expected, the local news had taken over the airwaves. A weatherman, almost unrecognizable beneath his protective clothing, stood outside city hall in downtown Buffalo. His clothes rippled and snow blew between him and the camera.

"Folks, don't fool yourselves into thinking that we somehow managed to escape these storms. All three are late to the party, but they're heading our way and are expected to arrive by noon. The governor has already ordered all of the major highways and thruways closed, and a travel warning is in effect. All incoming and outbound flights from Buffalo Niagara International Airport have been canceled until further notice, which you can imagine is causing quite a stir over there, and Niagara Falls International Airport is closed. The temperature is eight degrees below zero, and it isn't going to get any warmer, so stay indoors. I repeat, stay indoors."

Paul did some trunk twists and light stretching, then started a pot of coffee and pulled on his winter gear. The garage felt colder than it had the night before, and as the door rumbled open, snow blew inside. Pushing the snowblower forward to the edge of the garage, Paul heard the steady chugging of other machines. His neighbors shared his idea of clearing their driveways before the storms touched down, however insignificant that effort might prove in the greater scheme. Paul primed the engine and pulled the starter cord until the machine roared to life. Then he powered the blower into the snow that filled the driveway.

BLACKcreek

Lou steered the patrol car through the streets of Niagara Falls in a blighted area not far from the Seneca Niagara Casino, just minutes from the Falls. He and Gigi had already received word they needed to pull a double shift for storm support. As he turned the corner onto a side street, passing an Italian restaurant, Gigi leaned forward in her seat.

"Pull over," she said.

Lou pulled over to the snow drift covering the curb near the rear parking lot of the restaurant. "What is it?"

"Vagrant."

Lou zeroed in on a large cardboard box near a Dumpster. "Oh, for Christ's sake."

"Let's go."

Gigi got out before Lou could protest, so he had no choice but to get out and follow her.

"Son of a bitch," he said as the cold enveloped him. "Maybe he's dead. If he is, he can stink up the meat wagon instead of our car."

"You're a real humanitarian," Gigi said.

"If he's dead, we also get to go back to the station and fill out a report and get out of this. If he's alive, we have to haul his ass to a shelter."

The snow crunched under their feet. Gigi reached the Dumpster first. Lou saw the shapes of legs beneath a blanket protruding from the box.

"Hello?" Gigi said.

No one answered.

Lou joined her. "Hello? Police."

Gigi grabbed the box and pulled it, but the weight of its occupant held it down.

"Come on out of there," Lou said.

A faint moan rose on the wind. Gigi looked at Lou, who moved forward, seized the box in both hands, and tore the top in half. The tear veered off at an angle, and he had to tear it again. The box separated, revealing a man huddled beneath. He had covered himself with old newspapers, which his crossed arms held in place over his chest. At his ankles sat two shopping bags filled with filthy items that appeared charred. The man wore a dirty red cap pulled over gray hair, and his eyes blinked but he seemed to be looking at the sky, not at the police officers. His matted hair formed a single dreadlock that reached his knees.

"How are you feeling?" Lou said.

The man's lips parted and a moan escaped them.

"Sir, can you walk?" Gigi said.

Another moan.

Lou looked at Gigi, whose eyes reflected concern. The man probably had frostbite. Lou took his radio from his belt. "Dispatch, this is unit one-four, over."

"Go for dispatch, unit one-four."

Lou told the woman their location. "We have a vagrant in the parking lot who looks like he's been outside all night. Probable frostbite. Send an ambulance. Over."

"Copy that, over."

Lou reattached his radio to his belt. "We're going to get you some help, old-timer."

The man moaned again.

"I'll get a blanket from the trunk." Lou headed back to the car.

Ken felt a nudge in his ribs.

"The baby's crying," Jenny said beside him.

The baby always cried, at least between midnight and noon. "So? It's your turn."

"No, it isn't."

Ken checked the clock, then closed his eyes again. "I fed him at four. Now it's your turn."

Sighing, Jenny got out of bed. "You can't blame me for trying."

Ken had no trouble falling asleep again.

Jenny shook him awake. "We need diapers."

Ken rolled onto his back. "Why didn't you tell me that yesterday?"

"I thought there was another box."

Marcus gurgled, and Ken opened his eyes.

Jenny held the baby. "Is he wearing a clean diaper now?"
"Yes."

"Is there at least one other clean diaper?"
"Yes."

"Then wake me in an hour." He closed his eyes.

"It's going to take you that long to snowblow the driveway."

He opened his eyes again.

"You hear that noise outside? That's our neighbors taking care of business before things get worse. And when they are worse, you aren't going to be able to go anywhere."

Ken blew air out of his cheeks and sat up. His eyeballs hurt from lack of sleep.

Entering the house through the garage, Paul groaned as he removed his gloves. He opened and closed his hands, then rubbed his fingertips together.

Helen appeared in the doorway, wearing a robe and holding a mug of coffee. "Are you all right?"

"It's so frigging cold out."

"The kids are still in bed."

"Okay, then it's so fucking cold out."

"You didn't do Joanne's driveway."

"Helen—"

"It's her funeral today. Fran has to be able to get in and out of the driveway to pick Terry up and bring him back. Since we're not going . . ."

"I made a path from the street to the front door. That will have to do. I'm not going back out there anytime soon."

With a forced smile, Helen returned to the kitchen, leaving Paul to take off his coat and boots.

BLACKcreek

It took Fran twice as long as usual to reach Cayuga Island, and she lost control of the car several times. When she drove through her old neighborhood, she saw one man snowblowing his driveway, two houses down and across the street from her mother's. She started to turn in to the driveway when she saw only a path from the street to the front door had been cleared. She could not blame Paul Goodman for minimizing his volunteer work in weather like this. She honked the horn and waited. The front door opened and Terry appeared, wearing a long coat over a black suit. He made his way along the path, slipping and sliding in his shoes, his hands jammed into his coat pockets. By the time he opened the door and climbed inside, the wind had disheveled his hair.

"Good God," he said. "Now I remember why I moved away."

Fran stepped on the gas pedal, but the wheels spun. She rocked the car back and forth until the tires achieved traction and the car lurched forward. "No place is perfect."

"Where are Frank and the boys? Are they meeting us at the funeral home?"

"They're not coming. We decided it was better they stay home during this storm."

"Oh." Terry sounded disappointed.

"Hopefully you'll see the boys before you leave."

"Where are we going to eat?"

"I know a place not far from the funeral home."

"All the flights at the airport have been canceled. It will be a miracle if I get out of here tomorrow."

"At least you have a place to stay for free."

"Yeah, but if I'm not back Monday, I'll lose income. This isn't paid time off."

"I have a few hundred dollars to give you from Mom's account. She had me clear it out."

"That will help. Hey, what do you think we'll get for the house?"

Fran didn't want to discuss that now. "I don't know. Maybe eighty-five thousand. Maybe less."

"Split two ways, that's forty-two thousand dollars each."

Fran sighed. "Not exactly. Mom's will names me her executor, so I get an extra five percent off the top."

Terry looked at her. "You're going to take that?"

"I'll gladly let you do all that work if you want the extra money so badly, but it will probably mean having to come up here again."

"No, that's okay."

"Can we please just not discuss money today?"

"You're right. I'm sorry. I'm just trying to take my mind off things."

Driving over the bridge, Fran thought she glimpsed three figures scrambling through the snow covering the frozen creek below. At first she thought they were animals, because of their unnatural gait, but then she realized they were children, limping and shuffling from side to side. What the hell were they doing outside in this weather and on that creek? Then they were gone.

Adele stood bent over her desk with her slacks around her ankles while Will thrust into her from behind. She clawed at the desktop and turned her head away so Will could not see her face. The telephone rang.

"Don't answer," Will said.

This time she listened to him, and the phone continued to ring. Will drove her to orgasm, then felt an explosion. Laughing, Adele seized the phone and answered it, supporting herself with her elbows on the desk.

"Vincenzo Senior Homes."

Will slumped over her, setting his hands on the desk for balance.

"Hi, Jamie."

Jamie Mackelroy, Will's relief.

"Okay, I'll let him know. "

Jackoff Jamie.

"Bye." Adele hung up. "Looks like it's just you and me this morning."

Will straightened up. "Someone had better come in. We can't stay here indefinitely."

They cleaned up and dressed.

Will checked his phone for messages. The charge had died. "I'm going to run to the car for my phone charger."

"Okay." Adele fixed her short dark hair. "Let's have a smoke when you get back."

"Sure."

Bundled once more, Will exited the front office building and pulled the door shut behind him. The wind had blown snow into the walkway again, and he waded through it toward the main drive. A man in a pickup truck with a plow fastened to its front pushed snow from one side of the drive to the other. The sun would not rise for another half hour, and the sky seemed darker now than it had at nighttime.

Will traveled the drive rather than the sidewalk, the cold air hurting his lungs. He walked to the small staff parking lot at the side of the office house. The plowman had already cleared it. Only two vehicles occupied the lot: Will's Dodge Neon and Adele's Toyota Camry. Snow covered both vehicles. He brushed the snow clear of his driver's door lock, took off one glove, unlocked the door, and climbed inside the car. The temperature was as frigid inside the vehicle as outside, and vapor from his breath unfurled before him. He took his charger from the glove compartment, slid it into his coat pocket, and pulled his glove back on. He was not looking forward to working a double, but he needed the money for car repairs. As he walked back to the house with the wind at his back, he knew residents were waking, and he was going to be a very busy man soon. Maybe he could persuade Adele to make some rounds as well.

Adele! He could not believe he had fooled around with her twice. And he hadn't even needed to get her drunk. Maybe she really liked him. He looked forward to finding out. He hadn't had a steady girlfriend in over a year. As he neared the path his boots had made on his way out the front door, he stopped. Two houses ahead on his left, the curtains of a ground-floor side window flapped in the air. He could not imagine who would open his bedroom window in weather like this. Then it dawned on him who lived there: Denise Hornsby. He headed toward the house, concern building inside him.

BLACKcreek

Standing in his cluttered kitchen, Henri filled Panzer's dish on the floor with dog food, then made himself a cup of instant coffee. Panzer moved to the glass patio doors and wagged his tail.

"If I was you, I'd learn to use the toilet rather than go out in this."

He slid the door open and the dog ran outside onto the snow that covered the deck. Cold air raced inside, and Henri pulled the door shut. Panzer lifted a hind leg and sprayed one post of the deck, producing steam. Henri glanced at the Niagara River in the distance and his body turned numb. He could not see the opposite shore of the frozen river or sky anywhere: everything had turned solid white, and a wall of snow bore down on Cayuga Island. With his heart speeding, he shoved the door open again and Panzer gave him a confused look.

"Get in here!" Henri motioned for the dog to come inside. "Come on!"

Panzer trotted forward, and the wind increased, causing loose snow to rise from the ground. The dog came inside and Henri pulled the door shut. The immense wall of snow, as wide as he could see, advanced on the riverbank, and snowflakes swarmed like locusts on his property.

Will entered the apartment house and pushed the buzzer to Denise Hornsby's door. When she didn't answer, he pushed it again, reasoning that at her age the buzzer might not be loud enough to wake her. He used his key card to unlock the door and entered the dark apartment. Flicking on the overhead light, he keyed his code into the alarm pad, then unwrapped his scarf and took off his hat so Denise would recognize him.

The apartment was clean, which was the case with most of the units. Residents tended to move in with few belongings. He crossed the living room and entered the hall leading to the bedroom. The door was wide open, and even before entering he saw the empty bed. Walking to his left, he turned on the bathroom light, half expecting to find Denise in there. The bathroom was empty. When he entered the bedroom, he saw the curtains flapping outside like two flags on a pole. He turned on the light.

"Mrs. Hornsby?"

Circling the bed, he saw no sign of her, but shards of broken glass covered the floor. Someone had broken in. And then what? Taken her away with him? He remembered the Peeping Tom from a few weeks ago. None of this made sense. His eyes remained locked on the window as he backed out of the bedroom. He reached for his phone, then remembered its charge had died. Instead, he turned and ran.

Back inside after snowblowing his driveway, Ken used the bathroom and had a coffee.

"It's starting to snow," Jenny said in the living room as she breastfed Marcus. "You'd better go now."

Sighing, Ken stood. "Can you think of anything else we need? Anything at all. Because I'm not going out there again."

"Just Pampers."

Ken put his coat back on and zipped it. "Okay, get some sleep. I'll see you in a bit."

Using the side door, he entered the garage and got into his car. He used the remote control in the glove compartment to open the garage door, and as it raised, sunlight made it possible for him to see that the sharp edges he had carved out of the snow earlier with his blower had already disappeared. Keying the ignition, he set the radio to NPR. He backed out of the garage and closed the door, then backed into the street.

"There goes Ken," Helen said, standing at the picture window.

Paul joined her. "Where the hell is he going?"

"He's crazy, and so is Jenny for letting him go out."

As Ken pulled away from his driveway, he turned on his wipers. Big flurries. At least he had the street to himself.

"Here it comes," he said.

By the time he had completed the half circle around the island, the snowfall intensified and he decelerated. Within a minute, he found himself leaning over the steering wheel to peer at the bridge ahead. The view turned solid white, and his mind raced. Should he turn around or stop? If he stopped and waited, a snowplow might come along and crush him. He decided to proceed, albeit at a snail's pace, and try to turn around on the opposite end of the bridge.

"Easy does it," he said as he turned off the radio.

The car inched forward in the whiteout. Ken prayed he was still in his lane; a snowplow could easily ram him. He turned the wheel to the right just to be safe. The car lurched and bounced, and he knew he had veered off the road altogether. He stepped on the brake pedal, but the car slid forward—downward—and panic drove his heart faster as he imagined the creek below. The car stopped, blocked by the accumulated snow, but even as Ken exhaled, fresh snow slammed the vehicle from all directions.

NINE

When Will emerged from the apartment house, snow had begun to fall. The contractor had finished plowing and had disappeared, so Will was able to make better time running back to the main building. By the time he reached the office building, the snowfall had intensified. He unlocked the door and entered his code into the alarm pad, then ran to the office door, which he threw open. Adele rose from her desk as he ran inside and snatched the phone from her desk.

"What's wrong?" Adele said.

He pushed the buttons for 911. "Something happened to Mrs. Hornsby."

"What do you mean?"

"She's gone, and her bedroom window's broken."

Adele's face transformed into a mask of confusion.

"Police operator, where's your emergency?"

Will told the woman the location and address.

"What's your emergency?"

"One of our residents is missing. Her unit's empty, her bedroom window is broken, and there's glass all over the place."

"Do you wish to report a missing person?"

"Yes!"

"What's your name, sir?"

"Will Chance. I'm a caregiver here."

"What's the name of the missing person?"

"Denise Hornsby."

"Can you give me a description of the subject?"

"She's old . . ."

"Eighty-one," Adele said.

"Eighty-one," Will said. "Skinny, white, white hair."

"When was she last seen?"

"After dinner yesterday."

"Sir, an adult has to be missing for twenty-four hours before you can file a report."

"Look, last month we called you because she saw someone outside her window. You sent two cops then. Now that window's broken—there's glass everywhere. I think someone might have broken in from the outside and taken her. You'd better get someone over here now."

Adele opened her mouth.

The operator paused for what felt like an eternity. "Someone will be there shortly, sir."

"You'd better call in the FBI."

"Someone will be there shortly."

Will hung up the phone. "I hope they get here fast."

"Do you really think someone kidnapped Denise?"

"Kidnapped her or killed her."

"That's crazy. Who would want to kill an old lady?"

Will raised both hands. "I don't know! I just know what I saw, and I know there's no one here to help us."

Adele picked up the phone.

"Who are you calling?"

"Sharon. She's the supervisor, so she can get her ass over here and deal with this."

Gripping the steering wheel in both hands, Ken drew a deep breath and let it out. The front of the car was at enough of an angle that his chest pressed against the shoulder strap. One of the wipers had broken, and the other moved back and forth, pushing snow to one side only for more to take its place. At least the engine was still running. He looked out each window and saw nothing but white. He tried to remember where he had put his phone. His body stiffened. He had left it to charge while snowblowing the driveway.

"Oh no."

Snow continued to assault the car.

Henri stood staring at the patio doors with Panzer standing beside him. Snow packed against the glass, shutting out the early morning sunlight. The glass groaned against the pressure.

"Jesus," Henri said.

The tempered glass held, but the two kitchen windows exploded and snow blasted inside.

"Unit fourteen, this is dispatch. Over."

Gigi raised her hand radio. "Go for unit fourteen, dispatch. Over."

"We have a possible four-five-zero at Vincenzo Senior Homes." The dispatcher read the address.

"Copy that. Over." Gigi turned to Lou. "You don't think that's the old lady from the other night, do you?"

Lou shrugged. "We'll find out soon enough." He stopped the patrol car, did a three-point turn, and drove toward Black Creek Village.

"Here comes the snow," Gigi said.

Lou switched on the wipers. "We shouldn't even be out here now. We should be off duty."

"Think of the overtime."

The snow intensified as they reached the containment area.

"This is really nasty," Gigi said.

"We should have taken our second meal at shift change."

"We'd still be on the road. This would still be our call."

Lou turned left onto 95th. The view through the windshield turned solid white.

"Whoa," he said, slowing down.

"Jesus, pull over."

Lou guided the car to the curb. He stared at the whiteout. "This isn't good."

"Should we get out and walk?"

"In this? No fucking way. Do you want to get lost out there? We'll freeze to death."

"Turn on the lights. I don't want to get hit by a plow."

Lou activated the strobes atop the car. "Let dispatch know we're going to be delayed."

"Copy that."

Henri ran into the living room to escape the wind and snow blasting in his face, Panzer at his heels. He grabbed his coat and pulled it on, then his hat and gloves. He stood gazing at the snow filling his kitchen, then went into the garage, where he had plenty of wood. Shifting through the supply, he located two half-sheets of plywood and carried them inside one at a time.

"Get out of the way," he said to Panzer, who pranced before him.

He propped the first piece of plywood over one broken window, then took a hammer and long nails from a drawer and set to work.

Ken drummed his fingers on the steering wheel. He knew there was no reason to panic. He had driven off the road, must have slid down a sledding trail, and was stuck, but he had not reached the creek, and from memory he knew

149

scores of trees separated it from his car. He looked at the gas meter. The car had half a tank of gasoline. He turned up the volume on the radio to try to shut out the sound of the snow battering the car and reclined his seat to take the pressure off his chest. He would get some sleep and wait for a break in the storm.

"What the hell is taking them so long?" Will said, pacing the office.

Adele sat at her desk. "They're probably really busy with this storm."

"Too busy for a kidnapping?"

She rose from her desk chair and set one hand on his shoulder. "Come on, do you really think that's what happened?"

He felt himself getting angry. "What other explanation is there? Maybe a bear ate her."

She crossed her arms. "Gee, I don't know. Maybe her mind is in worse shape than we thought, and she went wandering off?"

He frowned. "What about the broken window?"

"I don't know. Maybe she broke it herself while she was outside?"

"She saw that Peeping Tom the other night . . ."

"*Thought* she saw a Peeping Tom. We don't know if that's true."

"Oh, man, what if there's some kind of Michael Myers running around the complex?"

"Preying on old ladies? I never saw a movie like that."

Will's jaw slackened as a thought formed in his mind. He snatched his winter gear from the desk and ran out of the office.

"Hey, where are you going?"

Will sprinted to the front door, pulled on his coat, and zipped it. Adele went after him.

"Will, where are you going?"

He pulled on his gloves. "There really could be someone out there."

"So what are you going to do? Find him and fight him, or take off and lose your job? Both ideas sound lame to me."

"I'm going to have a look around the grounds, is all. You get on the phone and start calling the residents, every single one of them, and make sure they're okay. Thank God there's no one else in Denise's building. That's probably why they went after her."

"Um, you're not exactly my boss. If anything, it's the other way around."

"I think we'd better get them all over here until the cops tell us it's safe."

"Where are we going to fit them all?"

Will opened the door, and the sight of the outside world caused both of them to stare. The blizzard had become a whiteout. Will knew he wasn't going anywhere, and no one was coming to them.

Stepping back, Henri admired his handiwork. Plywood covered both broken windows. Then he looked at the snow melting all over the floor. "Son of a *bitch*."

He walked through the house to his front door and took out the emergency snow shovel, which he carried back into the kitchen. He shoveled the snow, dumping it into the sink. When the sink overflowed, he ran hot water, melting it. Then he got a bucket and mop and set to work removing the water from the floor. Old Man Winter was not going to beat him, the prick.

Paul and Helen stood at the picture window, gazing at the whiteout that had engulfed the neighborhood.

"The governor has issued a travel ban throughout western New York," the anchorman on TV said. "That means all travel is forbidden—driving, walking, even sledding—except for essential personnel such as emergency responders."

A faint yellow light, blossoming and fading, marked the progress of a snowplow on the opposite side of the street.

"Happy Valentine's Day," Paul said.

"Happy Valentine's Day," Helen said.

Smiling at each other, they clasped hands.

"Just kiss her already," Evan said from the stairs.

"Yeah, kiss her," Helen said.

Paul kissed his wife on the lips.

"I don't believe this weather," Piper said, blowing past Evan.

"Don't say we didn't tell you so," Paul said.

Piper dropped onto the sofa with her arms crossed. "What's for breakfast, anyway?"

"Whatever you and your mother feel like making."

"How about whatever you and Evan feel like making?" Helen said.

"I have to go out and do the driveway again."

"You're not going out there in this."

"It's a losing battle, but I have to fight it."

"You'll do anything to get out of cooking."

"I hate my life," Piper said.

"Yeah, thanks." Sitting at the second desk, Will hung up the phone.

"What did they say?" Adele said.

"The storm is making it hard for the cops to get around. 'Sit tight.'"

"That isn't hard to believe."

Will looked at the window. Snow covered it.

"People have to understand just how dangerous it is out there," the weatherman on TV said. "Lake Erie and Lake Ontario had six *feet* of snow on top of the ice, and the Niagara River and surrounding creeks were just as bad. Then these three storms converged, creating winds of up to *sixty-nine* miles per hour. All that snow has to go somewhere, and we're seeing the result now. It's the classic example of lake-effect snow."

"Heh, he said sixty-nine," Will said.

Adele picked up her phone and pressed a number. "Mr. Rackfort? This is Adele in the front office. How are you today? That's good. Yes, it is horrible weather. No, the shuttle bus won't be coming through today. Yes, the travel ban applies to everyone but police, firemen, and ambulance drivers. That's why we made sure all of you got groceries before the weekend. I want to let you know that we're short-staffed today. It's just Will and I, and right now we can't even get out of the building. We just want everyone to know we are here." Adele hung up.

"Expect this to continue for three days," the weatherman on TV said, holding his microphone with one hand and keeping his hood on his head with the other.

"We're never going to get out of here," Will said.

"Overtime galore. There's food in the pantry and a working shower upstairs. As long as the heat and power stay on, we'll be fine." She picked up the phone and pressed another number. "Mrs. Boliek? This is Adele in the front office . . ."

Jenny snapped awake and Marcus stirred beside her on the bed. Without searching the house, she knew Ken hadn't returned home yet. Rising, she rushed to the window and opened the blinds. At first she thought so much snow had stuck to the window that she couldn't see through it. Then it dawned on her that the blizzard had intensified into a pure whiteout. Looking behind her, she saw it was past 10:00

154

a.m. She moved to the end table, picked up the phone, and called Ken's phone. His voice mail picked up.

"Ken, you've been gone more than an hour. Please call home and let us know you're okay."

After she hung up, she scooped Marcus in her arms and carried him downstairs to the living room, where she saw Ken's phone charging.

When Fran pulled into the driveway of the Bozek Funeral Home, a sheen of sweat covered her skin and her fingers ached from clenching the steering wheel. They had been halfway from the diner to the parlor when the storm had hit, and she had driven the rest of the way at five miles per hour. Thank God it was a straight shot. She made a left-hand turn into the parking lot and stopped the car.

"I have no idea if this is a parking spot," she said.

Terry looked over his shoulder. "I have no idea if the funeral home is still behind us."

Fran turned off the engine. "Are you ready to make a run for it?"

"As ready as I'll ever be."

"Take my hand when we get out?"

"Sure."

Fran pulled on her door handle, but the door wouldn't budge. "What the hell?"

Terry forced his door open, creating a curved impression in the snow. He got out, sank to just below his knees, and closed the door.

Fran saw a vague shadow as he circled the front of the car. The door swung open and he stood there.

"I don't think we'll be running anywhere." He held out a gloved hand.

Fran took it and he helped her stand. Her shoes sank in the snow, which clung to her calves up to her knees. "Oh, my God, it's cold."

Terry moved away from the car, pulling her with him, his face almost invisible through the falling snow. He slammed the door behind her. "Let's go."

They marched through the snow, Terry supporting Fran. Snow pelted them. Fran saw stark whiteness ahead of and behind her, as if they had ventured into some universal void. Terry walked ahead of her, pulling her along.

"That's the curb," he said.

Her left foot came down and stopped higher than her right. Freezing snow lashed at her face, and tears streamed down her cheeks. She wiped them away before they could freeze to her skin.

"Turn left now," Terry said.

The snow darkened ahead, taking on mass.

"The snow's just as deep on the stairs," Terry said.

The toes of Fran's right foot struck the concrete steps. Pulling Terry's arm with both hands, she climbed them. A glass door swung open and Terry pulled her inside the funeral home lobby. A whimper escaped Fran's throat as the door closed behind them.

"Oh, goodness," she said, patting down her hair. "That wind was fierce."

"I've never been through anything like that. I can't believe we even got here. That was some good driving on your part."

"Thanks."

A short man with an obvious toupee approached them.

"Good morning, Mrs. Kaminski. Mr. Wyler?"

Terry offered his hand. "Terry."

The funeral director shook his hand. "I'm Robert Bozek. I'm so sorry for your loss."

"Thank you."

"Well, I won't beat around the bush. This weather certainly is a predicament, isn't it?"

"It's a mess, all right."

"Quite honestly, I wasn't sure if you were going to make it."

"Well, why wouldn't we? This is our mother's funeral. I flew in from New York."

"I'm afraid burial is out of the question today and, if these reports are true, may be for some time."

"That's okay. I don't really want to stand outside during this anyway."

"Of course, we'll care for the deceased until burial is possible."

"I'm not sure how we'll even find Fran's car after the service in here."

Bozek's smile weakened. "Father Gibbens called, and I'm afraid he sends his regrets that he'll be unable to attend."

Fran looked at Terry.

"We're not going to have any kind of service at all?"

"This storm is an unfortunate development . . . an act

of God. The governor issued a driving ban, which the mayor reinforced. It's unlikely any mourners will be able to pay their respects. I'm terribly sorry."

Terry's own smile faded. "Yes, well, our mother can pass only once, can't she? We're paying for a funeral. The burial is one thing, but we expect a service."

Bozek glanced at Fran. "You have my complete sympathy in this matter."

"You also have our money or will have it."

"Of course, we'll offer the facility for an additional gathering when the burial is possible, and Father Gibbens will be sure to attend."

"All right," Terry said in a displeased tone.

"Won't you both come inside and make yourselves comfortable? Several people sent flowers. Your mother was well liked. Let me take your coats. I'm afraid none of my staff were able to make it in, but my wife is upstairs, making coffee and lunch for later. I don't think you'll be traveling anytime soon."

"That's very kind, Mr. Bozek," Fran said.

Bozek collected their coats and hung them on a rack, and they took off their hats and gloves and stuffed them into their pockets. The three of them entered the parlor, which reeked of fresh flowers.

"I'm at your service for as long as you're here," Bozek said. "Pay no attention to the time."

"Thank you again," Fran said.

Bozek offered a slight bow and retreated to give them privacy. Terry moved to the arrangement of plants and floral arrangements and looked through the cards. Most of the names meant nothing to him. He did recognize the name Goodman.

"Oh, look," Fran said. "Dan Bartkowitz sent flowers, and so did Jim Makowski. That's so nice."

Terry grunted. "What are we supposed to do with these, haul them home through this storm?"

"Oh, my. This one's from Henri Metzger."

"That old racist? Who'd have thought?"

"You just never know about some people. He and Mom lived on the same street for a long time. He came over to the house one day when I was there. He seemed really upset about Mom's condition."

"Probably just because he knows his time is coming too."

"Let's look at the casket."

Terry walked with Fran into the adjoining room, where Joanne's open casket resided on a pedestal. "Couldn't we have had a closed-casket ceremony?"

"I wanted people to be able to see her one last time."

"Fat lot of good that did."

They stopped at the casket. The corpse inside the box looked surprisingly like Joanne—a little more made up, a fancier hairstyle, but recognizable as a former human being.

"That isn't bad at all," Terry said in an agreeable tone. "Mr. Bozek is a master of his craft. Too bad we're the only ones who will know it."

Ken jerked awake with an explosive cough. He had no idea

if the storm continued to rage on, though he suspected that was the case. Snow covered the windshield and windows—dense snow, with no sunlight leaking through. The smell of gasoline hung heavy within the car. Carbon monoxide! He had left the engine running for heat and the radio, and the tail pipe must have clogged with snow.

He turned the ignition off and switched on the dome light, then pulled the door handle. Weight pressed against the other side of the door.

"My God." How much snow was there?

He threw his own weight against the door, and it opened a three-inch gap before grinding to a stop. Snow poured inside from above the door. He threw his body against it again, widening the gap by two inches. The snow poured over his arm and thighs. He threw his shoulder at the door again, below the window, and the gap increased by an inch. The next body slam produced no results, and the snow continued to pour inside. He could not squeeze through a six-inch opening.

Ken pulled the trunk lever and scrambled over his seat into the back of the car. He did not intend to die from carbon monoxide poisoning in his car. Kneeling, he lowered the partition separating the backseat from the trunk. The light in the trunk cast dim light over the assorted items there: an emergency car kit, a small army shovel, an empty Snapple bottle, a roll of paper towels . . . and a case of Pampers.

"Son of a bitch."

Shoving the items aside, he crawled into the trunk, then got up on all fours, forcing the trunk open and allowing snow to pour inside. He gulped fresh air, filling his lungs.

BLACKcreek

The snow had risen to trunk level, and the dense snowfall prohibited him from seeing more than a couple of feet. Clutching the army shovel, he twisted a ring on the end, raising the blade into position, then shoveled snow away from the outer trunk, his motions like those of a man paddling for his life. He dug out around the bumper, then reached down for the tailpipe and used two fingers to dig out the snow. Unable to see inside the pipe, he forced the shovel down and drove its handle into the pipe and pulled it out. Gasping, he backed into the trunk, then slammed it shut to escape the bitter cold.

When he climbed back into the backseat, his knees and shins were wet. He brushed the snow off the front seat, then got comfortable on the passenger side so he wouldn't get his butt wet too. His breath formed before him. Starting the ignition again, he cranked the heat. The snow was not letting up. He honked the horn long and hard, and continued doing so, praying someone would hear his call for help.

TEN

Brian lay awake in bed listening to the wind for almost an hour before he rose. Drawing back the curtains hanging over his window, he stared at solid white through the icy sheen on the glass. The sight did not fill him with optimism about getting Piper over to the house anytime that day. The thought of rescheduling for Sunday made him anxious, because the possibility existed that his parents might come home early. He wandered into the living room and drew open the drapes, unveiling the storm outside. Rooted to the spot, he searched for any break in the sheet of white. As far as he could tell, the falling snow raced past the picture window at a horizontal angle.

Picking up the remote controls from the coffee table, he powered on the TV and selected a local station. The weatherman stood superimposed over footage of Buffalo. The city was almost invisible through the snow.

"As you can see, I'm warm inside the studio," the weatherman said. "That's because the heavy snow, strong winds, and subzero temperatures have made it virtually impossible for our cameras to pick up an image outside, unless you want a close-up of my smiling face. The entire

Buffalo Niagara region is shut down. The governor has issued a travel ban, and at the moment, even fire, rescue, and police services are frozen. Folks, wherever you are, stay indoors. I repeat, do not go outside. This has the makings of being the worst storm to strike our area in over four decades."

Shaking his head, Brian went into the kitchen and poured Raisin Bran into a bowl. The landline rang as he took a gallon of milk from the refrigerator. He set the milk down and answered the phone.

"Hello?"

"Good morning, champ," Ron Darcy said.

"Hey, Dad."

"Your mother wanted me to call and check up on you. We're watching the news and she was worried."

"I'm fine."

"I don't want you going outside for anything, you hear? Just stay inside and watch TV or play video games or whatever. I don't know when we'll be able to make it back. It could be a few days. We'll worry about the driveway then."

"Okay."

"Hold on. Your mother wants to talk to you."

Before Brian could say anything else, he heard his mother's voice.

"Brian? Don't worry, sweetie," Rose Darcy said. "You've got plenty of food in the house."

"I'm not worried, Mom."

"Turn the heat up just as high as you like—don't worry about the presets."

"All right."

"We love you."

"I love you, too."

Rose said good-bye and hung up. Brian added milk to his cereal and carried the bowl into the living room.

Helen had just served breakfast to Evan and Piper when the garage door closed and feet stomped on the floor. Paul groaned, followed by the sound of a zipper being pulled. He staggered into the living room and lay spread-eagle on the floor.

"How did you fare?" Helen said.

"It's impossible. By the time I finished my second pass, the first path I made had already filled in. The wind must have dumped three feet of lake-effect snow, and it's still coming down."

"Someone in Salamanca already suffered a heart attack while snowblowing, and no ambulance can get to him. I don't want you going back out there. Just leave it be."

Paul sighed. "You'll get no argument from me. Any other news?"

"Two snowplows in Niagara Falls got stuck."

"Great!" He leaned up on his elbows. "Remember the winter of 2014? Some streets in Buffalo didn't get dug out for two weeks."

"Two weeks?" Piper said, her eyebrows rising.

"Yes!" Evan pumped one fist in the air. "I don't want to go to school for two weeks!"

"How fortunate that you have two parents who are

teachers, one of whom knows the curriculum, so you won't fall behind in your work," Helen said.

"Aw."

"Ha-ha," Piper said in a bratty tone.

A phone rang.

"That's mine," Helen said. She went into the kitchen and picked up her phone, which showed a photo of Alice Hines, Tommy Burgess's divorced mother. She raised the phone to her ear. "Hi, Alice. How are you?"

"I'm a little distraught, Helen. I went into work at midnight, and my relief called in sick, so my manager wouldn't let me go home." Alice worked at the Seneca Niagara Casino. "I told him I'd stay long enough for him to find someone else, and of course now no one can leave, and no one can get in. Tommy's home alone."

"Oh, no," Helen said.

"I really thought I'd be home by 9:30."

Helen walked over to the back door, as far away from her kids as possible, and looked out the window. She saw nothing but ice and snow, as if the shed no longer existed. "Have you spoken to him?"

"Yes, I just got off the phone with him. He's terrified."

"He'll be fine."

"I'm not so sure. I promised him I wouldn't tell anyone, but he's been in therapy for a few weeks now."

A twelve-year-old boy in therapy? "Is everything okay?"

"He's been having really bad nightmares, and every night he tries to stay awake so he won't have new ones. He's been losing weight, and his grades are suffering."

"How long has this been going on?"

"It started right before Christmas. I've tried to get him to open up about it, but he won't say a word about what's got his stomach twisted in knots. Whatever it is, he's extra scared now."

Paul entered the kitchen and took a glass from a cupboard.

"I wish there was something we could do to help," Helen said. "But you see what it's like out there. Paul wouldn't be able to see where he was going, and the snow is too deep. Maybe once it lets up . . ."

Paul turned the faucet knob on the sink. No water came out. "Shit."

"I know you can't go get him," Alice said. "No one can. But he's so scared. I was hoping maybe Evan could call him, and they could play video games online? Just some activities to keep his mind off things. I'm stuck here, and they're not going to let me keep checking on him."

Paul opened the cabinet under the sink. "Goddamn it."

"Of course," Helen said. "And we'll keep calling him, if you like."

"Would you? That would be great."

"I'll text you updates."

"I appreciate this so much."

"Don't worry about it, Alice. We're glad to help." Helen set her phone on the counter.

"The pipes are frozen," Paul said. "Even after I left the pressure on. Who was that?"

"Tommy Burgess's mother," Helen said. "She's stuck at the casino and he's home all alone."

Paul opened the cabinet under the sink and looked at the pipes. "That's some great parenting."

Helen crouched beside the cabinet door. "She said he's been having nightmares, and he's in therapy. She's worried about him being home alone."

Paul came out of the cabinet, a concerned look on his face. "Then maybe she shouldn't have left him alone, especially at night."

"I don't disagree, but she didn't have much of a choice. She's a single mother, and you know how that place treats its employees. If she doesn't do what they want, someone else will."

Paul stood, held out his hand, and helped Helen up. "I feel bad for Tommy, but what are we supposed to do? Their house must be a quarter mile away."

"I know, I know."

"What's wrong with Tommy?"

They both turned to Evan, who stood in the doorway.

"His mother's at work, and he's home alone and she's worried about him." Helen held out her phone. "I'd like you to call him and make sure he's okay. Then I want you to play some games online with him."

Evan stood still.

"Is something wrong?"

"Tommy doesn't really talk to me anymore. I don't think he wants to be friends."

"Why is that?" She knew Evan had something to say.

He shrugged. "I don't know."

"How long has this been going on?"

"A couple of months, maybe."

Helen looked at Paul. "That's how long Alice said Tommy's been having nightmares."

BLACKcreek

Paul turned to Evan. "What was that incident in the school hallway the other day?"

"I don't know. That's what I'm talking about. He's been acting weird."

Helen took a step forward. "You don't have any idea what that's about?"

Evan sucked on his lower lip.

"Evan?"

"Me and Tommy went out to play with Grant after school one day . . ."

"How long ago?"

"The first day we had snow."

"Okay, what happened?"

"We went to the creek."

"You know you're not allowed to do that," Paul said.

"We didn't cross the bridge. We just played hide-and-seek in the woods."

Helen raised one eyebrow. "And?"

"I was it. Grant jumped out and scared me. Then Tommy screamed, deeper in the woods. He came running out of the trees. I thought he was joking at first, but when he ran past us, I saw how scared he was, so me and Grant ran too. When we caught up to him, he just got hysterical and ran away from us."

"You didn't ask him what happened?"

"He wouldn't tell us. He ran straight home, and things haven't been the same since."

"You should have told us about this before," Paul said.

"I didn't want to get in trouble."

Helen motioned with the phone. "Make the call, and

stay in touch with him for the rest of the day."

"He doesn't want to talk to me. Why would he want to play games with me?"

"Be persuasive."

Rolling his eyes, Evan took the phone and carried it away.

"What do you think that kid saw out there?" Paul said.

"I don't know. But I feel really bad that he's stuck in that house alone now."

"We've got problems of our own right now."

With Helen still beside him, Paul took his phone from his pocket and called Ken.

"Hello?" a woman said after the third ring.

"Jenny? Paul. I was calling Ken. Are your pipes frozen?"

"Oh. I don't think so. Let me check."

Paul tried the knob on his sink again even though he knew nothing would have changed.

"Paul?" Jenny said. "Yes, our pipes are frozen."

"Damn, I was hoping it was just me, because then I'd have reason to hope I could fix it. If your pipes are frozen too, then it's got to mean the whole area. The last time that happened, we had no water for weeks. Do you guys have bottled water?"

"We're good on water, but Ken isn't here. I feel so bad—I sent him out into this storm for diapers, and he hasn't come back."

"How long ago?"

"Over two hours."

"He hasn't called?"

"He forgot his phone."

Paul knew that if Ken was anywhere with other people, like in a store or even a traffic jam, he would have called. "I'm sure he's fine. Let me know when you hear from him, okay?"

"Sure."

Paul hung up and looked at Helen, who stood waiting for an explanation.

"Ken's out in this storm somewhere, without his phone."

"Oh, my God."

Dan sat in his chair, rubbing Trapper behind his ears. On TV, the local anchors looked at the camera with grave expressions.

"If you're not happy to be stuck at home, imagine how people who can't get home must feel," the anchorman said.

The image on the screen cut to the whiteout.

"Motorists going to Canada and coming into the United States found themselves stranded at the Peace Bridge, the Rainbow Bridge, and the Lewiston Bridge. The unhappy travelers had to abandon their vehicles and seek shelter in the Customs office, in the Duty Free, and at Tim Horton's. We're told over one hundred people are stranded on each side of the border."

Dan grunted. His phone emitted a beeping sound,

something he rarely heard—someone had sent him a text. He shuffled some papers on the end table, located the phone, and read the text from Paul Goodman.

Water pipes are frozen. Stay warm.

"Oh, damn it." Dan stood and walked to the kitchen, wearing his robe over his pajamas. Trapper followed. Dan twisted the knobs on the sink. No water came out of the faucet. "Oh, for Christ's sake, City of Niagara Falls." He looked at the dog, which sat at his feet. "No water, boy."

Trapper wagged his tail.

"It's a good thing we've got all that snow outside. Why don't you go out and get some?"

Trapper yawned, something he did when he was hungry, and Dan chuckled. He bent over to pat the dog on the head, but before his good hand reached Trapper's skull, a deafening crash upstairs shook the house, and Trapper sprang to his feet.

"What the hell?" He half expected the ceiling to come down on top of him. "Oh, what now?"

Dan ran into the living room and up the stairs to his closed bedroom door. He hadn't closed it. Turning the knob, he pushed the door open, and his jaw dropped in slow motion. The roof had collapsed, and broken two-by-fours jutted into the ferocious sky like jagged teeth, their ends vanishing in the blowing snow. Three feet of snow had filled the room, burying his bed and bureau. The wind assailed his face. He stood there a moment, absorbing the cold air, then closed the door.

BLACKcreek

Jim Makowski was in his kitchen preparing an early lunch of mixed vegetables when his telephone rang. He went into the living room and answered.

"Hello?" he said over the hum of a space heater.

"Hi, Dad."

"Hello, Faith." His disposition brightened.

"We're watching the news. We're worried about you."

"Oh, don't bother. I'm fine."

"It looks terrible there."

"Spoken like a true Floridian. Oh, there's a lot of snow, but I'm not going anywhere, and I have good neighbors. We'll look after each other."

"But you have power and heat and everything?"

"No water, but power and heat."

"Oh, Dad . . ."

"If I couldn't figure out how to melt snow, you'd have reason to worry, but I still have some common sense."

"What are you going to do if you get snowed in for a while?"

"The same thing I do now: watch the idiot box and read the good book. The one thing I won't be doing is snowblowing my driveway until the weather gets back to normal."

"Well, I'm glad to hear that. Do you have plenty of food?"

"Sure, sure. And candles and kerosene for the generator in case I lose power." A beep came over the phone. "Hang on a second, dear. I've got another call." Switching lines, he saw Dan's name and number. "What is it, you Polack?"

"My roof collapsed, you Polack."

"How did you do that, you dumb Polack?"

"I ordered a storm with extra snow."

"Well, that was dumb. No surprise. You'd better bring your jammies over here."

"What about my dog?"

"Tell him to bring his jammies too."

"You need anything?"

"No, no, I'm good."

"I'll see you as soon as I finish digging the tunnel."

"Right." Jim switched back to his daughter. "Faith, I'm going to have to let you go. I'm expecting guests: a dog and his Polack. I'd better clean up first."

"I doubt your place needs cleaning, but I'll let you go. Have fun with your friends."

"Thanks for calling."

"Take care of yourself, Dad."

"Roger, things are only getting worse in Buffalo and Niag-ara Falls," the newswoman on the radio said. "Most snow-plows have been recalled, and three are missing in action. According to the reports we're getting, the south towns like Silver Creek, Dunkirk, and Fredonia are buried. The governor's declared a state of emergency and is calling on the National Guard for help, but what can they do? They're as powerless as the police and fire departments. One thing is certain: people will remember this storm for a long time to come."

Switching off the radio, Ken glanced at the dashboard clock and pounded the steering wheel. He had been trapped in the car for three and a half hours.

"Damn it!"

He tried the surviving wiper, which parted the snow on the windshield only to have more snow tumble into the fresh gap. He could wait no longer. He put on his cap and gloves, wrapped his scarf around his face like a bandit, and pulled the passenger door handle. The door opened three inches.

"Not again."

Turning sideways, he jammed his heels against the opposite seat and pushed, using his body weight to force the door open. Snow poured in over his head and shoulders, and he groaned like a weightlifter achieving a new goal. The door ground against the snow. When he was satisfied he had created enough space for his body to escape, he jerked the keys from the ignition, shoved them into his pocket, and climbed into the snow, which pressed against him. Standing upright, he burst through the accumulated snow, free from his sternum down, but the falling snow pummeled him. Gazing at three feet of snow on the roof of the car, he closed the door.

Using the car as a guidepost, he slid toward the trunk, leaning into the powerful wind. Then he maneuvered around the trunk to the middle of the rear bumper. He took out the keys, unlocked the trunk, and removed the army shovel. Facing away from the car, he estimated the road was straight back, but without traffic sounds it was hard to tell. Taking a deep breath, he started forward, digging the shovel into the snow, which rose above his hips. The snow was heavy, both to lift and to walk through. Soon his arms ached and his lungs hurt. The wind pounded him, pushing him back and biting his face, and the snow stung him like hail. He had never tried to walk in such a gale force before, and he had not even gone ten feet before he collapsed face-first in the snow. For several seconds, he felt like a man drowning in a swimming pool. For all he knew, the road to the bridge was only another ten feet away. Groaning, he realized he could not make it. He turned around on all fours and crawled back to the car. Unable to see more than a few feet ahead of him, he followed the path he had created, his knees digging into the packed snow. When he reached the bumper, he pushed to his feet and moved around the car to the passenger door.

He found it harder to squeeze back into the car than it had been to get out, and he half collapsed over the seats. Sitting up, he pulled the door shut and brushed snow off himself and the seat. He switched on the ignition, sagged into the seat, then reclined it as he had the other. He drummed his fingers on his wet thighs, trying to remain calm, then bolted upright and pressed the horn again.

ELEVEN

Dan struggled through the snow separating his house from Jim's, a laundry bag stuffed with clothes slung over one shoulder and Trapper's leash clutched in his good hand. He wasn't worried about the dog running off but about getting lost in the whiteout. The wind slammed him from behind, pushing him down into the waist-deep snow. He had to toss the laundry bag in front of him to free his hand and push himself upright again. Wind roared in his ears and flung snow at him. He had boxed in the Navy, and he felt as battered now as he had many times in the ring.

Trapper did not bark, but Dan felt the animal pulling on the leash behind him. Dan scrambled through the snow, almost swimming as much as walking. His hand connected with something solid, and he knew he had reached the first of the bushes in front of Jim's picture window. Gasping, he tugged on Trapper's leash.

"We're almost there," he said, confident the dog heard him over the wind.

Jim's voice reached his ears, but he could not make out the words.

"Coming, Mother!" He fell over again, stood, stumbled, and swam.

"You should have brought a cane," Jim said.

Dan plowed forward, staggering into Jim's arms.

"Get in there."

Jim guided Dan to the front door, which Dan fumbled to open, dropping the laundry bag in the process.

"I got it," Jim said.

Trapper jumped ahead of Dan and pulled his owner inside. The house seemed dark even with a reading lamp on by Jim's reclining chair. Glancing at the dark TV screen, Dan still heard the wind after Jim closed the door.

"What took you so long, you Polack?" Jim said.

Dan wiped his nose on the sleeve of his coat. "Jesus, it's cold out there, you Polack."

"Language."

Dan got down on one knee and unhooked the leash from Trapper's collar, freeing the dog, who whined. "Why don't you have the news on?"

"It was on when I went outside to wait for you. The satellite must be covered."

Dan's knee cracked as he stood. "Then you'd better go out there and brush it off."

"You brush it off." Jim looked at the laundry bag. "What's in here?"

"Clean underwear and dog food."

"Trapper gets the spare bedroom, you can have the kitchen floor."

"I'm obliged."

"Come on, Trapper, let's go upstairs and get you settled."

BLACKcreek

Jim carried the laundry bag upstairs, followed by the dog, followed by Dan.

After lunch, Paul and Helen sat on the sofa watching television. Beside them, Evan played games with Tommy on Helen's phone. Piper sat alone on the loveseat, texting Brian.

"If you thought the drone footage of the falls was something, we have something that will really amaze you now," said the local anchorwoman on TV.

Photographs filled the screen depicting an immense wall of snow that made the city skyline beneath it look insignificant.

"That's the band of snow that has paralyzed Niagara County, Erie County, and parts of Chautauqua County."

"My God." Helen turned on the sofa. "But it's clearing up out there."

Paul turned as well. "That's still a blizzard."

"But I can see across the street now. Look—there's Henri!"

Narrowing his eyes, Paul made out Henri operating his snowblower in his driveway. The wind snatched the snow shooting out of the blower's chute and blasted it in a different direction. "If I ever needed proof of Henri's insanity, I have it now."

"He's just the old man and the sea."

"Something's wrong with my phone," Piper said in an irritated voice.

"Same here," Evan said.

Paul took out his phone and verified there was no signal. "The relay towers must be down."

"How am I supposed to text Brian?" Piper said.

"Try e-mailing him on your laptop," Helen said. "Or use the landline and call him."

Piper rolled her eyes and stomped upstairs. Helen turned to Evan. "E-mail Tommy. You can find a game to play on the computer."

Evan went over to the computer hutch.

"We just got a report that the roof of Cosentino's supermarket in Niagara Falls has collapsed from the weight of the snow," said the anchorwoman. "As many as sixty people were inside seeking shelter. Eleven suffered injuries, none of them serious, which is fortunate since no one can reach them to provide help."

"Do you think our roof's safe?" Helen said in a low voice.

"I think so," Paul said. "Don't forget, those supermarkets have flat roofs and those giant air conditioners."

"Thank goodness we don't live in a supermarket."

Sitting at the hutch, Evan worked the keyboard. "I got Tommy."

"Excellent," Helen said.

"Isn't it great that we get to spend time together as a family like this?" Paul said.

Helen chuckled, then jerked her head back to the window.

"What?"

"Henri isn't out there now."

Paul turned around for a better view of Henri's house. "Good. He must have wised up and gone inside."

"The garage door is open, and I don't see the snowblower in there. It must still be outside."

Paul narrowed his eyes. Panzer stood in Henri's picture window, barking and turning in circles. "I don't know how you can see inside that garage."

"My eyes are younger than yours."

"Maybe he went inside to take a leak and he's coming back out when he's done, or maybe he just needed to get warm for a few minutes."

"What if he had a heart attack?"

"You're overreacting."

"He's old, he chain smokes, and he's been out there all winter."

Paul stared across the street. The snowfall intensified again. "I don't see it."

In the picture window, Panzer pawed at the glass, still barking.

"Look at Panzer. Something's wrong. Henri may need help. I wish I could call Jenny—maybe she can see him from her bedroom window—but I don't even know her landline number. I'm going to e-mail her." She walked over to the hutch. "I need to get on there for a minute. Tell Tommy you're taking a short break."

Evan exited his game and reopened his e-mail. He keyed in a message, pressed send, and vacated his seat for Helen.

Paul leaned closer to the window as the wind picked up outside. He hoped to see Henri exit the house into the garage, but that didn't happen. By the time Helen returned to the sofa, the whiteout had resumed.

"Mom, you've got an e-mail!"

Helen hurried back to the laptop. She read her message and replied to it, then rejoined Paul. "Jenny can't see anything."

Paul gestured at the window in response.

"She still hasn't heard anything from Ken."

"Do you know how hard it's going to be for me to get over there?" Paul said.

"Not if you take the snowmobile."

"In zero visibility? That's even more dangerous."

She stared at him.

Frowning, he stood.

Sitting in the front seat of the squad car, Lou stuck a piece of gum into his mouth and chewed it. They listened to emergency calls come over the radio, and only in a few instances did officers respond to them.

"Give me a piece," Gigi said.

"It's nicotine gum. You were never even a smoker."

"I don't care. I need something to chew on."

He handed her a piece and watched her figure out how to tear open the small square package.

She popped the gum into her mouth and chewed it. "Not bad. It's waking me up."

"It's as addictive as cigarettes and costs more."

A rumble tore through the sky, causing Gigi to snap

her head toward the windshield. "What the hell was that?"

"Thundersnow," Lou said.

"Oh, Jesus, what next?" She faced him. "No one's coming for us."

"Nope."

"Then we have to walk."

Lou gestured at the windshield. "I'm not walking in this."

"That retirement community is less than a quarter of a mile away."

"And if we miss it, there's nothing else for a mile. We'll freeze to death."

"We'll freeze to death eventually if we stay here too, because we'll run out of gas." She looked behind her. "Colvin isn't a quarter of a mile away, and there are houses on the opposite side of the street. We're bound to hit something."

Frowning, Lou jerked on his door handle. The door would not open. He lowered his window, looked outside, then turned back, his hair covered with snow, and raised the window. "The snow is up to the door handle. We'd have to climb out the windows. Then what? Do you know what it's like to walk through three feet of snow? In subzero temperatures? With wind like this? We'll never make it. I won't, anyway." He slammed his palm into the steering wheel.

"What I wouldn't give to see a Saint Bernard with a barrel of brandy around its neck right now," Gigi said.

A rumble rose in the distance. Light flashed where the sky should have been.

"Thunder comes *after* lightning," Lou said.

Gigi leaned forward. The rumbling grew louder. The sound continued with no change in tempo.

"That's not thunder."

The rumbling became a roar. The light ahead blossomed and faded, backlighting the falling snow.

"Get out!"

Gigi lowered her window. "What about you?"

Lou slammed the horn with both hands. The roar bore down on the vehicle, splashing yellow light in their direction. Gigi scrambled out her window. Lou screamed, and then his world turned upside down.

"Susan, police and rescue units throughout Niagara, Erie, and Chautauqua counties are requesting that anyone with a snowmobile volunteer them for service," a reporter stationed inside Buffalo City Hall said. "Wherever you are, if you think you can safely make it to your local police station or firehouse, authorities encourage you to do so."

Eating chunky canned soup, Korbel watched the television newscast with glazed eyes. At least the governor had stopped talking from the safety of Albany. When the mayor's face filled the screen again, he switched the channel to Cartoon Network. Anything beat watching politicians cover their asses. He had given up on waiting for Skipper to come home. If his beloved dog had survived on his own until this morning, then this storm had surely killed him. The only hope he held on to was that someone had found the mutt and taken him in. But Skipper wore tags, and Korbel had left flyers in every store within miles. The thought that someone could have abducted his pet to compete in dog-fights occurred to him not for the first time, and he wished now that he had purchased a GPS tag for Skipper's collar.

A loud bang drew his attention from the television. It had sounded like thunder, only with a metallic echo, and he pictured two garbage trucks colliding. He rose, raced onto the porch, and looked out a window. He saw nothing, so he opened the door. Wind and snow rushed inside. Shielding his eyes, he peered ahead but saw nothing through the field of white. Probably just thundersnow, he supposed. Then a second, similar crash rose on the wind.

As Gigi climbed out the squad car window, the roar of the snowplow became deafening, and she sensed the vehicle's mass just beyond its hood. Planting her heels atop the door, she felt a great vibration through her heels. The wind blew her hat off and she leapt into space, unable to see the snow just a few feet below her. The sickening sound of a collision, the twisting and grinding of metal, echoed around her even as she dove headfirst into the snow. The ground seemed to shake as the snow swallowed her, and she thought she heard Lou screaming over the shrieking metal. The snow had an instant numbing effect on her body. Using her gloved hands, she pushed her upper body up, putting her weight on her feet until they touched ground solid enough for her to stand. Snow reached her hips, as if she were wading in a pool. She staggered forward, her face stinging, then turned around.

Snow rose from the ground at the same time it fell from the sky. The patrol car had disappeared. A boom echoed to her left, causing her to flinch, and she glimpsed the vague outline of an immense, shadowy shape. The snowplow, she knew. But where were Lou and their car?

She moved forward, raising her knees high, but she was unable to bring her feet above the snow. "Lou? Lou!"

Gigi tried to run, but the effort only served to bring her down into the snow, where she struggled to get up again. She developed a shuffling rhythm that enabled her to jog. Oh, Jesus, why hadn't she convinced Lou to abandon the vehicle earlier?

Panting, she reached the rear of the snowplow and realized it had turned over on its side. She did not hear the engine over the raging wind. Feeling her way along the underside of the oversized truck enabled her to move faster, the smell of oil, grease, and diesel fuel filling her nostrils.

"Lou? Lou!"

She circled the enormous blade on the front of the truck. She leaned against it, and hot metal warmed her hand. She reached the cab. The emergency light on its roof had ceased to flash. A spiderweb of cracks obscured the windshield. She punched her elbow through the upper corner of the decimated glass, which felt like hard candy. Sticking the fingers of both hands through the hole she had created, she pulled down on the glass, tearing it away like a large piece of cardboard. The driver of the plow looked up at her. Somehow, he had become pinned in the middle of the cab.

"What the hell happened?" Gigi said.

The man winced. "I got lost. My GPS wouldn't work in the storm . . ."

"You hit a cop car! Where did it go?"

He shook his head and blood seeped out of his mouth. "It flew past me . . . I swerved . . . turned over . . ."

Gigi leaned inside for a better view. A long metal stick shift disappeared into the man's belly, impaling him. He held onto it with both hands to keep from moving.

"Help me . . ."

She had to find Lou. "There's a medical kit in my car."

"Wait . . ." The man coughed and more blood came out of his mouth.

Gigi moved around the truck, peering through the whiteout. Her foot kicked something heavier than snow. Crouching, she picked up a handful of salt. The contents of the truck's payload had spilled out when it tipped over. She stood and searched the blizzard, then moved away from the snowplow in a direction that made sense to her. The snow reached her hips—then her thighs, then her knees. Something had cleared a path for her. A shadow formed, then a silhouette. The car came into view: upside down, dead silent, and low to the ground, because its roof had caved in and flattened out.

"Lou!"

Gigi circled the car to the driver's side. A left arm, lying in a pink puddle shimmering with shards of broken glass, protruded from the wreckage. The blood had melted the snow. Gigi sank to her knees, touched the lifeless hand, and vomited. When she had finished, she wiped her mouth on her sleeve and spat stomach acid. She rose on wobbly knees. There was no way she was getting the trunk open, let alone getting inside the patrol car. Reaching for her radio, she realized she had left it near her seat. She waded into the snow and made her way back to the snowplow in a daze, feeling nauseated. The same wind that buffeted her kept her from losing consciousness. Anger swelled within her: anger at the storm and anger at the snowplow driver. That anger dissipated when she reached the cabin of the truck. The man had slumped over, his arms dangling toward the door on the road.

"Mister?"

She raised his head and stared into lifeless eyes. She moved into the cab for shelter from the wind. A bright orange knit item had been stuffed between the seats. Taking it, she stared at the eyeholes of a ski mask. She pulled it on, exited the cab, and made her way through the maelstrom toward the street, her thighs aching and cold.

TWELVE

Helen, Piper, and Evan stood at the top of the stairs while Paul carried Piper's old pink sled up from the basement. He also held two ski poles and wore an orange snowmobile suit.

"You're kidding, right?" Piper said. "Why don't you just ski?"

"The wind will blow me over." He opened the door leading into the garage. "Besides, if Henri's out there, I may have to haul him back here on this. Mrs. Goodman, I'll need your assistance."

Entering the garage, Paul pulled down his ski goggles. Helen joined him, putting on her coat.

"If I can manage it, I'll check on Jenny too," Paul said.

"Please be careful."

Paul grunted.

"We have to make sure he's okay. Whatever else he is, he's our neighbor."

Paul pressed the wall switch and the garage door ground open, revealing the whiteout. The snow looked four feet deep, and some of it spilled into the garage. He walked over to the lever extending from the apparatus that opened the door and pulled to disengage it.

"Now I'll be able to open it manually when I come back. I'll be hungry. Maybe we should have an early dinner."

She gave his beard a playful scratch. "It's your turn to cook, so don't waste any time then."

Smiling, he carried his ride to the edge of the garage. "You're going to have to shovel the snow I knock over before you can close the door."

"I've shoveled snow before."

Paul set the pink sled on the snow, and the wind blew it sideways. He snatched its rope and pulled it back. "Whoa."

Helen joined him. "Do you want a push?"

"Nope. But you can hold this for me."

Helen held the back of the sled with both hands. Paul backed into the garage, then took a running start and dove toward the sled. He landed on it and his momentum launched the sled over the snow and into the wind. When the sled slowed to a stop, he grabbed the ski poles, drove them into the snow, and pulled himself forward. Behind him, Helen grabbed a shovel and scooped the fallen snow. Paul pulled the ski poles free, swung them forward, then drove them into the snow ahead of him. The garage door rattled down behind him.

It didn't take long for snow to cover Paul's goggles. He wiped them clear, then resumed his trip. Not that clearing them made any difference: he couldn't see more than a few feet ahead. The muscles in his arms grew tired, and he wished he had found more time for his swim workouts. He knew when he had reached the edge of his driveway because he saw the vague silhouette of one of the two trees that flanked it. Gathering the poles once more, he steadied himself, catching his breath. He didn't believe a snowplow would come through—none had been by for hours—but he preferred to be safe. Closing his eyes, he listened to the wind and falling snow. Hearing nothing else, he opened his eyes and pulled himself forward, crossing into the snow-filled street. This time he pulled the poles out faster, increasing his speed. The cold ate through the layers of fabric covering his body. Picturing the street without snow, he estimated five or six pulls should bring him to Henri's driveway, and another five or six should bring him to the house. He felt tired after four.

Kneeling on the sofa, Helen peered out the picture window.

"Mom, you can't see anything out there," Piper said from the loveseat.

"It doesn't hurt to try." Helen did not want to alarm her children by admitting she was watching for a snowplow.

The mayor of the city of Niagara Falls took his turn on TV. "We've received a number of reports of people in western New York suffering heart attacks while shoveling or snowblowing their driveways. Do not shovel or snowblow your driveway! What's the point? The streets are buried, so no one can go anywhere. And even if you find a way, the travel ban is in effect for drivers and pedestrians alike. Stay home, stay indoors, and stay safe."

"Does Dad think Mr. Metzger had a heart attack?" Evan said from the computer hutch.

"I don't know what he thinks," Helen said, regretting having sent her husband out into the deadly storm.

Paul was just beginning to think he had missed Henri's driveway when he heard a scratching sound beneath the sled, which slammed into the bottom frame of Henri's picture window. The impact echoed in the air and reverberated through Paul's body. He slid forward on the sled as it bounced backward and stopped on the other side of a bush. The tips of branches with pine needles protruded from the snow like tentacles reaching up from the sea. Gazing at his reflection on the glass, Paul chuckled—then recoiled when a snarling face with yellow teeth replaced his own countenance. Panzer must have leapt onto a sofa, lunging at the window in attack mode. Even through the glass and under the howling wind, the barking startled Paul. Setting the poles at his sides, he raised his goggles, then his hands.

"Easy, boy. It's just me." He liked the dog more than he did Henri and had patted its head more than once.

Panzer continued to snarl, his lips pulled back and his teeth jutting out.

"I'm just here to help."

Paul repositioned his goggles, retrieved the poles, and managed to turn himself parallel to the window. He pulled himself forward, harder now that he faced the wind. Snow struck his face, but instead of cleaning the goggles, he lowered his head and soldiered through the storm. His arms quivered and he groaned as he pulled himself past the front door. Relying on his memory, he angled himself toward the garage, and within seconds a dark rectangle appeared before him. He pulled himself toward the opening, then slid down a slope of snow into the garage, alongside Henri's pickup truck. The sled stopped on the concrete. He rolled off it onto his back and panted.

Raising the goggles, Paul focused on the crossbeams in the ceiling. Smelling oil, he sat up, allowing his arms to hang limp in his lap. Gardening equipment, tools, and broken furniture cluttered the garage. He got up, brushed snow off his legs, and walked to the garage door. The handle of Henri's snowblower protruded from the snow, which had almost filled in the path the man must have carved along the driveway. If Henri was on the ground, he was buried. Making his way around a desk turned on its side, Paul pounded on the door to the house.

"Henri!"

Panzer barked on the other side of the door. Paul checked the doorknob: it turned in his hand, but he was afraid to open the door for fear the dog might attack him. Instead he located a garden shovel and went outside. Standing in snow up to his hips, he prodded the snow with the shovel's wooden handle, searching for Henri. A piece of red fabric caught his eye. Using the shovel, he lifted a hat with earflaps and fur lining. Henri had worn the hat every winter day Paul had seen him. Something red marred the white fur lining.

Paul returned to the garage and set the hat down on the desk. Keeping the shovel in his hands for protection, he opened the side door. Panzer darted out, raced past him, and tore out of the garage, jumping into the snow and disappearing. Paul ran after the dog. Wading into the snow, he saw the dog leaping and running through an almost filled path that led to the backyard. Paul frowned. Had Henri gone out back? He followed the trench. At the rear corner of the house, he stopped. Panzer vanished in the falling snow.

Paul cupped his hands around his mouth. "Panzer!"

The wind howled in response.

"Panzer!"

Paul continued to follow the path for a dozen steps. It headed toward the river, and he knew that was where the dog had gone.

"Awkward," Terry said. He and Fran sat alone in the funeral parlor's viewing room.

"We should have postponed," Fran said.

"You're right. I'm sorry. I just wanted to see her off."

Fran touched his hand. "I understand."

Bozek entered the parlor and stood before them, his hands clasped. "You're both welcome to stay as long as you like, either here or in our family residence upstairs. Officially, the service has concluded. The weather hasn't improved at all, and the travel ban is in effect, so I encourage you to stay."

Terry looked at Fran.

"Frank will kill me," she said.

"What does he expect you to do? The roads are impossible."

"I agree," Bozek said.

Fran offered a weak smile. "You don't know my husband."

"We've plowed our parking lot and, since this is a main street, the city plows have been through, so at least you can get out of here. After that, I don't know."

"It's your call," Terry said. "I know I won't be back in New York City anytime soon anyway."

After conducting a thorough search of the sloppy house to verify Henri was not there, Paul filled a roasting pan with dog food and set it in the garage for Panzer, who had not returned. He lowered the garage door halfway, then set Piper's sled on the snow and climbed onto it. This time the sled sank into the loose snow, and he had a harder time getting started. But with the poles in hand, he pulled himself toward the Johnsons' house. For the first time since he had embarked on this trip, he had the wind to his back, and when he pulled himself forward he slid almost as fast as if he had been going downhill.

Neither Ken nor Jenny had left their garage door open, so he pulled himself over to the front door and pushed the doorbell. A few moments later, the inside door flew open and Jenny stood at the storm door. She narrowed her eyes, a quizzical expression replacing the look of hope that had just been there. Paul raised his goggles and her features relaxed.

"I can't open the door," she said through the glass.

Paul pointed. "Open the garage."

Nodding, Jenny closed the door. By the time Paul had managed to turn around, the garage door opened. He pulled himself over to the crest of snow that had risen against the door, and it collapsed beneath him, forming an instant cushion for his fall. The sled slid a couple of feet and stopped, and he rose.

Standing in the side doorway, Jenny activated the door closer.

Paul used the sled to scoop up fallen snow and toss it outside before the door closed. Removing his goggles and gloves, he joined Jenny, who stepped back from the door. Inside the basement stairway, he took off his gloves and rubbed his hands.

"Have you heard from Ken yet?"

Closing the door, Jenny shook her head. "Our landline just died. All I've got now is the Internet on my laptop. I'm worried."

"I'm sure he's fine."

"Then why didn't I hear from him when that was still possible?"

"You'll get your landline back soon. Everything is going to get better."

Inside, the baby cried.

"It's going to get worse before it gets better. The stories on TV are terrible. Come on in."

BLACKcreek

Stomping snow from his boots, Paul followed Jenny through the kitchen and dining room and into the living room, where she had left Marcus in a playpen. She picked up the baby and slid a bottle into his mouth, bouncing him.

"What are you doing out here, anyway?"

Unzipping his coat, Paul revealed a pouch slung over one shoulder. He unhooked the strap bag and held it out. "Diaper delivery. Helen has a collection of cloth diapers she uses for rags. They're all clean."

Jenny took the bag and set it on the sofa. "Thank you. Hopefully it won't come to that." She sat next to the bag. "You didn't come over here in this storm just to bring me diapers. Helen was worried about Henri. How is he?"

Paul sat beside her. He did not want to worry her with the truth, but he saw no choice. "He wasn't in the house."

"Was his truck there?"

"Yes."

"And his dog?"

"He ran outside when I opened the door. He's still out there somewhere."

"Oh, no. That dog drives me crazy with his barking, but I'll miss him if anything happens to him."

"Not Henri?"

She rolled her eyes. "That man's a bigot and a terrible neighbor. He doesn't speak to us, you know."

"I know. He's not a likeable fellow."

"But you came out in this to check on him."

"Helen's orders."

"I wish he'd move, but I don't want anything to happen to him."

"He must have left on foot."

"Without that dog? I can't imagine it." She bowed her head and her shoulders shook.

Paul touched her shoulder. "Listen: Ken is going to be okay."

Turning her face from him, she looked out the window. "I wish I believed that."

"I don't like the idea of you being here alone. Why don't you come over to our house? We've got room."

Looking at him, she forced a smile. "How would you get us over there?"

"I'll put you both on the sled and drag you."

"That doesn't sound like fun for any of us. Thanks, but I want to be here in case Ken comes home. Do you want some coffee?"

He stood. "No, thanks. I've got to get back. Do you have a generator if the power goes out?"

She shook her head. "Just the fireplace."

"Firewood?"

"On the side of the house."

"I'll bring some in just to be safe. Do you know how to light it?"

She nodded. "Have you ever seen an albino deer around here?"

The question caught him by surprise. "No. Why?"

"Because I did, a couple of months ago. Right out back."

He smiled. "I blame Hooker Chemical."

She returned a smile that did not convince him.

"Hi, Marcus." He rubbed the baby boy's head. Marcus looked at him but continued sucking his bottle.

BLACKcreek

"Thank you," Jenny said.

Dan and Jim sat at Jim's kitchen table, playing poker while the radio station WBFO updated them on storm news. Jim watched Dan studying the cards in his hand.

"For Pete's sake, will you make up your mind?"

"I'm thinking," Dan said. "It isn't easy playing with one hand, you know."

"Your hand's got nothing to do with your brain."

"Sure it does. The human brain sends signals to every muscle in the body. I ain't got none in my right hand, so those signals go unanswered and create confusion."

"That's ridiculous."

Dan shrugged. "Maybe if you'd let me smoke in here I could screw on my thinking cap."

"The one with mouse ears?"

"Don't be a hater."

"If you need to pollute your lungs, do it outside."

"You'd like that, wouldn't you?"

"I'd like you to play your blasted cards."

"It's okay if you swear in your own castle."

The doorbell rang and Trapper looked up from the floor.

"You expecting company?" Dan said.

"I was about to ask you the same thing. Maybe you invited the whole neighborhood over."

"Maybe I did."

Jim rose, though stooped over, and crossed the living room. He opened the foyer door, turned on the light, then opened the front door without stepping down. A man holding a pink sled stood outside the storm door. The wind jerked the sled and Paul Goodman braced his legs and pulled it back. Jim opened the storm door and Paul staggered inside.

"Did the mailman deliver my mail to you by mistake again? If so, you can keep it. You only got my bills last time."

"Can I borrow a cup of sugar?" Paul said.

"I don't keep any. Brings in the biggest damn ants I've ever seen. What did you do, use that fancy sled to clear the snow in front of my door?"

"I'm a teacher. They trained me to solve problems."

"Come on in."

Paul closed the front door, leaned the sled against the foyer wall, and stomped snow from his boots. Then he brushed it from his snowsuit and hat.

"Don't forget your beard."

Paul rubbed his beard. "That's ice—it will have to melt first." He unlaced his boots.

"Take those off inside so you don't get your socks wet. Lay them by the heater."

"That's mighty neighborly of you." Paul entered the living room and Trapper went over to him.

"Come to play a hand?" Dan said from the table.

Paul set his boots on a plastic mat by the heater and patted Trapper on the head. "I'm snowboarding home, kind of like the swimmer in John Cheever's story."

"Burt Lancaster," Dan said.

"Right. Helen sent me across the street to check on

Henri. One minute he was blowing his driveway, the next he was gone, with his blower outside and the garage door open."

Jim frowned. That didn't sound right.

"He's not in the house, and he left his dog inside. The driveway isn't clear, and his wheels are in the garage."

"Maybe he ran out of cigarettes," Dan said. "He'd walk through a storm like this if he ran out of smokes. So would I."

Paul shook his head. "I found a carton inside. The only tracks I saw went around the house and disappeared in the direction of the river. I wasn't about to follow them."

"Neither would I," Jim said.

Dan got a funny expression on his face.

"Anyway, when I went inside, his dog got loose," Paul said. "He did follow the tracks, and he didn't come back. Keep your ears open, will you? If Henri comes back he's going to be pissed at me."

"You don't think he's coming back?" Dan said.

"Something isn't right about this. Why would he leave his garage door open and that snowblower outside like that?"

"He loved that snowblower more than he did his wife."

"There's one more thing. I found his hat in the snow, near the blower. That one with the big flaps. It might have had blood on it."

"Either it had blood on it or it didn't," Dan said.

"Okay, it did."

Jim looked down. "That isn't right."

"Ken Johnson is missing, too. He went out in the storm this morning and hasn't come back. Jenny's alone with the baby over there."

"Boy, you're just full of good news," Dan said.

Jim set one hand on Paul's shoulder. "Thanks for letting us know. How about some hot tea?"

"I think I'll take you up on that."

"Have a seat, youngster."

Paul sat on the sofa with a groan. He pointed at the dark television. "You guys don't want to follow the news?"

"Cable just went out," Dan said.

"Jenny said the phone lines are down too. She was depending on her Internet."

"We still got the radio."

"True."

"My roof caved in from all the snow."

"Oh, Dan, I'm sorry to hear that."

"This winter just keeps getting better."

"Let us know if there's anything we can do to help. I mean it."

"I appreciate that."

Jim returned with a steaming mug on a saucer, which he set on the coffee table. "Here you go. Drink that down. I'll be right back."

Paul cupped his hands around the mug, warming them. "That's better."

When Jim returned the second time, he held two walkie-talkies. Sitting on the sofa, he handed one to Paul. "These are high-end radios. I want you to take one with you so we can stay in touch. We'll use channel three."

Paul looked at the radio. "Maybe I should take this to Jenny."

"Well, that's up to you. I feel bad for her. But I wouldn't

recommend making that trip again. You've got to get all the way across this dumb Polack's lawn just to get home, and you'll be going into the wind, unless you plan to stay here until it changes direction."

"Sure, stay and play a few hands," Dan said. "This dumb Polack won't play for money. I need some real competition."

Paul glanced out the window. "I can't. I have to get back. Helen will be worried." He sipped his tea. "I'll finish this, though."

Fran drove the Subaru at five miles per hour, with the wipers going full speed. She had turned off the radio and sat hunched over the steering wheel.

"This is worse than it was before," Terry said.

"I'm sorry, but I couldn't spend the night in a funeral home."

"It's going to take us an hour and a half just to get back to Mom's house at this rate. I think you should stay there—this isn't safe."

"I might do that. We'll see when we get there."

A circle of snow turned yellow in the distance.

"Watch out for that snowplow," Terry said.

"I see it," she said in an edgy voice. What she did not see was the road ahead or anything on the sides. She had no sense of her place on the road. And still the snow fell.

Another snowplow passed them, moving left to right. Through the falling snow, it might as well have been a battleship. Fran turned right and accelerated.

"What are you doing?" Terry said, his voice rising.

"That plow's getting on the LaSalle Expressway. We can follow straight to the exit near Cayuga Island."

"But the travel ban—if cops see us . . ."

"Who can see anything in this snow? We'll be right behind the truck." She slowed down when salt pouring out of the truck spattered the windshield. "See that? Now we're going a nice, steady twenty miles an hour."

"You're more resourceful than I remember."

"I'm a survivor."

Ken's eyelids fluttered open and he focused on the dark patch of snow over the sunroof. He had fallen asleep again. Hell of a way to catch up. Raising the seat, he checked the dash clock: 3:04 p.m. The sun would be setting in a couple of hours. He did not want to make the trek home in darkness, without the benefit of what little heat the sun provided. He did not want to go at all, but he saw little choice: he wanted to die in his car least of all.

"Stupid way to go," he said out loud.

He pushed the horn long and hard a few times, then exhaled. He knew this much: this was his last winter in western New York. Some way, somehow, he intended to take his family to a warmer climate. Taking a deep breath, he switched off the ignition and pocketed the keys. Then he pulled on his hat and gloves and crawled over his seat into the trunk. The lid bobbed in the wind while he grabbed the military shovel. Crawling to the edge, he used his free hand to raise the lid and recoiled.

A figure stood three feet away from the vehicle, half visible in the snowfall. At first Ken thought the bulky man wore rescue gear; then he thought it was no man at all but an animal covered with fur. But as his eyes adjusted to the faint light, he discerned lumpy gray-and-orange flesh and a human scowl. The figure, which stood over six feet tall, lunged at the car with surprising speed, shifting his weight from side to side. Ken pulled the trunk down, but the monstrous figure caught it and flung it up again. Ken tried to flail at the thing, but there was no room to maneuver, and his attacker seized his coat and yanked him out of the trunk.

Suspended in the air, feeling naked in the wind, Ken flailed his limbs. His assailant jerked his face close to his own and roared. He had pinkish eyes, and his foul breath made Ken retch, and inside his open mouth he saw two rows of crooked teeth on each jaw. The ferocity of the humanoid creature's roar caused Ken to scream. In response, the thing hurled him at the ground. Ken landed in the snow on his back, sinking two feet beneath the surface with his limbs spread apart. The thing strode over to him, its legs wide apart, filling Ken's field of vision, and reached out for him. Ken swung the short army shovel at the monster's forearm as hard as he could, the blade cracking bone and eliciting a pained cry from his target. The impact of the blow sent Ken's arm back into the snow. The creature gripped the wound with his free hand, and Ken swung the shovel blade at him again. This time the edge of the blade chopped off two of the creature's fingers, producing twin fountains of blood that splattered Ken and the snow. Now the monster snarled at him like a rabid dog. It plucked the shovel from Ken's hand and raised it high over his head. Ken pictured Marcus as the shovel whistled toward his head.

THIRTEEN

Korbel searched the channels on his old boom box for local news, but all the news stations came with static that made them unintelligible. A knock on the door made him pause. Who the hell would be knocking on his door in this storm? Whoever it was knocked again. Rising from the sofa, he went to the desk against the wall, opened the drawer, and took out the Smith & Wesson M&P pistol he kept there. He had bought the weapon for self-defense following his discharge. The knocking continued as he moved to the front door.

"Who is it?" he said in a loud voice.

"Police," a woman said.

Raising his eyebrows, he looked at the weapon in his hand. "Just a minute."

He looked through the peephole in the door. None to his surprise, he saw nothing. The woman on the other side of the door pounded the wood.

"Hurry," she said.

Tucking the .22 in the back of the waistband of his jeans, below his sweatshirt, Korbel twisted the lock above the doorknob and opened the door as wide as the chain lock permitted.

Peering around the edge of the door, he looked down at an orange ski mask. Snow covered the mask and the woman's coat.

"You don't look like no cop."

The woman pulled off her ski mask, revealing dark features and dark hair pinned tight to her skull. Her eyes filled with tears. "Please help me."

"Badge?"

"Oh." She brushed snow from her coat, revealing a shield pinned to the navy blue fabric.

"Uh-huh. How about some ID?"

"Are you really going to make me take off my gloves so I can get it? I'm so tired and cold."

"What do you want?"

"Just to come inside . . ."

Korbel looked around outside, unable to see anything beyond her. "Then I want to see your ID."

The woman bowed her head in defeat. She pulled one glove off, then looked at Korbel. Her eyes rolled up and she fell backward into the deep snow covering the steps.

"Oh, damn," Korbel said. He closed the door, removed the chain lock, and threw the door open.

The woman stirred in the snow, moaning. She did not get up. Korbel ran outside. The wind tore at his clothing as he hopped down into the snow. Crouching over the woman, he jammed his hands beneath her to get a good hold of her, then pulled her upright. Her head rolled on her neck.

"Hang on. You're going to be okay." Throwing her right arm around his neck, he attempted to walk her up the steps but fell to his knees. "You're going to have to help me a little, though."

BLACKcreek

The woman moved her legs, which accomplished little. Korbel hauled her up the steps and inside, where he laid her on the porch's carpet and shut the door, which he locked. He dropped to his knees beside the woman and gave her face a gentle slap.

"Hey, wake up."

Her eye opened. "Thank you."

The wind hammered Paul as he used the ski poles to pull himself on the sled alongside Dan's house. Snow covered his goggles, blew away, then more snow accumulated. The muscles in his arms ached. It took longer to swing the poles into position, longer to pull himself to them, longer still to jerk them out again. He didn't think he would make it. Paul set one pole beside him in the sled and grabbed the remaining pole with two hands, then pulled himself toward it. The physical burden eased, but his ability to steer the sled in a straight path decreased, and when he pulled the single pole out of the snow, the wind blew the sled backward. He resumed using both poles.

Light flashed overhead, followed by thunder. Undeterred, he pulled himself into the storm. The routine tested the limits of his strength, and he found himself staring down at the snow as he put his arms through the wringer. The force of the wind decreased, and only when he pulled himself headfirst into the side of the garage did he realize he had arrived home. The house blocked the wind, and a sob that sounded like a laugh escaped his lips.

But the house did not protect him from the cold. Bowing his head, he rested for a moment, then gathered his strength and turned the sled sideways and pulled himself to the corner. Another turn back into the wind, and he pulled himself alongside the garage door. He rolled into the snow, and the wind took the sled. Raising his head, he watched it skitter along and vanish. Kneeling on wobbling knees in the snow, which reached his chin, he grabbed the handle on the door and heaved it up. Snow spilled onto the concrete, and he landed inside.

The door leading into the house opened and Helen ran out, followed by Evan and Piper.

"Oh, my God, are you okay?"

"Close the door," he said, but his jaw felt numb and he didn't know if she understood him.

Helen grabbed the rope tied to the bottom door handle and pulled it down with an echoing crash that rivaled the thundersnow.

"What took you so long?" Helen said, crouching beside him.

He gave her an incredulous look.

"Never mind." Taking him by the arm, she helped him sit up. "Is Henri okay? What about Jenny?"

"Just help me inside."

"Get his other arm," Helen said to Piper, who obeyed. Mother and daughter helped him to his feet, supporting him as he limped toward the door.

Evan opened the door. "Are you okay, Dad?"

Paul nodded and grunted. When they reached the

top of the basement stairway, he collapsed. He raised both hands, and Helen pulled off his gloves. He raised his right foot, and Piper worked on his bootlaces.

"Dad, your shoelaces are frozen."

He raised his left boot and Evan went to work on it. Helen squeezed his hands and pain shot through them. When both boots thudded on the landing, he sat up. "Help me out of this snowsuit."

Helen unzipped the long zipper, which ran up one leg, across his chest, and down his opposite arm. He tried to take it off, but his hands hurt too much.

"Stand up," Helen said.

He obeyed his wife and she pulled off the snowsuit. The walkie-talkie thumped on the floor and Evan picked it up.

"Cool," Evan said.

"Where did you get that?" Piper said.

"Turn it on," Paul said.

Evan switched on the power.

"Press the big button on the side."

Evan pressed the button with his thumb.

"Goodman to Makowski," he said. "Now release the button."

Evan did.

"Go for Makowski," Jim said.

"The eagle has landed."

Gigi sat huddled in a blanket on Korbel's sofa, sipping the

hot chocolate he had made for her. He'd used milk because the pipes had frozen again. She had cried after telling him about her partner and the driver of the snowplow.

"That crash must have been what I heard earlier," he said, sitting in his desk chair. "I thought it was thundersnow."

"I need to call my dispatcher," Gigi said.

"Can't. Phone lines are down, and so are the relay towers. Cable's out and the pipes are frozen. This is some resort town. No wonder Niagara Falls is such a tourist destination. We are 100 percent cut off from civilization."

"Lou's family needs to know what happened to him. So does that plowman's." She sipped her cocoa. "We were responding to a call about a missing person. Some old lady at the assisted living community on the other side of the containment area. I wonder if she turned up . . ."

Korbel stood. "How about some dry clothes? I've got long johns and sweat suits. Clean, of course."

"Thanks. I'm soaking. Do you have a dryer?"

"Doesn't work. You can leave your clothes over the vents, though. Maybe stick your shoes in the oven."

"Sounds good."

"Um, I don't want you to get the wrong idea, but I have a gun in my trousers. I didn't know who you were."

"It's your house. There's nothing illegal about that."

"Right." He opened the desk drawer. "I'm just going to take it out and put it in here, okay?"

She nodded.

He reached behind him, took out the .22, and laid it in the drawer, which he closed.

"I guess you believe I'm a cop now," Gigi said.

"That must have been some walk."

"It was terrible. I've never been in anything like that before. The snow just kept getting higher and higher."

Korbel shook his head. "You've been through some shit, pardon my German. Do you want something stronger to drink? I've got beer and whiskey."

"Maybe I'll take you up on that after I dry out."

"Sure." He went into his bedroom.

"Do you mind if I try the radio?"

"Make yourself at home, and good luck."

"Thanks. And thank you for saving my life."

He smiled. "I didn't do anything but open the door."

"That isn't true. I appreciate what you did for me, what you're doing now."

"You're welcome." He went upstairs to find her some clothes.

In their bedroom, Paul lay on the bed with his feet touching the floor, and Helen peeled off his jeans.

"What do you think happened to Henri?" she said.

"Maybe he took a long walk off a short pier, as Archie Bunker used to say."

She dropped his jeans and started on his long johns. "That isn't funny."

"I don't know why he would take a stroll down to the river in this weather and leave Panzer behind."

"I feel bad for Jenny."

"So do I. But what could I do?"

"Thank God you made it back. I'm really sorry I sent you out there."

"You were just being a good neighbor."

"But a shitty wife."

He opened his legs a little wider. "I can think of a way you can make it up to me."

"Are you trying to guilt me into a blow job?"

"It is Valentine's Day."

Snorting, she stood, went to the door, and pushed the button lock on the knob. "Aren't you going to take that cold underwear off?"

Paul folded his arms behind his head.

Helen returned to the bed. "So that's how it is, huh?"

"Yep."

Sliding her hands up his thighs, she curled her fingers around his waistband and tugged off his briefs, then tossed them onto the floor with the rest of his clothes. She touched his flaccid penis, shrunken from the cold. "This is going to take a lot of work."

"We've got time."

"Uh-oh." Fran hunched over the steering wheel, peering ahead as the wipers worked at full speed.

"What is it?" Terry said.

"I lost him. He must have run out of salt."

Now Terry leaned forward. "Well, slow down for

Christ's sake."

"Then I'll lose him for sure."

"Please slow down. We're almost there. I know it. The ramp must be up ahead."

"All right . . ." Fran eased up on the gas. "But if we get lost now, it's your—"

A sharp crash echoed in the car as a rock the shape and size of a baseball embedded itself in the middle of the windshield, sending fissures through the rest of the glass. Fran screamed and let go of the steering wheel.

"Jesus!" Terry seized the wheel and jerked it toward him.

The car veered off the road and rammed through a snowbank while Fran continued to scream. Then it rolled over and slid down an incline upside-down, and Terry screamed too.

Gigi emerged from the downstairs bathroom layered in long johns, sweats, and gym socks. She had unpinned her hair, allowing it to frizz. "I feel so much better, no matter how awful I look."

Korbel thought she looked just fine. He pointed at the coffee table. "I made us some sandwiches. Fixings on the side. I've got some soup on the stove."

She sat beside him on the sofa. "You're probably tired of hearing me say thank you, but I really don't know what I would have done if you hadn't opened the door for me.

I tried two other houses before yours. No one answered, even though the lights were on. In one house, I saw a movie playing on a TV."

"What was it?"

"Something with Adam Sandler."

"Yeah, people are pretty stupid around here."

She smiled. "Because they like Adam Sandler?"

"Naw, because they wouldn't at least see who was knocking at their door. I remember when I was a kid, if someone got their car stuck in the snow, he didn't even have to ask for help. People just came out and did the right thing. Now everyone's afraid of being robbed by a crackhead."

Gigi took a bite of her turkey sandwich. "Can you blame them?"

"Nope. This city's fallen on hard times, and things just seem to get worse. What made you become a cop?"

"I noticed the photos of you in uniform on the wall. What made you join the Army?"

Korbel shrugged. "It was a job."

"Same here. I've been on the job two years, and I'm twenty-six. When I'm forty-four, I can retire."

"Not bad." Korbel tried his sandwich. "As long as nothing happens to you before then. You chose a dangerous profession in a dangerous city."

"Where did they send you, if you don't mind my asking?"

"Oh, they sent me to Iraq and Afghanistan."

"Then you chose a dangerous profession in a dangerous part of the world."

"True, true."

"I know I'm not supposed to ask, but I feel like we're brothers-in-arms. Did you see any action?"

"Yeah, a lot of it. You?"

"Some. Today was the worst, though."

"I'm sorry about your partner."

"Thank you."

"I lost friends too."

"I'm sorry."

"I lost my dog this week."

"That's sad."

"Yeah."

They finished their sandwiches without further conversation.

The upside-down Subaru slammed into the snowbank at the bottom of the hill, and both airbags deployed. When they deflated, white powder floated inside the dark car, like the snow outside. Real snow pressed against Terry's window and the windshield. His neck ached even though the seat belt prevented his head from striking the roof.

"Are you all right?"

"I think so," Fran said, but he heard hysteria creeping into her voice.

Pressing the palm of his left hand against the roof, he unbuckled his seat belt and dropped, then rolled onto his knees. The engine coughed but continued to run. Feeling along the cold metal beneath him, he located the dome light and switched it on, illuminating the interior from below.

"Are you hurt?" he said.

"No," Fran said between sobs.

Terry slid one arm between her back and the seat and pressed his free hand against her left collarbone. "Grab the steering wheel with your left hand, then use your right hand to unbuckle your seat belt. I've got you."

Fran reached up to her buckle with a trembling hand. "I feel like Shelley Winters in *The Poseidon Adventure*."

"Only you're going to make it out of this boat alive."

She pulled the buckle and fell into his arms, and he lowered her onto the roof and eased her legs straight back. For several seconds she covered the dome light, and light spilled around her silhouette. He helped her onto her knees, and she yelped in pain.

"Oh, my God, what the hell happened?" she said.

Terry turned to the windshield. The snow reflected the headlights and filled the cracks in the windshield with light, silhouetting a round object embedded in the glass.

"Is there a flashlight in here?"

"There's a penlight in the glove compartment."

Terry moved the deflated airbag out of the way and opened the glove compartment, dumping its contents onto the ceiling. He picked up a black metal cylinder. "This is called a Maglite."

"Whatever."

Pressing the rubber button on the back of the Maglite, he shone the light on the rock cannonball in the windshield. He touched its hard, cold surface. "Someone threw or shot this into the windshield."

"On purpose?" Fran sounded horrified. "Maybe the plow kicked it back at us."

"Maybe." But the plow had been nowhere near them. "In any case, we have to get out of this car now." He handed the Maglite to her. "I'll dig us out. You keep the light on me and follow."

"We'll freeze to death out there."

"No one knows we're here. In half an hour, this car will be completely covered, and no one will find us even when the storm is over. We're leaving now." He turned the ignition off but left the headlights on. "Switch places. I think your side will be easier to get out."

Grunting, Fran maneuvered around him, and he moved forward on his knees. Locating the door handle, he gave it a pull and opened the door, the metal scraping snow. Fran shone the light outside.

"We're in luck—the car crushed the snow down."

He climbed out of the car and stood. As Fran moved closer to the door, she saw he stood in snow up to his thighs. He held his hand down and she squeezed it; then he helped her stand. A bitter cold gust slapped her face, and her hair blew around her.

The icy wind stung Terry's face as he looked around. He saw nothing but snow falling in every direction.

"The expressway's up that way," he said, pointing. "We don't want to go up there."

"Why not?"

"If anyone sees us, it will be because they hit us or a snowplow cut us down. We were close to the exit." He turned the other way. "That means civilization is this way."

"You don't know that."

"I'd bet on it."

"That snow is three or four feet deep! I'm wearing a *dress*."

"It's real simple, Fran. Either you suck it up and meet this challenge, or you'll die. I really don't want to stick around for another funeral."

"Then you'd better plan on carrying me."

"Through this snow? Not happening. No offense, but you're not the toothpick you were before you had kids."

"You can be a real asshole, you know that?"

"At least I do whatever needs to be done when it needs to be done."

"Like you did with Mom? *I* took care of her, not you. You stayed in that stupid city with your stupid job because you're ashamed of where you grew up, you stuck-up . . ." Fran sucked in her breath and pitched forward, disappearing from his view.

"Fran?" Groping the air before him, one hand closed around a metal rod one inch thick.

Fran made a sound below him, like a person might make after vomiting.

"Fran!" Sliding both hands down the rod, he kneeled in the snow. His gloved hands found her back. The rod protruded from it. Pink steam rose into his face. "Frannie!"

Spying a circle of light in the snow, he dug out the Maglite and aimed it at his sister. The metal rod had gone through her back and out her sternum, impaling her. She held onto the rod with both hands, blood spilling over them.

"*Frannie!*"

BLACKcreek

With his free hand, Terry raised his sister's head so she faced him. Her eyes blinked at him but she said nothing. Then her hands fell away from the rod and her body slid down it into the snow, which turned red.

"Jesus Christ," Terry said in a low voice. Someone had thrown the rod into his sister like a javelin. The same person who had hurled the rock into the windshield. He scrambled backward, away from his sister's corpse and the Subaru, just as another rod struck the body of the car, a clanging sound echoing through the snowfall.

Terry turned and ran but came to an immediate stop as soon as he reached the snow beyond the car. It really was four feet deep. Panicking, he dug at it, then realized he still held the flashlight, its glow giving away his location. He clicked it off and jammed it into his pocket, then half-crawled and half-ran through the snow. Something sliced through the snow to his left—another rod, he imagined— and he angled to his right. If he could get far enough, the whiteout would mask his location. He fell forward, snow numbing his face, and crawled for a few feet before rising and resuming his trudging run. His shoes slipped in the snow and he recovered his balance. He imagined whoever had murdered Fran—whoever wanted to murder him— held an advantage.

His knee struck something hard but flexible, and he realized he had run into the fence that separated the incline of the expressway from Black Creek Village. He scaled the fence and, when his feet touched its metal piping, dove forward, saving himself some work. Snow struck his face, numbing his flesh and keeping him alert at the same time.

He tunneled forward, rose, and pushed on. His heart pounded in his chest and every breath pained his throat and lungs.

When the ache blossomed in his chest, he assumed he had suffered a heart attack from all the effort. His legs gave out and he fell forward. A new explosion of pain forced him to recognize he had been impaled in the same manner as Fran. Like her, he grabbed the makeshift spear protruding from his sternum to keep his body from sliding down the cold metal. He fell over sideways, sinking deep into snow. The pain ebbed and he knew his body was going into shock. Gazing up at the sky, he watched snowflakes rain on him like frozen meteorites. A street sign loomed above him. He had almost made it!

Reaching into his overcoat pocket, he took out the Maglite and clicked it on. That was the easy part. Aiming it at the sign was another thing. After several attempts, he shone the light on the metal sign. Reading it from an upside-down position, he saw that he had reached the inter-section of Frontier Avenue and 101st Street: Love Canal. Laughing, he coughed up blood.

FOURTEEN

Ken stirred, fighting to wake up. The left side of his face felt swollen, and nausea clung to the inside of his stomach like a wet towel. He snorted snot up his nostrils, then coughed and tasted blood. What the hell had happened to him? His brain tingled. His left shoulder throbbed. The fiend with two rows of teeth on each jaw brought the shovel down . . .

Ken's eyes opened, and that simple act ignited pain across his forehead. Darkness swam around him and he felt the urge to vomit. He tried to move his hands and realized they had been bound.

"Are you awake yet?"

A man's voice.

"Don't worry. I'm tied up too. At least they didn't gag us."

Ken tried to sit up, but everything hurt. His legs and butt touched the ground; his back did not.

"Your arms are tied up over your head. Dig your heels into the ground and push with your legs."

He blinked several times despite the pain that set his face on fire. His arms stretched above him, his hands reaching for a ceiling impossible to see. Turning his head to one side, he spat acidy saliva. Blood trickled out of his nose again.

Digging his heels into the ground, which felt like cement, he used his legs to propel his buttocks beneath his hips and at the same time used his arms to pull himself up. He had almost achieved a sitting position when one heel slipped and he went back down. Electrifying pain radiated through his left shoulder and arm, and he grunted.

"Jeez, talk about pathetic."

Gritting his teeth, Ken planted his feet flat on the floor and pushed again. This time he settled on his butt with his legs stretched before him. A lantern hung on the opposite wall, casting a dull glow over the immediate space. Dripping water echoed. A menagerie of foul odors assaulted his senses.

"Where are you?" Ken said.

"Right in front of you."

"I can't see you."

"I could say the same about you."

The voice sounded familiar. "Do I know you?"

"We're neighbors, dipshit."

Henri. Ken chuckled. The chuckling grew out of control, blossoming into outright laughter. Soon Henri laughed too. Their laughter echoed around them.

"What the hell have we gotten ourselves into?" Ken said.

"A world of shit."

Ken's eyes adjusted to the darkness. Henri became a vague impression ten feet away, sitting in the same position as him, his arms raised over his head. "Where are we?"

"You tell me." Henri shouted at the darkness, "Show yourselves!" His voice echoed. "If I had to guess, I'd say a mine or a tunnel. But I don't remember ever seeing either in our neighborhood."

"Are you hurt?"

"One of the fuckers bit off my ear. He ate it too, while they beat me down."

"There were more than one?"

"Two. You think I'd let one take me out? Goddamned freaks."

"It only took one to take me."

"You're a teacher, not a fighter."

"Kind of you to say. What did your two look like?"

"Ugly as sin. My dog drops turds that look better and smell better. They wore animal skins. One was bald; the other had patches of long hair on one side of his head. The bald one had sharp ridges all over his forehead, like he had a dinosaur skull or something. The one with the hair had lumps all over his whole head, like tumors. What about yours?"

"His head was kind of lumpy too. I got a look inside his mouth, and he had two rows of teeth."

"Jeez, I didn't notice the teeth on my guys, except when the one bit off my ear; then they were red."

"Pink eyes?"

"Pink, maybe white. Freaky."

"So there are three of them . . ."

"More than that, probably—a whole tribe of 'em. I seen some of them once before, two summers ago, walking along the riverbank at night. Hunting party, I guess now. I only saw them from a distance—I didn't know how freaking ugly they were. But they had kids with them. That was what I noticed. One of them must have seen me, because they scattered and I never saw them again. I bet they were out there a bunch more times, though, hiding like vermin. I bet those little bastards are just as ugly as the big ones, too."

Ken saw Henri better now. Blood covered one side of the man's face and beard. "Did the ones who took you say anything to you?"

"I don't think they could talk. They just grunted. Seemed to understand each other, though."

Ken gathered his feet under him and stood. The pain in his head flared again.

"What did he do to you?" Henri said.

"He hit me over the head with my own shovel."

"Next time carry a gun."

Ken attempted to loosen his bonds.

"Don't bother. They understand knots."

Ken continued anyway. "This rope is cutting off my circulation. You think these are our neighbors?"

"Distant neighbors. I went in and out of it when they brought me in. I know they dragged me along the river to the creek."

Ken gave up on the ropes. "I drove my car off the road near the creek."

"That was stupid."

"Yeah, I agree."

"There must be a cave somewhere along the creek, a secret entrance they use to enter this tunnel that allows them to get from where they live to where we live."

Ken returned to the floor. "And where do they live?"

"Where the hell do you think we are?"

"Enlighten me."

"We're under Love Canal, genius."

The Goodmans sat around their table, focused on a board game while dinner cooked. Evan drew a card from the deck, then surveyed the colored pieces on the board.

"Hm. Now let me see . . ."

"Don't you dare, you little creep," Piper said.

Evan picked up his man and knocked Piper's over. "*Sorry*."

Piper rolled her eyes. "I hate playing with him."

Evan laughed.

The timer in the oven went off and Helen stood. "That's my cue." She went into the kitchen.

Paul drew an eleven and had one of his men switch places with Piper's sole man on the board.

"Dad!"

"Sorry, honey."

Piper crossed her arms. "This is a conspiracy. What a weekend."

"It could be a lot worse."

"How?"

A rumbling noise caused Paul to stiffen: someone had raised the garage door. He traded looks with Piper and Evan.

"Who's that?" Evan said.

"I don't know. Let's see."

The three of them stood and went to the side door, which Paul opened. The garage door closed with a bang and a figure in a ski suit lumbered toward them, a heart-shaped box of chocolates in one hand.

"I hope you don't mind if I leave my Cat parked in front of the garage," he said, gesturing to the snowmobile visible in the frame of the garage doorway.

"Brian!" Piper ran past Paul into the garage and hugged the young man. "Oh, my God, I can't believe you came."

"Neither can I," Paul said into Helen's ear.

"I couldn't stay away. I had to deliver this." Brian held up the box. "Happy Valentine's Day."

Piper looked at the box and ran her fingers over the envelope taped to it. "Thank you." She gave him a quick kiss on the lips.

Paul frowned, and Helen squeezed his arm.

"That's so romantic," Evan said in a singsong voice.

"There's no way we're letting you go back out in this," Helen said. "You'll have to spend the night here. Right, Paul?"

"We have a spare room," Paul said. Now he would have to stay up all night.

"That's great. I really appreciate it."

"Well, come on inside so we can close this door," Helen said.

They moved into the house, where Brian took off his boots and ski suit.

"How was the drive?" Paul said.

"Rough. I had to go super slow because I could only

see a few feet in front of me. I started out in the street, or where I thought the street was, but I nicked a couple of cars that were buried under snow. I triggered their alarms and everything. So I switched to people's lawns. It's not like I was tearing up their grass or anything, right? All that falling snow made me dizzy."

"All to bring me chocolate," Piper said.

"That's right."

"That was the last condom," Will said as he zipped his fly.

"Then that was the last time," Adele said, brushing her hair.

"We're officially into the dinner hour. What are we going to eat?"

"Look in the fridge upstairs."

"Okay."

Will closed the door behind him and crossed the hall to the stairway. He flicked on the lights upstairs, then started his climb. The muscles in his legs and groin ached, and his eyeballs felt as if they had been drained. By the time he reached the top of the stairs, he felt exhausted. He took out his key card and opened the only door.

Like the downstairs office, two units had been combined to create a bigger space for management. He turned on the lights and entered, then passed desks, tables, and storage units to the kitchen, where he opened the refrigerator. He and Adele had already eaten cold cuts, so he ignored the wrapped sandwich meats. Closing the door, he checked a cabinet and selected two cans of soup. He found two pans in a lower cabinet, poured the soups into them, and lit the stove. Then he went back into the main room and stood at a window facing the rear of the property. Throwing the locks, he raised the window and stared into a solid sheet of snow that had built up on the ledge. A chuckle escaped his lips and he elbowed the sheet. Most of the snow collapsed outside, but some spilled onto the floor. He didn't care.

Eighteen hours was long enough to spend on the job, overtime or not. He took his cigarettes from his shirt pocket, shook one loose, and lit it. He exhaled out the window, but the wind blew smoke right back into his face.

Then the lights went out.

Seated on the sofa, Korbel and Gigi sipped whiskey from mismatched glasses. The wind outside did not let up, and the reception on the radio came and went.

"I never expected to have a cop as a houseguest," Korbel said.

"I never expected to be stranded in a stranger's house in Love Canal during a snowstorm. How much food do you have in the house?"

Korbel felt the discouragement showing on his face. "Maybe enough for three days, if we're careful."

"That should get us through the storm, at least. But it could be weeks before they dig us out."

BLACKcreek

"The phones should be working way before then. At least you'll be able to tell your people what went down."

"Lou and that driver are still out there . . ."

"Frozen stiff, pardon the expression."

"All because of snow. I want to move to Florida."

Korbel grunted. "The streets are *really* crazy down there."

"I'll deal with it. I don't ever want to see snow again."

The lights went out, shrouding them in darkness.

"Uh-oh," Korbel said.

Tommy Burgess lay on the sofa in front of the flat screen TV, watching a DVD that belonged to his mother. He had wanted to watch his copy of Rob Zombie's *Halloween II*, but it had occurred to him this was a poor choice while home alone. His mother had told him there was an old version of the movie, and he had tried to watch it with her but had lost interest because there was no blood or guts in it. He did not remember the title of the movie he had chosen as a substitute, but it was a comedy about an unmarried woman who was jealous that her best friend was getting married. It was pretty gross, like a movie for guys, and he laughed quite a few times.

It felt good to laugh. He hadn't much since the incident in the woods near Cayuga Creek two months ago, when he had been startled by the great wild animal crouching in the bushes with its back to him, watching Grant sneak up on Evan. He did not remember much about the creature's body, which was covered with fur, but he had a vivid recollection of its fangs: two rows of them, crooked and yellow. Its eyes were pink, with a white film over them. As soon as it turned toward him, he knew it wanted to hurt him. He knew this with absolute certainty, and he ran as fast as he could to escape it. He expected the creature to chase after him, galloping on all fours, and ran as though his life depended on it, leaving his friends behind after a cursory warning. This is why he had been unable to speak to them since: he was ashamed of his cowardice, and Grant had humiliated him for it in school.

Tommy had suffered from nightmares ever since, and his mother forced him to see a psychiatrist. He told Dr. Carpetyan everything, because he knew that was how he was supposed to get better, but he left his sessions feeling the kind-faced psychiatrist hadn't believed a word he had spoken. Worse, he suspected Dr. Carp blabbed everything to his mother, who had become overprotective.

But where was she now? Stuck at work, in the casino. And here he was, with no phone or Internet service. Thank God for the Blu-ray player.

Thunder rumbled. While the cable had worked, the newsmen called it thundersnow.

The lights went out, and he sat up. The house had turned pitch black: not even the lights on the Blu-ray player functioned. The hum from the refrigerator in the kitchen stopped, casting the house in silence. Turning, he climbed onto the sofa and drew back the drapes for a look outside. He stared into darkness: the streetlights had gone out too. That meant a blackout, which meant the heat had gone off.

His heart beat faster. He would freeze to death. The fireplace hadn't been used in years, and his mother had said the chimney needed to be swept before it was used again, or the house might burn down. He would have to bury himself in all the blankets he could find. But how would he find them in the dark? He didn't know if his mother even kept a working flashlight in the house.

Lightning flashed, illuminating the falling snow and silhouetting the figure of a bulky man standing at the window, staring inside. Tommy glimpsed lumps on a barren head. He recoiled even as the lightning faded, falling backward off the sofa with a piercing cry.

Paul observed Brian and his daughter during dinner, the way they stole glances at each other when they thought no one was watching, and the way their hands lay on the table, close to each other but never quite touching. Young love.

"Have you chosen a college yet, Brian?" Helen asked.

"I'm going to Buff State. Communications and media studies."

"Interesting."

"Weren't you even tempted to go somewhere else, to be on your own?" Paul said.

Piper shot him a look.

"Not really," Brian said. "All of my friends are here, and most of them are staying. My family's here." He paused. "And Piper."

Not the answer Paul wanted to hear.

"I'm staying at home, at least next year."

"That's a relief," Paul said.

"Dad!" Piper said.

"I think it's nice when young people stay close to their families," Helen said.

"Moving away for college is part of the experience of growing up," Paul said.

"How would you know? We both went to Niagara University."

Piper laughed, then Evan, and Paul joined in.

Then the lights went out.

The emergency lights kicked on, casting oval-shaped pools of light on the walls. Will flicked his burning cigarette out the window, then pulled the window down. If the power had gone out, then so had the heat—and the heat in all the units. The residents would freeze to death.

He entered the kitchen, where the twin circles of blue fire on the stove continued to burn, and moved the pots of soup to the unused burners. If he turned the gas off, he might have trouble relighting the pilots. At least if he left them on, the kitchen might stay warm. He went back into the main room and made his way to the exit, somewhat unsettled by the eerie lighting. As he opened the door and made his way downstairs, his mind formulated a plan that he did not like at all. Hurrying to the office, he tried to think of an alternative course of action. None came to mind.

Adele had already put on her hat and coat when he entered the office, which seemed like an entirely different place with the emergency illumination. The lighting cast long shadows over her face.

"The heat's off," she said. "The residents . . ."

"We're going to take care of them. We have to go outside and split up. You take one side of the drive; I'll take the other. We'll go to each house and round up the residents."

"Then what? There's no way any of them can walk through this snow."

"No, but we can put them all in one apartment in each building so they can keep each other warm, and we can light all four burners on the stove to give them some heat. Do you have a lighter?"

She nodded. "It will take us all night to go door to door like that in this."

"What other choice do we have? This isn't even about our jobs; it's about keeping these people alive."

"I know. This is bullshit—Sharon should be here to deal with this."

"Well, she's not. It's just you, me, and sixty seniors." He thought of Denise. "Fifty-nine." He went to the coat rack. "Put on as many layers as you can."

A window in the back wall exploded and Adele screamed.

The emergency flashlight left charging in the wall cast a circle of light on the ceiling. Paul rose from his chair and unplugged it. The flashlight dimmed and he switched it on again. Moving back to the table, he aimed the flashlight at the kitchen cabinets. "Bring out the candles."

Helen went into the kitchen and opened a cabinet. Paul aimed the flashlight inside the cabinet, and she grabbed several candles, which she brought to the table. She made a second trip for more and a box of kitchen matches, which she handed to Piper.

"Get started." She turned from Piper to Paul. "What now?"

The walkie-talkie squawked in the living room.

"Jim for Paul, over."

Paul used the flashlight to locate the walkie-talkie on an end table and picked it up. "Go for Paul. Over."

"Did you lose power? Over."

"Affirmative. Over."

"Roger that. Do you have a source for heat?"

"We've got a fireplace and a cord of firewood. You?"

"Generator. We're good. Over."

Paul brought the walkie-talkie into the dining room and set it on the table, where Piper had already lit half a dozen candles, creating the ambience of a cathedral. "Put one of those in the downstairs bathroom, on the back of the toilet tank. Put one in the kitchen and two in the living room."

"Okay," Piper said.

Helen pressed a button on the thermostat mounted on the wall and its screen lit, thanks to triple-A batteries inside it. "The temperature's already dropping."

"Can I help, Mr. Goodman?" Brian said.

"Yes. I want you and Evan to get your coats on and help me carry the firewood inside. Helen, use the matches to light the burners on the stove."

"Right."

Silhouetted with their faces glowing in the soft candlelight, they got to work.

Using Gigi's smartphone for light, Korbel led her into the kitchen. He stopped at the stove and handed the phone back to her, then took a lighter from his pocket. He turned on the gas for each of the four burners, then sparked his lighter to ignite each one.

"At least we have some heat," he said. Then he moved two kitchen chairs before the stove. "Have a seat. I'm going to get some blankets."

She held out the phone. "Take it again."

"Thanks."

He made his way through the darkened house and up the creaking stairs.

Will looked at the cinder block that lay on the floor, surrounded by broken glass, and the blinds that had been ripped from the window frame.

Adele backed away from the window. "What the hell?"

"The wind didn't do that." Will took slow, measured steps across the room, his flashlight trained on the window, falling snow glowing in its beam. "Hello?"

"Careful, Will."

His boot crushed a shard of glass, and the piercing sound made him wince. Reaching the window, he called out again.

No one responded.

He leaned outside. "Hello? Do you need help?"

Still no response.

He turned to Adele. "Maybe someone's hurt out there."

Adele opened her mouth as if to speak, but a scream came out instead. A powerful arm encircled Will's throat and jerked him off his feet. Clawing at the arm, he saw Adele covering her mouth with both hands even as his attacker pulled him kicking through the window.

Bitter cold gripped him. His attacker lunged away from the building, raising Will over his back. Will saw the falling snow above him; then his attacker hurled him into the snow on the ground, and an icy numbness spread through his body. He intended to get up and fight, but before he could move, something long and metal pierced his right buttock and emerged through the skin above his groin, skewering him like a fish on a spear, and he screamed.

FIFTEEN

Adele stood shocked by what had just occurred. Then she shook her head and ran to the window. Outside, a bulky man covered in fur raised a metal spear with both hands and drove it into Will, who squirmed in the snow. The assailant pulled his spear back and blood squirted out of Will's body. Will screamed and the spear descended again. And again. And again. Will's frantic movements sprayed steaming blood over the snow. He turned onto his back, raising one hand toward his attacker, his eyes pleading for mercy. The attacker drove the spear into Will's chest. Will gazed at the figure with an expression of disbelief. Blood poured from between his lips, and he stilled.

Adele covered her mouth so she would not scream, but Will's murderer turned to her anyway. Between the dim light and the snowfall, she registered only enough of the man's features to know his face was deformed. Then she fled, running for the office door, which she hurled open. She sprinted toward the front door, her mind grappling with the incomprehensible nature of what had transpired. Reaching the door, she turned the locks and threw it open, then stopped. A drift of snow five feet high blocked her exit.

A whimper escaped her throat as she spun around. The murderer emerged from the office, the bloody spear in his hands. Tufts of hair dangled over the tumors covering his face. He moved toward her, and she glanced at the top of the stairs, her only chance for escape.

Then something jerked her head back into the snow and cold metal sliced her throat. She screamed through two mouths, blood gurgling from both of them. Foul body odor filled her nostrils as Will's killer advanced on her, the emergency lights highlighting his pink eyes. Covering her ruptured throat with her hands, she sank to her knees. She did not live long enough to see the face of her killer.

Tommy ran into his dark bedroom and closed the door. He pushed the button lock and backed up. The wind howled. Who had been standing outside the window?

The monster from the woods.

Downstairs, a window shattered.

Using a long match, Helen lit the paper beneath the log in the fireplace. Piper had set up another half-dozen candles, and the group stood watching the first log smolder. The wind descending the metal chimney sounded like screams.

"I think you've got this in hand." Paul turned to Brian.

BLACKcreek

"I need you to help me get my snowmobile out."

"Why?" Helen said.

"I've got to get Tommy. He must be scared out of his mind, and he's got no heat."

"What about Jenny and the baby?"

"I made sure Jenny's set up. She'll be okay for now. But I'm not leaving that boy on his own."

"You said it was too dangerous before, and that was in the daytime."

"Brian made it, and he lives farther away than Tommy. I can make it too."

"You can just take my snowmobile," Brian said.

"Thanks, but no thanks. Anything could still happen out there, and I'm not on your insurance. I'll have to use my own Cat."

"I'll go, then."

Paul didn't know whether to be touched or offended. "Then I'd worry about both of you."

"Then let's do it."

Chrs circled the house, unconcerned about leaving tracks. The wind and the snow were his allies when it came to secrecy. The boy had seen him in the flash of lightning, but that didn't matter. He knew the child was alone. Easy prey. All he had to do was reach him.

Chrs hugged the side of the house and moved sideways through the deep snow, protected by the layers of deer hides

241

he wore. His skin remained warm and dry, his appetite high. Mthr and Fthr had argued about whether he should be allowed to hunt on his own. Mthr said yes; Fthr said no. The old man wanted him to hunt with his brothers, but he had been staking out the house and knew the boy inside was often left alone. This was the first year Grndmthr had agreed to let the tribe hunt top dwellers in their homes, and he intended to prove himself.

The locks on the doors were stronger than others he had broken, and the door on the side of the garage was metal and lacked glass panes, so he chose the kitchen window. No neighbors could see him through the falling snow; none even tried. Using his spear, and with the frozen river to his back, he shattered the window twice. The shards rained into the snow and inside the house, clattering on the dishes in a metal sink. Then he used the spear to clear the jagged remains of the glass from the window frame. He could not climb into the house with the spear, so he tossed that through the window space and listened to the ensuing clatter. He did not worry that the boy would pick it up and use it against him; the child would be too frightened by the noise. The succulent, tender child.

Seizing the frame with both hands, he jumped off the ground and pulled himself up at the same time, his feet stomping the siding. Climbing in his layers of fur proved difficult, but hunger and the need to prove himself drove him onward. When he had achieved enough height, he pushed his shoulders inside and shimmied his legs.

He aimed his left shoulder where he knew it would find the sink, plastic breakfast bowls easing his fall, and his legs

slammed onto a countertop. He rolled into the space, landing on the palms of his gloved hands, and waited until the
vibrations in the floor faded before rising into a crouch. His
eyes adjusted to the darkness and he skittered across the
floor, collecting his spear. He dropped the bag he carried
slung around one shoulder before the refrigerator, intending
to raid it on his way out, then moved through the house,
sniffing the air for the boy. The place reeked of artificial
scents. He moved up the stairs.

Paul heaved the garage door open while Brian shone the
flashlight on him. Brian gaped at the glittering snow that
reflected light at him. It reached five feet high and covered
Brian's snowmobile several feet away. Fresh snowfall swirled
in as if through a funnel.

"Are you sure you want to go out there?" Brian said.

Paul pushed the snowblower and a few other objects out
of the way, then climbed into the pickup truck that held the
snowmobile. He started its engine, switched on the dome
light and headlights, then scanned the radio stations before
landing on local news.

"Western New York is buried thanks to the monster
storm known as Snowzilla, with the cities and suburbs of
Buffalo and Niagara Falls coping with up to five feet of snow
so far. Residents are snowed in, and emergency services
are unable to function. The snow is expected to continue
through Sunday, and Governor Cosgrave has extended the

travel ban until then."

Paul backed the truck up to the edge of the driveway and got out. Brian joined him at the rear of the truck. The tailgate, which had been lowered to accommodate the snowmobile, had sliced into the snow. He proceeded to unfasten the straps and tie-downs that held the snowmobile in place.

"If this wasn't in the truck, you wouldn't be able to get it out," Brian said.

Paul slid out the sections of the aluminum ramp and extended them from the back of the truck into the snow covering the driveway. The wind rattled the ramp pieces. Paul handed the truck keys to Brian.

"When I leave, put the ramp back into the truck and pull it up. If you want to use it to bring your Cat into the garage, feel free."

"I think I'll leave it out there," Brian said. "It's not going anywhere."

Paul climbed into the back of the truck and picked up a red helmet off the floor. He put the helmet on, switched on its headlight, then unlocked the brake of the snowmobile and pushed the machine backward. He rolled it out, pushing it up and over the curve of the ramp. The treads rolled over the ramp and the snowmobile slid onto the snow. Paul held his breath, fearing the snowmobile would sink, but it did not. He walked along one track, ducking beneath the garage door, and the wind slammed him. Within seconds snow covered the snowmobile and his snowsuit.

Stepping off the track, he swung one leg over the snowmobile and sat astride it, losing sight of Brian through the snowfall, though the flashlight in Brian's hand remained visible. He started the engine, which roared to life, and switched on the headlight, illuminating the snow before him and Brian in the garage. Taking off his right glove, he programmed Tommy's address into the GPS. Then he pulled his glove back on and got ready. When the snowmobile lunged forward, he leaned to his left, steering it in a half circle that missed the front of the house and took him into Joanne's driveway, where he slowed to a stop. Gazing into the whiteout, he imagined the view of his neighbors' houses across the street without snow: Henri's at a forty-five-degree angle to his left, and Ken and Jenny's beyond that. He gave the snowmobile gas and moved into the street at five miles per hour, driving blind. Leaning to his right, he made for Henri's house—he hoped.

He knew he had succeeded when the glass panes of the garage door reflected the headlight back at him. He parked the snowmobile six feet from the door, jumped off, and lumbered through the snow, each step sinking deeper. By the time he reached the door, the snow reached his sternum. Locating the handle, he raised the door, the headlight filling the garage with harsh light and projecting the shadows of himself and the falling snow across the floor. The dog food he had left for Panzer lay untouched in its bowl. Without bothering to go inside, he went back to the snowmobile and climbed onto it.

"How long do you think they've been down here?" Ken

said, twisting his trunk back and forth to loosen his bonds.

"Love Canal was evacuated in '78," Henri said. "Not everyone left. Some people who did allowed their houses to be torn down; others insisted they be left standing. Even then there were stories about squatters moving in. I bet some of them moved down here when that became impossible."

"That was forty years ago. More than a generation."

"Who knows how many of them came down? Eating, drinking, and breathing the shit that was buried down here, fucking and making little monsters that grew and fucked and made more little monsters, each more fucked up than the last."

"I can see you've given this some thought."

"Love Canal's roosters never came home to roost, because they never left in the first place."

Ken did not wish to accept any of the old racist's beliefs, but in his present situation he needed an ally more than he did a debate rival. "I feel heat. Where's it coming from?"

"Coals all over the floor."

"What do you think they want to do with us?"

Henri snorted. "What do you think? They want to eat us. White meat, dark meat, it doesn't matter to them. This is still going to be a long winter yet, and they're hunters."

Ken's stomach churned, and he thought of Jenny and Marcus. "This isn't how I plan to go out."

"Me neither."

A bang echoed, and Henri sat up straight.

"Listen."

Distant voices murmured.

"They're coming."

Jenny opened her front door, a flashlight in her hand. Paul shielded his eyes with one gloved hand, then pointed at the garage door. He couldn't see if she nodded or not, and then the door closed. He drove in a circle, pulling close to the garage as the door opened, then got off and waded forward, the snowbank he reached collapsing into the garage. Standing in the side door with Marcus in one arm, Jenny palmed the wall button and the door started down.

Paul removed his helmet. "Did you get your fireplace going okay?"

"Yes," she said in a tired voice. "I set up a little camp around it. How long do you think it will be before the power comes back on?"

"I honestly don't know. But we want you and Marcus over at our house. I'm going around the bend to get Tommy Burgess because he's home alone. I'll bring him back to my house, then come for you and Marcus, so you have time to pack."

"I want to go with you, but I can't. If Ken comes home . . ."

"If Ken hasn't come home by now, he won't be back until this storm is over. The travel ban is still in effect, there's five feet of snow on the streets, and this isn't supposed to let up until Sunday night."

The resolve in her expression weakened.

"No arguments. You have to think about yourself and Marcus."

She looked at her baby. "I'll need to bring so many things . . ."

"If I have to make two trips, I will. Hell, I'll even make three. Get started." He put his helmet on and faced the door, waiting for it to rise. As soon as it had, he jerked the handle dangling from the automatic closer's track, disengaging the door.

A pinprick of light deep in the tunnel grew brighter, closer. Loud voices and laughter echoed, indecipherable from the distortion.

Swallowing, Ken pressed his back against the wall.

Figures appeared in the darkness. Three of them, one carrying a lantern.

Ken couldn't make out any details, except that all three appeared to be male, and each one carried something over his shoulder. As the trio grew closer, and their lantern added light to that provided by the one hanging on the wall above Henri, Ken saw they wore similar but not identical outfits of animal fur. He recognized the one who had assaulted him, and he assumed the other two had captured Henri. One had a lumpy bald head, the other tufts of hair on one side of his skull. They walked with similar limps and seemed comfortable and at home, paying no attention to the bound men. Their approach also allowed him to see that he and Henri sat upon raised tiers, while the three men walked on a lower tier between them.

The additional light enabled Ken to discern two long tables standing end to end against the opposite wall, with two-shelf bookcases under each one. Rather than books, tools occupied the shelves. One of the men threw his cargo on top of one table with a loud thump that echoed. Ken stiffened when he saw the dead woman. The other man threw another body onto the next table, which produced a louder echo: a dead man.

Ken's heart beat faster. The man who had abducted him, and who held the lantern, turned in his direction. Fear paralyzed Ken. Blood flowed from the man's ear so that he matched Henri. He made an abrupt turn toward Henri and tossed his prize at his feet. Ken recognized the dog's corpse even with his throat torn out and his beautiful fur slicked with blood.

"Panzer!" Henri twisted his body. "You killed my dog, you fucking asshole."

Crouching and leaning forward, the man pointed at his own bloody ear. "Bt m'fckng r!"

Henri curled his lips back. "Good! I'm glad he bit it off! Now we're even!"

The man gave Henri a backhanded slap that echoed, and Henri kicked at him, his boots connecting with the man's jaw. Ken winced at the sound of the impact, and the man's roar rebounded off the walls. Moving to the table, the man drew a long-handled knife from one of the shelves beneath the nearest table.

"Hld hs fckng hd," he said to the other two.

The man with no hair lumbered toward Henri.

"Get the hell away from me!"

The man seized Henri's head. Henri struggled, but the man held his head still. Ken feared the man would break his neighbor's neck. The man with the knife handed his lantern to the third man and advanced on Henri, whose face turned scarlet.

"Fuck you, asshole!"

The man with the knife tried to pry Henri's jaws apart, but Henri clamped his teeth together, angry grunts escaping through them. The man pressed the tip of the knife's blade against Henri's teeth. Ken wanted to look away, but he couldn't. A whistling sound came out of Henri's nostrils and his eyes bulged with fear. The man gave the knife a shove, forcing Henri's mouth open and driving the blade upward. Henri screamed, and Ken imagined the blade slicing into the roof of his mouth. The man reached inside Henri's mouth with his thumb and forefinger. The blade prevented Henri from biting down. The man drew Henri's tongue out of his mouth, slick with blood. Henri gagged and pleaded at the same time. The man pulled his knife out of Henri's mouth, then used it to sever the tongue. Ken squeezed his eyes shut as Henri gurgled and screamed. Then he heard chewing, and the laughter of the other two men.

Chrs closed his fingers around the knob of the bedroom door, but it would not turn. Stepping back to kick the door, he wedged the metal rod that served as his spear between the two walls of the hallway. He pushed on it, but it did not budge. Anger swelled in his chest, and with a roar he pushed on the rod so hard its ends tore through the walls. Facing the stairs, he hurled the spear downward and heard it chew through the foyer door. Drawing his bone-handled knife with one hand and a flashlight with the other, he kicked the flimsy bedroom door open and stormed into the room.

The intense darkness caused him to pause. He switched on the flashlight, but the batteries produced only a dim yellow circle on the unmade bed. His lips peeled back, and as he licked his two long front teeth, acidy drool spilled onto his chin. He turned in a complete circle, moving the light over the walls, which had been covered with posters. The light settled on the open closet, revealing a clothes hamper and footwear on the floor. Sniffing the air, he took a step forward, then dove beside the bed and snarled underneath it. His flashlight revealed nothing but dust bunnies and candy wrappers. Jumping to his feet, he charged at the closet and threw the hamper over his shoulder. He growled as he tore into the clothes hanging from the rod, slashing them with his knife. The boy had tricked him, and he would pay.

Jenny zipped the rolling suitcase filled with clothes and essential baby items, the bedroom illuminated by the soft glow of the lantern she had set on the bureau. Downstairs, Marcus cried. She had left him sleeping in the bassinet near the fireplace, where he would be warmest. The bedroom was already too cold to sleep in. Swinging the suitcase off the bureau, she grabbed the lantern with her free hand

and moved around the bed. She slammed her left shoulder against the door frame, wincing as Marcus continued to cry.

"I'm coming," she said.

The lantern cast golden circles on the ceiling as she descended the stairs, the darkness parting before her outstretched arm. Marcus stopped crying, which struck her as odd. As she neared the bottom of the stairs, where the front door reflected orange flames from the fireplace far across the room, she heard a female voice whispering. She knew that was impossible, but something did not feel right. Stepping onto the carpet, she turned around the stairway and froze, her mind processing the tableau before her. An adult figure stood between her and the bassinet, silhouetted by the fire and wrapped in a blanket. Jenny dropped the suitcase.

The figure turned to her: a white woman, her long hair highlighted by the fire glow. Her smile revealed toothless gums. She cradled Marcus in her arms.

Jenny swallowed. "Please. I don't care who you are or what you're doing here. Take whatever you want. Just please put my baby down."

The woman raised Marcus in her arms. Her pale eyes looked pink. "B'b?"

Jenny assumed the woman could not speak because she had no teeth. She took a step forward. "Yes, that's my baby. My baby boy. Marcus."

The woman's smile broadened. "Mrcs."

She was deranged, Jenny concluded. Probably homeless.

As Jenny took a step forward, the woman darted around the bassinet to the opposite side, clutching Marcus to her bosom, panic in her eyes. She moved in a lopsided manner, shifting her weight. Jenny froze so Marcus would not be harmed. The woman's new position allowed the fire to reveal her features in greater detail. Her nose had been broken more than once, scars crisscrossed her face, and scabs seemed part of her natural skin texture. She wore layers of fur hides, not blankets.

"Okay, just calm down," Jenny said. "Just take it easy. No one is going to hurt you, and I don't want my baby to get hurt. It's cold outside; I get that. I don't know how you got in here, but that's okay. You're welcome to stay until the storm blows over. Make yourself comfortable, stay warm, eat. Just put my baby down in that bassinet before he gets hurt."

The crazed look in the woman's eyes softened. She looked down at Marcus, then lowered him toward the bassinet. Jenny let out a slow exhale. The woman froze with Marcus held just above the bassinet. She looked at Jenny and her eyes turned cold. Jenny's mouth opened. The woman returned Marcus to her bosom. Jenny's body wilted. She wished Ken was here.

"Let's just be calm, okay? Let's talk like two rational adults."

"M b'b nw," the woman said in a strangled voice.

Jenny's heart rate quickened and her voice quivered. "Please . . ."

The foyer door burst open behind Jenny and a hulking figure strode toward her, a long hunting knife in one hand. Crying out, Jenny flinched. Like the woman, this man wore layers of fur, and he moved with a double limp. Screaming, Jenny ran toward the bassinet, where the woman hissed at her like a giant cat. Jenny veered toward the fireplace and snatched a forged steel poker from its rack. Pivoting on one heel, she swung the poker like a baseball bat with all her strength. The poker struck the wild man on the side of his skull, the rake at the end rupturing a grayish tumor. The man jerked his head back, the poker wedged in his head, and Jenny staggered forward, refusing to let go. His pink eyes rolled up as he moaned, and he sank to his knees and fell face-forward to the floor.

Jenny's chest rose and fell. She jerked the poker out of the dead man's head with a splitting sound and turned toward the bassinet. The woman leapt into her face with a growl, and Jenny fell back with a startled cry. The woman had set Marcus in the bassinet, and now she straddled Jenny's stomach, raising a long knife over her head. She brought it down, burying it in Jenny's chest cavity. Jenny gasped with incomprehension. The woman pulled the knife out, and raised it again. Dark blood dripped from its blade. Jenny opened her mouth but nothing came out. Marcus cried, and the knife came down again.

SIXTEEN

After the three monsters—Ken refused to think of them as men—had left, Henri wept in the shadows. Ken felt wet between his legs and realized he had urinated in his pants. He felt no shame over this, but he feared his wet trousers would speed his demise in the cold tunnel.

"Henri, I know this is a stupid question, but are you all right?"

Henri responded with a wail.

"Okay, I'll do all the talking for both of us, then. If you need to chime in, hum once for yes and twice for no."

Henri sobbed.

"We've got to get the hell out of here. I'm still working on my ropes. Are you still working on yours?"

A moment of silence. Then Henri hummed once.

"Good. Don't give up, brother. Keep at it. Whoever gets loose helps the other one, right? It may take both of us to get out."

Another moment of silence.

Followed by a single hum.

Gritting his teeth, Ken twisted his wrists back and forth, wiggling them and ignoring the pain of the rope burns.

"Those animals were speaking English. All consonants, no vowels. I don't know if it's their idea of a code or if they were educated by an imbecile."

Henri's three hums sounded like "I don't know." Ken understood him as well as he had their captors.

"If you're right and these people are cannibals, and we're on their menu, then this must be the equivalent of a meat locker. I don't know who those two sorry sons of bitches on the table are, but they must be up first since they're already dead. Our hosts are keeping us alive so we don't spoil. So we've got some time to get out of here. We just have to keep our wits about us."

Henri hummed once.

"I'm sorry about what they did to you. That wasn't right. When we get out of here, we'll make sure they pay."

The hum Henri made sounded angry.

"I don't blame you."

Henri stopped moving and made a hum similar to the sounds Boris Karloff had made as Frankenstein's monster. Ken froze.

"What is it?"

Henri did not respond. Ken listened. The echo of voices heading their way.

"They're coming back." Despair crept into his voice.

The pinprick of light reappeared in the distant darkness.

Chrs threw mattresses against the walls and box springs on

the floor and tore clothes from their hangers. He knew the boy was hiding here somewhere. His flashlight died, and he stuffed it into his pocket. Where the hell had the brat gone? He cocked his head, listening. It occurred to him the child had tricked him: he'd never been in the bedroom. He had locked the door and closed it from the other side. He hadn't gone upstairs but downstairs, into the basement. And during the time it had taken Chrs to ransack the room, the boy might have fled outside, into the storm. Grunting, he stalked back to the bedroom doorway and the stairway beyond.

In Jim's garage, near the door, Dan stood shining a flashlight on his friend as Jim hunched over the generator. An extension cord ran from the generator into the house. Jim switched the power button to the on position and the generator chugged to life. Then he pushed in the choke, and the motor roared.

"Go open the door," Jim said.

Dan aimed the flashlight in the opposite direction and pressed the button for the garage door, which rose. Wind and snow blew inside. Jim joined Dan at the door to the house, and they stood watching the generator cough exhaust at the opening, then blow back inside.

"I don't know," Dan said in a skeptical tone.

Jim took Dan's wrist and aimed the flashlight at the garage's side door. He walked over to it, pushed the two bolt locks, and swung it open. The snow outside reached higher than the doorknob. He returned to Dan.

"That should keep us breathing."

"Your garage is going to fill up with snow."

"One day at a time, you dumb Polack."

"The furnace is going to have to work overtime to keep the house warm."

They went inside. The extension cord connected to the generator ended in a four-way box at their feet, with four extension cords plugged into it. One ran to the oven in the kitchen, two ran to lights in the living room, and the last ran to the furnace in the basement. Light shone from the living room.

"What do I care?" Jim said. "This is a life-or-death emergency."

He closed the door. A small hole had been drilled at the bottom of the door to accommodate the cord.

"Let's get that pilot light lit." He went downstairs with Dan trailing him.

"Watch your step, you dumb Polack," Dan said.

"You too, ya dumb Polack."

The wind rocked Paul on the snowmobile. The falling snow in the headlight disoriented him. A dark shape loomed before him and he leaned to his right to avoid it: a thick oak tree. At least he knew he was following the sidewalk. The Burgesses lived on the opposite side of the street from his house, with the river behind them. He moved to his right, searching for the house while he waited for the GPS to alert him.

Two monsters appeared this time, one carrying a lantern, and both carrying prey slung over their shoulders. They dumped the bodies of a young man and a young woman on the floor. Ken swallowed. These were different killers than the previous three. How many of them were there? One looked at him with pinkish eyes. His lower jaw was long and narrow—not human. Ken averted his eyes. The other monster had a hunchback and walked with a double limp. He moved to a bell mounted on the wall above the tables and rang it, paying no attention to the bloody corpses below him. Then both of them skulked off the way they had come, like rats.

Chrs moved with great care through the pitch-black basement, taking slow steps and making as little noise as possible. He felt his way along the walls and around the washing machine, dryer, water tank, and furnace. He bumped into a pool table and then an out-of-tune piano with broken keys positioned in one corner. He did not smell the boy. Anger flushed him. The boy *had* tricked him.

Sitting on the living room sofa with the two lights on, Jim picked up his walkie-talkie. "This is Jim for Paul, over."

Dan sagged into the sofa behind him. A moment passed.

"This is Evan. My father went out on the snowmobile to rescue a friend of mine. Over."

Jim and Dan looked at each other.

"Jim, this is Helen, over."

"Go for Jim, Helen. Over."

"Paul went to get Tommy Burgess, one of Evan's friends. His mother is stuck at work, and he's home alone with no heat. Over."

"How far away is he? Over."

"The far side of the bend." She paused. "Over."

"Have him check in as soon as he gets in, over."

"Roger that."

Evan's voice returned. "Over and out."

Jim set the walkie-talkie on the table, then turned and looked out the picture window, which served no purpose. "It doesn't seem right."

"What's that?" Dan said.

"We're sitting here with heat and electricity, and Jenny Johnson is across the street with a baby, and all she's got is a fireplace."

BLACKcreek

Leaning right, Paul drove the snowmobile into the driveway. He could not see the house. Leaning left now, he pulled parallel to the entrance, just a few feet from the house. The numbers nailed on the vinyl siding confirmed the address. Snow reached the picture window and just touched the storm door handle. He circled the front yard, hoping the garage had a side door. It did not.

Because of his proximity to the wooden fence that surrounded the back property, he motored through the open gate into the backyard to turn around. He came to a sudden stop. To his left, the curtains in the kitchen window billowed in the wind like twin flags. A sick feeling settled in his stomach. Someone had broken into the house.

He pulled forward, alongside the deck, and killed the engine. Standing on the snowmobile's seat, he leapt off and made an almost silent landing in the snow on the deck. It was easy to step onto the wide wooden railing, and because the house sheltered him, it wasn't too hard to maintain his balance in the wind. The headlight on his helmet illuminated the snapping curtains and lit up long icicles. Bracing his hands against the siding, he reached out with his left leg and set his foot on the window's edge. He practiced bending his right leg a few times, then pushed off the railing. For a moment he stood straight, perched only on his left foot. Then he threw his arms up and caught the eight-inch-high ridge of ice that had formed along the gutter on the flat roof over the kitchen. He set his right foot on the window's edge and held tight, then took a moment to feel secure before making his next move.

Careful to maintain his balance, Paul lowered one hand

and gripped the inside of the upper window frame. Then he did the same thing with his other hand. He lowered his body, his butt hanging in the air, so he faced the missing window. Then he stepped through the space and leaned inside. His headlight moved across the floor like a searchlight mounted on a prison watchtower. Broken glass and water from melted snow reflected the light. Looking up, he listened for movement, but the wind outside drowned out any noise inside. He moved sideways onto the counter and lowered himself onto the floor. Easing open a silverware drawer, he searched its contents and withdrew a steak knife. Then he closed the drawer and moved through the cold dark house.

In the living room, he found a mess on the coffee table: cereal bowls, plates bearing the remnants of pasta, and plastic drinking glasses. Tommy had probably spent the entire day on the sofa. But where was he now? Turning left, he aimed the flashlight at the stairs. Something caught his eye to his right. Aiming the headlight low, he frowned at a metal rod protruding from the front door. Moving closer, he slid the knife into his pocket and used both hands to pull the rod free. Its end had been ground into a point. He leaned on the heavy spear, using it to stand, and aimed the headlight upstairs. He swallowed. This had become a matter for the police. Too bad there was no way to reach them.

"Tommy?"

While he waited for some sign of the boy, he sensed rather than saw movement to his left, in the direction from which he had just come. Turning his head so the headlight passed over the room, he glimpsed the snarling face of an animal, a terrifying visage glowing in the light. Long translucent hair hung from the top of the figure's head but only in patches. Sores and blemishes covered his skin, stretched over a skull that bore angles and curves with little relation to human anatomy. The eyes were sunken, the nose upturned to reveal gaping nostrils, and the teeth appeared to have been filed into jagged points.

The figure disappeared, and Paul aimed the headlight at the floor just in time to see it scampering, clad in animal skins of some kind, out of the light. Paul aimed the headlight even lower, this time catching the thing—a man—in the light as it leapt straight at him, its open mouth like that of a wild animal. The man collided with him, knocking him into the corner. The fall to the floor saved him from the knife, which flashed above him and scraped the wall.

Paul kicked the disfigured man in one calf, and when the man arched his back, Paul shoved him onto the stairs. The man faced him, snarling, with bloodlust in his pink eyes. Seeing no alternative, Paul drew the steak knife from his pocket and dove at the man, who kicked Paul's chest, driving him through the air and crashing against the door. The knife slipped from Paul's fingers, and a second later he joined it on the floor.

The man scrambled a few stairs up, then turned and got to his feet. Paul felt on the floor for the steak knife. The man leapt high above him, rimmed in light from the headlight, his knife seeking a target. Paul's hands located the spear instead of the knife, and he swung it up. The man landed on it, driving its back end against the door and impaling himself through his chest with a shocked scream. He slid down the length of the spear, slicking it with his blood, until he came face-to-face with Paul, who gazed in horror at his bluish, monstrous features. Seizing the dead man by the collar of his fur, he stood and shoved him sideways. The sharp end of the spear struck the floor, and the man slid down it, then lay still with the spear sticking straight up.

Paul retrieved the steak knife and aimed the headlight at the dead man on the floor. In addition to the furs, he wore a necklace that appeared to have been fashioned from human fingers. Paul aimed the headlight at the top of the stairs.

"Tommy? It's Mr. Goodman from school. Evan's father. Come on downstairs, son. It's safe."

A long moment passed before Tommy appeared at the top of the stairs. "Is he gone?" the boy said.

Paul glanced at the corpse on the floor, then back at Tommy. "He's dead."

"Good." Tommy came down the stairs.

Paul held out his free arm, and Tommy hugged him without prodding.

"Are you taking me home with you?"

"Yes, but not just yet. I have to do something first."

The ropes chewed into Ken's flesh as he continued to rub his wrists against each other like two sticks used to start a fire. Across from him, Henri grunted, doing the same. So focused on the chore at hand, Ken had run out of comments.

BLACKcreek

Voices echoed in the darkness. Ken faced the tunnel to his left, then realized they came from his right—the opposite end.

Two lanterns appeared this time, bobbing along. Fear crept up Ken's spine.

Three figures came into view, accompanied by female voices. As they grew closer, Ken saw five beings in total: three adult women, an adolescent girl, and a younger girl of five or six. All of them wore furs and bone-white jewelry. They shuffled in the center trench, creating the illusion their legs had been cut off. Henri whimpered.

The females hobbled past them and moved to the tables, stepping around the two corpses on the floor. All of them had long translucent hair that made them appear aged. The leader seemed twice as old as the other adults, who might have been in their twenties. Ken counted three generations, each progressively uglier than the one before it.

"Lt's gt bsy," the oldest said, her grunts reminding Ken of those made by a gorilla.

"Wr gng t't wll," one of the younger women said. She had a big nose.

"Wnt mt s'bd," the remaining younger woman said. She spoke out of one side of her mouth, as if her jaw had been broken.

The oldest woman—the grandmother, Ken supposed—took a thick rope with a noose on one end from under one of the tables. She placed the noose around the feet of the male corpse and tightened it, then fed the rope through a pulley mounted on a wooden crossbeam in the ceiling. Using both hands, she pulled on the rope, raising the corpse's legs, which made snapping sounds. She continued to pull the corpse from the table. It swung upside down in a circle, and the first daughter—Ken named her Big Nose—steadied it. The corpse's arms separated from its sides, aimed at the ceiling at unnatural forty-five-degree angles. Ken did not recognize the man, who wore a black suit beneath his overcoat.

Grandma wrapped the end of the rope around an anchor mounted on the wall. Big Nose grabbed a metal bucket from beside the table and placed it beneath the hanging corpse's head. Crooked Jaw pulled a hunting knife from beneath her fur and slit the dead man's throat, pouring his blood over his face and into the bucket.

Grandma tightened a second noose around the ankles of the corpse on the other table, while Big Nose tended to the body of the dead young man on the floor. Grandma pulled her rope, raising the legs of a dead woman who wore sheer stockings beneath a black dress, as if she had dressed for her own funeral. Within minutes, three corpses hung from the ceiling, their blood draining into buckets.

Crooked Jaw took a fourth rope from under the table. It did not have a noose, so she had to fashion one. Looking away from the horrible scene, Ken focused on Henri, missing an ear and half his tongue. The little girl climbed on top of the second tier that Ken sat upon and moved before him, blocking his view of Henri. When she came into the light, he flinched. Grime covered her face, and her long hair was matted. Both of her lazy eyes were pink, and her mouth drooped on one side. She had a hump over one shoulder, and her fingers stretched to an unnatural length. She was younger than Ken's students, but he recognized an innocent curiosity within her. She smiled at him, and he saw several gaps where teeth belonged.

"Gt 'wy frm hm!" the older girl said with a hiss. She had the same lazy eyes and jaw as the little girl, who scampered away.

Crooked Jaw looped the new noose around the ankles of the female corpse on the floor and hoisted it into the air. The corpse turned in a circle, closer to Ken than the others. He did not recognize her either, and for that he was grateful.

Grandma moved to the first corpse she had strung up and seized the collar of his overcoat. She tugged the coat free of his shoulders, then pulled it off his arms. She held the coat before her, studying it, then tossed it aside. Next she removed his suit jacket and tossed that aside. Unsheathing her knife, she cut off his necktie, then the buttons from his bloody shirt. Curling the fingers of one hand around the cuff of a trouser leg, she slit the pants down to the man's crotch, then drew the knife up the other leg, and tossed the rag aside. The corpse hung naked except for the man's soiled underwear. A dozen entry and exit wounds pocked his flesh, and dried blood caked his skin. Grandma tore his briefs apart with her bare hands, chuckling at his flaccid penis. Big Nose and Crooked Jaw laughed, and the older girl joined them.

A deep barking sound reverberated off the walls, silencing them and causing Ken to recoil. A man with long hair and a filthy beard shuffled out of the darkness, coming from the same direction they had, and loomed between Ken and Henri. The older girl ran behind Grandma, where she cowered with the little girl.

"Wht's ll ths tlkng?" Grandpa said. He had broad shoulders and stood taller than them despite his age. "'M fckng hngr!"

Grandma made a sucking sound between her teeth. "Wr ll hngr."

"Thn stp ymmrng nd strt ckng!"

Grandma waved him off. "G'bck t'bd, ld mn. W'v gt wrk t'd."

Sneering, Grandpa seized Big Nose by the wrist. The female shook her head and rubbed her belly in a circular motion with her free hand. Ken gathered she was pregnant. Grandpa spat on the floor, then grabbed Crooked Jaw and spun her to face the table. He dropped the furs from the lower half of his body and the foul odor in the air increased. He hiked up Crooked Jaw's fur dress and shoved himself inside her, grunting. Crooked Jaw leaned on her arms, taking his angry attention without complaint. Clucking her tongue, Grandma drove her knife into the pubic area of the naked corpse and drew the blade down to his collar bone, splitting him open.

SEVENTEEN

Paul pulled the spear out of the dead man and tossed it aside. It thumped on the sofa, and it occurred to him Alice was not going to appreciate the bloodstain it left. He seized the man's wrists and dragged him into the dining room. Tommy followed.

Paul heaved the dead man into a sitting position, threw the lifeless arms over his back, lifted the corpse off the floor, and dumped it on the dining table with a crash that caused Tommy to flinch.

"I'm sorry," Paul said, his chest heaving. He took out his phone and turned on its flashlight function. "Take this."

He handed the phone to Tommy, then moved closer to the corpse. Warts, scars, and lesions covered the dead man's misshapen face, which had a third cheekbone. Squeezing the cleft chin, Paul pulled the lower jaw down. Two rows of teeth glistened with saliva on the lower jaw. Paul leaned down and looked inside the mouth.

"Give that to me."

Tommy handed him the phone, and he aimed it inside the gaping maw at two rows of teeth on the upper jaw. He handed the phone back and stood straight. Grabbing the man's left wrist, he raised the forearm and narrowed his eyes. What appeared to be fur-covered hands were actually gloves. He tugged the glove from the hand and allowed the arm to drop back to the table. The glove's fingers had webs between them, and stitching ran along the lengths of the fingers. Deer hide had been sewn onto the dried skin of a human hand. Paul tasted bile.

"What is it?" Tommy said.

"Nothing." Paul tossed the obscene glove onto the table and proceeded to open the flaps of fur, revealing knives and bones that could be used as clubs. He took the phone from Tommy and began taking photos with it.

"I saw another one of these in the woods," Tommy said.

Paul looked at the boy. "A different one?"

Tommy nodded. "The one I saw didn't have any hair on his head, but he had those same bumps all over."

Paul pointed at the dead thing's face. "These are tumors. Cancer."

Paul moved to the end of the table and raised the corpse's legs. He grabbed the fur-covered boots by the ankles, then pulled them off. The legs swung at their knees, and he grabbed them at the ankles again. The same type of dried human skin that had been used to fashion the gloves had been utilized for thick socks as well. Paul declined to remove them, but what he saw startled him even more: both ankles appeared to have been rotated, so the feet pointed inward at each other.

"What are those?" Tommy said.

"Club feet."

"Can we go now?"

"Yes."

BLACKcreek

Korbel and Gigi sat huddled together in the kitchen, wrapped in blankets and passing the whiskey back and forth while the blue flames in the stove's burners illuminated the kitchen and provided warmth.

"Happy Valentine's Day," Gigi said in a dazed voice.

"You too."

Grandpa groaned and arched his back, then slumped over Crooked Jaw. He reset his furs, then turned to the other women as they flayed the corpses hanging from the crossbeam.

"Hrr'p."

Looking at the ground, he picked up Panzer by his collar and heaved the dog's carcass onto the table, then walked away. The older girl emerged from hiding behind Grandma.

"Tk cr'f th dg," Broken Nose said.

The girl shuffled over to the table, opened a drawer, and withdrew a knife, which she used to cut the dog open. On the floor, Henri kicked his feet in a spasm of fury, driving his heels into the floor and cursing with his mangled tongue. Ken watched the women trade annoyed looks.

"Stop it, Henri," he said.

Henri continued to wail. Crooked Jaw moved over to

him with her knife.

"No!" Ken lunged at his ropes.

Crooked Jaw jerked Henri's head back. He barked at her in a defiant manner, and she cut his throat. Ken's body numbed. Henri's scream turned into a strangled gurgling, and his head slumped forward. A broken whimper escaped from Ken's lips. Crooked Jaw whirled on him, aiming the knife at him as if scolding a child. Ken held his breath, sweat beading on his forehead despite the cold, and Crooked Jaw rejoined the other women, who returned to their work.

Piper, Brian, Evan, and Helen sat around the living room coffee table, which they had moved closer to the fireplace. All four of them wore their winter coats. A light moved across the picture window.

"I think your father's home," Helen said. She stood and buttoned her coat, then pulled on her hat. "You keep playing without me."

Brian stood too. "I should come. He'll need help bringing the snowmobile in."

Piper stood as well. "I'm going too then."

"I'll wait here," Evan said without enthusiasm.

In the garage, Helen raised the door and watched Tommy emerge through the blowing snow. He slid down the snowbank and into the garage, followed by Paul.

"Tommy, are you okay?" Helen said.

Nodding, the boy threw his arms around Helen, who

gave Paul a questioning look.

"He's had an ordeal," Paul said. "So have I." He turned to Brian and Piper. "Would you two mind taking Tommy inside?"

Piper walked over to them. "Sure." She held out her hand. "Come on, Tommy."

Tommy took her hand and she led him inside, followed by Brian.

"I just killed a man," Paul said.

Helen's eyes widened. "An accident on the snowmobile?"

Paul shook his head. "I wish. He broke into the Burgesses' house and was trying to get at Tommy. He had a knife and a spear. He attacked me, and I picked up the spear . . ."

Helen shook her head. "Wait a minute—what?"

"He wasn't normal. He looked like a freak and acted like a maniac."

Helen held her hands to her temples. "Start from the beginning."

Paul recounted his tale, vapor billowing from his mouth.

"It was self-defense," Helen said.

"Of course."

"We have to tell the police."

"How? Set a house on fire? Who would come? We're on our own. Henri disappeared, and Tommy said he saw another one of those things in the woods. I'm going to get Jenny and bring her and Marcus over here."

Helen considered it and decided against arguing. "Okay."

"I told Tommy not to say anything until I get back. Go manage that situation."

"Right."

She watched him climb out into the snow, and when she couldn't see him anymore, she closed the door.

"What's that?" Dan said.

"It sounds like a snowmobile." Jim stood up from the sofa and pulled back one curtain.

A headlight moved across his front yard. "Looks like Paul."

The headlight turned toward the window, then stopped and shone inside.

"What does he want?" Dan said.

The headlight blinked on and off.

"I think he wants to come inside."

"So let him in."

They put on their coats and went into the garage, where the generator roared. A figure emerged through the falling snow and tumbled into the garage, bringing snow with him.

"You look like Robert Perry," Dan said. "Sorry, the North Pole's already been discovered."

Paul got to his feet and raised his goggles. "I need your help."

"Shoot," Jim said.

"I need you to come across the street with me."

"What's going on?" Dan said.

"I brought Tommy Burgess back to my house like I said I would. Something happened over there—something bad. The police will need to be involved." He repeated his story for them.

"That's kind of hard to believe," Dan said.

"I thought you'd say that." Paul took out his phone and showed them his photos of the man he had slain.

Dan took the phone, studied the photo, and showed it to Jim.

"According to Tommy, there's another one out there. I think there could be more."

"I'll get my gun," Jim said.

Helen sat on the sofa. "Come here, Tommy."

Tommy walked over to her. He had been sitting, watching Piper, Brian, and Evan play Sorry, his expression blank.

"Mr. Goodman told me what happened. Sit with me."

The boy climbed onto the sofa with her, and she put her arms around him and kissed the top of his head. "Everything will be okay."

Evan looked at them. "What's wrong with him, Mom?"

"Nothing, sweetie. Go back to your game."

Paul drove the snowmobile to the end of the driveway with

Jim hanging on behind him. He was glad it was almost a straight shot to Ken and Johnny's front door, because he did not look forward to making turns with the taller, heavier man onboard. He stopped at what he estimated to be the end of the driveway, then motored the vehicle across the street at a slow speed. Snow blew into his eyes and he wiped it away. The machine climbed an incline, which he knew to be the Johnsons' driveway. When they crested the incline, he decelerated even more, then stopped the machine altogether. He killed the engine and looked over his shoulder at Jim, who nodded.

They got off the snowmobile and Jim sank to his knees. They lumbered toward the garage door. Paul groped for the handle in the snow. He raised the door, and once again the snow collapsed beneath him and he rolled into the garage. Jim waded in after him.

Paul stood. "Ready?"

"And willing," Jim said.

Using the flashlight, Paul led Jim to the side door. He rapped on the door with his fist. They waited, and he rapped again. Cupping his hands around his mouth, he called out, "Jenny?"

"Locks on side doors like this aren't very secure. I suggest kicking the door right above the knob. You may not even break it."

"I don't think I can get my leg that high in this suit."

"Then step back."

Paul moved aside. Jim studied the door for a moment, then gave it a good kick. The door flew open. Darkness beckoned.

"Wait." Jim reached into his pocket and drew a .38 revolver. "Okay, now."

Paul led the way. They climbed the steps to the hallway, which led into the living room. Flames crackled in the fireplace.

"Jenny?" Paul said.

The bassinet was empty. As they entered the room, Paul saw two figures on the floor.

"Jenny!" He ran to her side, but what he saw made his mouth open and the blood rush from his head.

Jenny lay on the floor, her torso covered with dozens of knife wounds. Her open eyes did not blink. The carpet around her had soaked up her blood, and when Paul moved closer his boot made a squishing sound.

"Jesus," he said. "Jenny . . ."

Jim pointed at the second corpse. A fire iron protruded from the man's head. He wore layers of fur, like the man Paul had killed. "This one's even uglier than the one that attacked you."

Paul looked at the corpse with the misshapen head. "What do you think? Did they kill each other?"

The flames crackled before Jim spoke. "Maybe. But if they did, where's the knife he used to kill Jenny?"

Paul stared at the old man. "The baby's gone."

"Let's go get him."

In a small mudroom located near the back of the house,

they discovered the intruders had sneaked in through a window facing the river. The glass in the window had not been broken; the window had simply been left unlocked.

"I'll take you to my house first, then go get Dan," Paul said.

"That won't work."

"Why not?"

"Because we're going to need a lot more guns."

Ken hung his head. He did not wish to watch the progress of the women as they butchered the four people and the dog. The sounds of cutting, sawing, and snapping sickened him. Nor did he wish he to stare at Henri's corpse. Broken Nose relieved him of that horror when the pregnant woman looped one of the nooses around Henri's ankles and secured it.

"Gv m'hnd," Broken Nose said.

Crooked Jaw joined Broken Nose, and the two women pulled on the rope. Henri's legs rose into the air, his back slid across the floor, and then he swung out of view. Tears rolled down Ken's cheeks as he listened to blood pouring into another one of the metal buckets. He sobbed, unable to distinguish the sounds of fabric tearing from those of flesh ripping.

Closing his eyes, he imagined a street in New York City. He had been there many times. Towers stretching overhead and the smells of hot dogs with onions filling his nostrils. Horns honking. Brakes squealing. People chatting on phones. A siren wailing. A helicopter roaring overhead. The sun beating down on his forehead.

Dan stood in Jim's garage with his arms spread wide. "What happened?"

Jim picked himself up off the floor as Paul slid down the slope of snow behind him.

"Get your hat and get on that snow scooter," Jim said.

"Am I going for a ride?"

"We got trouble."

"What happened?"

Jim entered the house and closed the door behind him.

"We're going to my house," Paul said. "Jim's getting his guns."

"Let's go," Dan said. "But Trapper's coming too."

Ken snapped his head up. Lost in his mental reconstruction of New York City, he had actually managed to fall asleep. The females had left, taking their spoils with them. Henri's bloody clothes had joined the others' in the pile. His muscles ached from the cold, so he stood and stretched despite the discomfort it caused.

A baby cried in the darkness. He realized this sound had awakened him. He turned toward where the females had come from, where their camp must have been. The echoing cries came from the opposite direction, so he looked that way. A lantern glowed far down the tunnel. Good Lord, they had snatched someone's baby. As the lantern grew closer, the baby's cries grew familiar.

A figure clad in the same fur hides approached, the lantern in one hand and a baby in the other. Tears formed in Ken's eyes. The figure drew closer: a woman with a scarred face and matted hair. The baby was wrapped in several blankets secured by a leather strap. The woman glanced at him as she neared the table.

"Marcus?" Ken said in a quivering voice.

The woman passed him and he lunged at her, trying to see the features of the baby.

"Wait—that's my baby."

The woman looked at him. Her pink eyes were crazy, even by the standards of these cannibals. She kept walking.

"You've got my son!" A tingling sensation swept through his body. "Come back! What have you done to my wife? Please, that's my son!"

The darkness swallowed the lantern's light. Ken fell to his knees, weeping as Marcus's cries echoed.

EIGHTEEN

"Excuse me, kids."

Evan and Tommy cleared off the sofa, and Jim dumped the canvas army bag full of weapons there. The stocks of rifles protruded from the open end of the bag and ammunition cartridges rattled against each other. Helen cleared the dining room table, which they had pulled into the living room, closer to the fireplace. Jim joined Paul and Dan at the table; then Helen pulled out a chair and did the same. Trapper lay on the floor at Dan's feet.

"Are you sure you want the kids hearing this?" Jim said to Paul.

"They'll be fine," Helen said. "So will I. We're all entitled to know what's going on out there."

Jim offered a slight bow.

Paul had laid several maps out on the table. "Henri disappeared earlier today. I found tracks leading toward the river. Panzer ran in that direction and didn't come back. I didn't follow because the snow was so deep."

"I wouldn't have either," Dan said.

"Right now, we don't know what happened to either of them. We do know that at least two of these *things* entered the Johnsons' house through a back window, which also faces the river. Jenny was killed, and she took one of them with her. Marcus is missing."

Helen shook her head. "Jenny died trying to protect her baby. I would have done the same thing."

"Ken is missing, but I assume he's somewhere safe."

"Why do you assume that?" Jim said.

"Because Jenny sent him to the store for diapers before the storm hit. He must have gotten off Cayuga Island before the weather became impossible to travel through. Hopefully he's holed up somewhere warm."

"But Jenny never heard from him, even before all forms of communication went down," Helen said.

"Nevertheless, he isn't *here*."

"Neither is Marcus."

Paul met his wife's gaze. "I want to stay focused on this island. Next, one of these things tried to get Tommy, for no discernible reason. Again, it broke in through a back window that faced the river."

"Let's back up for a moment," Jim said. "You keep calling these perpetrators 'things.' Explain that, and I'll offer my theory why the river is the common factor."

Paul took out his phone, brought up the photos, and set it on the table. "These are the shots I took of the intruder I killed—"

"Stop saying that," Helen said. "The way you described it, he killed himself. And if he didn't, it was self-defense."

"She's right," Jim said. "Be careful how you describe your account."

"—and of the one we believe Jenny killed. First, let's look at their clothes. They both wore animal hides, deer fur.

282

Human skin for undergarments. And they carried weapons and wore jewelry—for lack of a better word—made in part from human bones. Purely from a sociological and cultural level, they are not from our society. Next, look at their physical properties. Both were male, and both suffered some identical genetic defects: they had two rows of teeth on each jaw and they had club feet. Identical birth defects. Humanoid, yes. But human? I don't think so. They descended from humans like us, but they're something else: genetic mutations."

"Mutants," Dan said.

"Exactly."

"I blame Hooker Chemical."

Jim rolled his eyes. "Here we go again."

"I think he's right," Helen said.

"So do I," Paul said. "They shared other defective traits, like tumors and lesions all over their bodies, and pink eyes, like albinos. Whatever they are, they're not normal. Let's face it: we all know where they are. Love Canal is only two miles from here. All those toxic chemicals went into the ground, and a lot of them came back up. The documentation exists: more than a third of the population there suffered chromosomal damage."

"*Hooker Chemical*," Dan said.

"Which brings us to my theory," Jim said. "The linking factor between Henri's disappearance, Jenny's murder, and the attempted assault on young Mr. Burgess is the river. These goons must have come from there. Not directly, but they use it for safe passage—*secret* passage."

"The river people," Dan said.

"What's that?"

"Henri once told me he saw people walking along the riverbank at night. He called them the river people."

"Why the river, though?" Paul said.

"Because it leads to Cayuga Creek," Jim said.

"That's where Tommy says he saw one of these *goons* a couple of months ago," Helen said. "Maybe they have a camp somewhere in the woods."

"I don't think so." Jim took off his eyeglasses and wiped the lenses with his shirt. "The woods along the creek, at least on our little island, barely qualify as woods. It's really just an embankment, and the playground is right there. These goons were adults. They had to grow up somewhere unnoticed. Someone would have seen them."

"Someone did see them." Helen glanced over to the coffee table and the floor around it where Tommy sat with Evan, Piper, and Brian.

"But he didn't report it. Someone, sometime, would have."

"A cave, then?" Helen said. "Right off the creek?"

"Or a tunnel."

"Jesus, that's it," Dan said.

"There are abandoned sewer lines all over the area," Dan said.

"That's an old wives' tale," Paul said.

"I remember when they dug that new sewer line at Love Canal. That's when they broke through the seal and let some of that toxic crap out. It stands to reason that if they built a *new* sewer line, there must have been an *old* one."

Helen leaned forward. "Dan's right. An old sewer line

or some other kind of abandoned tunnel could lead from the creek right back to Love Canal."

Paul inhaled. "Even if that's true, we'd never find it in this storm, because no one's stumbled across it *without* the storm."

"They must have hidden the entrance," Helen said.

"The cops will have to find it when the storm blows over," Dan said.

"Or when spring comes?" Paul said. "There isn't time for that. Henri and Marcus are both missing now. I hate to think what our goons wanted with them or with Tommy."

"It's been a long, cold winter," Helen said. "They need a food supply."

"That's exactly what I was thinking."

She faced each man in turn. "Maybe they were desperate and the storm emboldened them to come out. No one could see them during this"—she gestured at the picture window—"even in the daytime."

Piper stood. "Will you listen to yourselves? You're being ridiculous. And creepy. You're going to scare Evan and Tommy."

Evan did look scared. Tommy looked determined.

"You're all welcome to play that board game," Helen said.

Piper sat back down.

Paul looked at the two men. "We have to do something."

"Where would we even look?" Dan said.

"At the source," Helen said.

"In Black Creek Village," Paul said.

Ken gnawed on his ropes, took a break to spit fibers out of his mouth, then gnawed some more. He did not know what had happened to Jenny, and he tried not to think about it, but he knew his son was here, somewhere, underground. He intended to free him from these monsters.

Why had they kept Marcus alive?

For the same reason they had kept *him* alive—for future feeding.

A faint sound echoed. Looking up, he saw lantern glow heading his way. He spat more rope fibers out of his mouth and sat on his butt. The lantern grew closer. He recognized Broken Nose. She carried the lantern in one hand and a bowl in the other. Drawing closer to him, she set the lantern on the ground and drew a knife from the folds of her fur. Did she intend to kill him? He swallowed, and rope fibers made him gag.

Getting down on one knee, she aimed the point of her knife at his crotch. "Ndstnd?"

He nodded. "I understand."

She raised the bowl to his lips, and he saw it had been made from the top of an animal skull. A dog skull, maybe.

"Drnk," she said.

He lowered his eyes to the slop in the skull bowl. It resembled ground beef and water. He shook his head.

"Drnk!"

"No," he said.

She raised the knife from his crotch to his throat. "*Drnk.*"

He glared at her. Why did she want him to eat so badly? To fatten him up, he reasoned. Or at least to keep him from wasting away while they feasted on the others. She stepped back in one quick movement and rested on both heels, just beyond his reach if he tried to kick her. She raised her hands before her face and bent them at the wrists like paws, then panted.

They had served him Panzer in a bowl, either because they knew he would not eat, or they refused to share, human meat.

"All right," he said. "Bring it here."

She scooted back to him, returned the knife to his crotch, and raised the bowl to his lips. The touch of the bowl made him cringe. She raised it further, allowing the meaty liquid to seep into his mouth. He swallowed it. At least it got rid of the tickling sensation left by the rope fibers. Broken Nose grinned. What would it be like, he wondered, to take her child from *her*?

She raised the bowl to his lips and he took in a mouthful of the slop and chewed it before swallowing. He told himself it was only chili, but in the end he would have eaten it anyway, whatever it was, because he needed his strength to kill every one of them.

"You're jumping to one hell of a conclusion," Dan said. "It's a mighty leap from Cayuga Creek to Black Creek Village."

"It makes sense," Paul said. "I'm guessing these goons were both in their twenties. That would make them second-generation Love Canal residents—or third generation, depending on how their microsociety developed."

"But if that's where they live, why aren't they kidnapping and killing people there?"

"Because then the odds of them being traced would be greater," Helen said. "If they live underground somewhere near Love Canal, in Black Creek Village, they use the tunnel to reach the creek, and the creek to reach the river, and the river to reach right across the street."

Dan gestured with his arms. "We don't even know if there is a tunnel!"

"But you said there is."

Dan looked at Paul. "Say something to her."

"We also don't know they haven't killed anyone in their own neighborhood," Paul said. He rifled through his maps and put one on top. He indicated different points. "This is Colvin Boulevard, and this is the containment zone. We've got these side roads around the field, and the buildings where the pumping station used to be in the middle. Not to mention parks between the streets, and these fields over here."

"Maintenance people work in those two buildings," Dan said. "Or mad scientists."

"That doesn't mean our goons couldn't be living underneath it. Or over here"—he pointed off to one side of the field. "There are still a few abandoned houses where the canal used to be. Maybe the goons lived in one of them before they went underground. If so, they might still be using the house—the best of both worlds."

Dan drummed his fingers on the table. "So? What do you want to do? Go out there now, in this, to see if there's an entrance to an underground camp where mutants are holding a baby and an old racist prisoner?"

Paul held his gaze. "It couldn't hurt to look."

"You ever heard of frostbite?"

"I have a snowmobile and so does Brian. If he's agreeable, we could take them both for a ride."

"Or we could just ride them to a police station."

"The police will never believe you," Helen said. "They won't risk the lives of any cops just to take a look until it's too late."

"She's right," Jim said. "I know how they think. I used to be one of them. I still am, I guess."

"Of course they won't believe you," Dan said. "Because it's a cockamamie idea in the first place."

Paul pointed at his phone. "The truth is in my phone and in the Johnsons' house and over in Tommy's house. I'm going, with or without backup."

"Maybe we should just be worrying about our own neighborhood. What if those things come back? We have to warn people."

"They won't come back now. Two of their own are dead, remember? If they're as clever as we think, they won't risk being discovered again for a long time."

"I'm going too," Jim said.

"You're both crazy," Dan said.

Brian stood. "You can use my snowmobile, but I'm driving it."

"No!" Piper jumped to her feet.

"We can't ask you to do that, son," Paul said.

"I insist." Brian approached the table. "Do either of you know how to drive one?"

Jim and Dan looked at each other, then shook their heads.

"Then you need me. No one's learning how to drive a Cat on a night like this."

"Only three of us can go," Paul said. "We need to save some seat space for Henri, if we find him. Dan, since you're not exactly gung ho about this, you stay here and keep my family and Tommy safe."

"You'll get no argument from me," Dan said.

"*Help* keep us safe," Helen said.

"Then it's settled," Paul said.

Jim stood his two hunting rifles on end. "I only brought four. I wasn't counting on the young man joining us, but I'm not comfortable giving him one anyway."

"I want one of those to stay here," Helen said.

They stood around the table, where Jim had laid the weapons out.

"Then you shall have it."

"Don't worry. I can shoot that," Dan said. "This stump isn't entirely useless."

"Don't worry, because you won't *need* it," Paul said.

"I have my .38 revolver." Jim handed a holstered Glock

.22 to Paul. "You carry that."

"Is this legal?" Helen said.

"No, but who will know? No one will see us, and we already know there's a valid reason for your husband to be armed, whether we encounter trouble or not."

Paul pulled the .22 free of its holster and studied it.

"Have you ever fired anything like that before?" Jim said.

"I've never fired any gun before," Paul said.

"Wonderful. It's like a pocket camera. Just point and shoot."

"What about me?" Brian said.

"That isn't going to happen."

"What if there *is* trouble?"

"Stick close to the grown-ups."

NINETEEN

They stood in the garage, watching Brian clear the snow from his machine outside. Neither the snow nor the wind had let up, and multiple beams from phones, flashlights, and headlights crisscrossed the space.

"Take care of yourself, you dumb Polack," Dan said.

Jim gave him a disdainful look. "Who are you calling Polish? I'm a wop."

Dan smiled.

Helen hugged Paul. "We need you to come back."

"I will." Paul looked at Evan and Tommy. "You listen to your mother. And you listen to *his* mother."

"Don't do anything stupid out there, Dad."

Paul mustered a smile. "Have I ever?"

"There's a first time for everything."

"This whole thing is stupid." Piper stepped before her parents. "Daddy, if anything happens to him out there, I swear I'll never forgive you."

"Piper," Helen said.

"It's okay," Paul said. "She's old enough to speak her mind." He looked at his daughter. "Some things are worth taking a risk for. Brian understands that."

Tears filled Piper's eyes. Brian's snowmobile started, and she ran to the edge of the garage. "Brian!"

Unable to get off the snowmobile, Brian waved.

"Poor kid," Paul said.

"What about me?" Helen said.

"Don't go shooting at shadows." Paul kissed her mouth.

"I love you," she said.

"I love you."

"Let's get going," Jim said. He wore an orange hunting vest over his parka.

Paul walked to the edge of the garage.

"Take care of him, Dad," Piper said, staring straight ahead at Brian.

"I intend to." Paul clapped Jim's shoulder. "Let's saddle up."

Paul put his helmet on, then stepped into the blizzard and trudged through the snow, each footstep carrying him higher than the one before. He climbed onto the snowmobile and started its engine. Jim climbed the deep snow and got on behind him, his rifle slung over one shoulder. The snowmobiles drove off and vanished into the whiteout.

The snowmobilers traveled single file at five miles per hour, with Brian following Paul and Jim close enough to see them. They took the streets this time to avoid the possibility of colliding with a tree. Jim reasoned that few cars had been left at the curb, and those that had were covered in snow;

they only had to worry about SUVs and pickup trucks, sticking out of the frozen waste like the Statue of Liberty at the climax of *Planet of the Apes*. Even when he wiped snow clear of his GPS, Paul had to lean close to see it. He found the journey as disorienting and surreal as its purpose.

They followed Rivershore Drive downhill, and Paul knew the street had become South 86th Street when they moved uphill. The headlights on his helmet and snowmobile illuminated the snow falling in front of him, and the headlights of Brian's helmet and machine illuminated the snow falling at his sides. It felt like traveling through a star field in a science fiction movie playing on a giant 3D screen.

A knot formed in his stomach as his snowmobile leveled off. Snow six feet deep rose above the railings of the bridge. If they did not match either of the lanes, they could lose control and crash into the ice twenty-five feet below, and if they did not travel close to the dividing line between the lanes, the snow might crumble beneath them with the same results. The slower speed gave his anxiety extra time to spread. The falling snow became hypnotic, and for several moments Paul did not feel the cold. Even time blurred. If Helen was right, somewhere below them lay the entrance to the tunnel used by the mutant goons.

Behind him, Brian honked his horn, and Paul blinked. Scanning the snowfield ahead, he realized he had begun to lean to his right. He threw his body to the left, aiming the snowmobile in that direction. Jim's grip around his waist tightened, and the old man cried out, his panicked voice echoing. The snowmobile dipped in the rear, and Paul's heart skipped a beat as he imagined the right tread spinning in empty space. He gave the machine gas, urging it forward, and exhaled when the machine angled left. Once the snowmobile leveled off, he leaned right, straightening their course. They descended the other side of the bridge, and he knew they had cleared it when the ground leveled off again. Jerking his head to look over his shoulder, he saw Brian close behind.

Paul passed a street sign for Buffalo Avenue on his right, sticking three feet out of a snow drift, and he leaned to his right, following the commercial street. Somewhere on either side of him, invisible through the snow, were the pizzeria, coffee shop, and drugstore he frequented. Most of the two-story buildings had shops on the street level and apartments upstairs. They passed beneath a traffic light bouncing on its cable in the wind. The snowmobile's front ski skidded over something, slowing its speed and causing him to lunge forward and Jim to lunge into him, and the treads created a deep thumping sound with a metallic echo beneath them. The snowmobile had gone over the roof of an SUV buried in snow, giving a violent shake that sent vibrations through Paul's body. Then it tracked over snow once more, and the ride smoothed. Paul leaned right, just missing the upper portion of a buried city bus. From that point on, he used the roofs of buried trucks on either side of the road as guideposts for the middle of the avenue.

He kept track of the street signs they passed as well, some on the left and some on the right, all of them only a quarter visible above the snow. The signs seemed alien when viewed from above. Picturing the fork in the road ahead, he leaned to his left. Wiping the GPS's screen, Paul relied on it to guide them to 95th Street, which would take them to Colvin Boulevard. They had entered Black Creek Village.

Helen and Piper carried sleeping bags, blankets, and pillows downstairs. Jim's generator roared in the garage.

"We'll stay down here," Helen said. "We may have heat in the whole house, but we only have electricity down here, and not a whole lot of it."

Dan looked up from the coffee table, where he and the boys played Sorry. "This generator's only supposed to run for two hours on, then two hours off. Get everyone settled down, and I'll give it a break for a couple hours."

"You can have the sofa bed, Dan. I'll bring a cot down for myself. Piper, you can have the loveseat if you want, or you can sleep on the floor near the fireplace with Evan and Tommy."

"Gee, thanks," Piper said.

"I have a better idea," Dan said. "You and Piper take the sofa bed, and I'll take the cot. Trapper can sleep on the floor with the boys."

"Are you sure?" Helen said. "That cot isn't very comfortable . . ."

"And I'm big and fat?" He chuckled. "That cot will be better for me. If I'm going to get up every two hours to go into the garage to turn the generator on or off, I don't want to get too comfortable. Just a light doze. Believe me, you don't want to try to sleep with my snoring. You'll all be up all night."

"Let's all brush our teeth and get to bed, then."

Paul brought his snowmobile to a stop where the sign for 95th Street protruded from the snow. Brian pulled up alongside him, close enough so they could hear each other over the wind. They took off their helmets and the snow beat their faces.

Paul pointed past Brian's nose. "You can't see them, but the retirement community is up on the left."

Jim leaned closer and shouted to be heard over the wind. "I sure hope they're okay."

"So do I. We can check on them when we're done." Paul pointed to his right. "The containment area should be right over there, and Colvin is straight ahead. If we get into any trouble, just remember there are houses over there. Let's circle the entire area first, then cut along Frontier and Wheatfield."

"Then what?" Brian said.

"I can think of only a few abandoned houses still standing. We start with those."

Ken gave up on chewing through the rope that bound him. His teeth ached and his jaw throbbed. Sitting back on his heels, he whipped his right arm back in anger, bottling a cry of frustration inside him. His hand came free and he fell backward, his arm flailing. Only the rope remaining around his left wrist prevented him from falling onto the lower level of the tunnel. He blinked at his bound hand, trying to comprehend what had just happened. Then it came out of the knotted rope as well.

He examined his wrists. The tissue around them, as well as the back of his right hand, had been rubbed raw. It felt wet, but in the dull glow of the lantern, he saw no blood. Rope fibers stung his skin. Rising on wobbly knees, he stretched his body and snapped his joints. He looked in both directions and knew he could escape. But then what? Recalling the deep snow that had engulfed his car in the woods, he knew he would never make it home to check on Jenny, let alone to a police station. And would the cops even believe him? He supposed he could dial back his version of events, but even then, he doubted they would send a SWAT team out into the snow to look for the tunnel. Could he even find it again himself?

He reached into his pocket for his house keys. His captors hadn't even bothered emptying his pockets, so confident were they of his helplessness. On the keychain was a mini-flashlight from his mechanic. He pressed the round button on one side and the tiny bulb cast a brilliant light. Stepping onto the lowest level, he walked to the table where Panzer had been butchered and shone his light on the instruments upon the shelves. He selected a knife with a long blade and slipped it into one coat pocket, then took another and slipped it into the opposite pocket. He picked up a meat cleaver and weighed it in his hand, its blade dark with blood. Without giving his options further thought, he set off into the darkness where Grandpa and the females had gone, in search of his son.

Paul pulled over to the right on 95th Street, and Brian pulled up beside him. Once again, they removed their helmets.

"What is it?" Brian said.

Paul gestured to a vague silhouette ahead. "Something's over there. We'd better take a look."

They put on their helmets and drove closer to the shape, which grew larger the closer they got. Paul turned off his snowmobile's engine and took off his helmet, pulling the rim of his hat over his ears.

"Looks like a truck of some kind," Jim said.

"Come on." Paul climbed off his snowmobile and stepped into the snow, sinking to his knees. Jim and Brian followed. They waded closer to the truck.

"It's a snowplow," Jim said. "Never saw one flip over on its side like this before."

They circled around the plow's immense blade, which had been covered in snow, and stopped before the cab. The windshield had been torn out, and snow filled the cabin. Paul pawed at the snow, which poured out like salt, and the lifeless, frozen features of a man came into view.

"Poor son of a bitch," Paul said.

"I wonder what happened to him," Jim said.

"Does it matter?" Brian said.

"Given the reason we're out here? Yes."

Paul continued to dig at the snow, and Jim helped him. It turned deep pink, then red.

"Oh, man," Brian said.

Their efforts revealed the driver had been impaled on the truck's long stick shift.

"This was an accident, not murder," Paul said.

"Let's make sure that's all there is to it before we leave," Jim said.

Moving their hands along the surface of the overturned truck, they waded around it through the snow. Paul tripped over something solid and fell forward, but he caught himself with his hands.

"Salt," he said, rubbing the crystalline mineral between his gloved thumb and forefinger.

They scrambled up the spilled salt, which the wind had reshaped into a giant mound. They stood upon the mound, gazing at the slope wall that descended into the truck.

Paul turned around. "The fence for the containment field must be right there. We just can't see it."

The others turned as well, and a metal spear sliced into the salt at their feet.

Tommy could not sleep. The sounds of the strange house disturbed him, compounded by the wind howling outside and the sound of snow striking the windows. The fire kept him warm, but the light it gave off added to his restlessness. Mr. Bartkowski's snoring sounded like the engine of a school bus. A battery-operated clock on the wall ticked away the seconds. A low knocking in the kitchen persisted with a steady rhythm. He frowned. What was that?

Sitting up in his sleeping bag, he saw Trapper a few feet away on the floor, his head raised in the direction of the kitchen. Evan slept on the other side of the dog.

"What is it, Tommy?" Helen said in a tired voice across the room.

"I hear something in the kitchen. Something's trying to get in."

Ken followed the tunnel, his keychain flashlight offering just enough light to penetrate the gloom. He had not expected the tunnel to reach so far; he felt as if he had already walked the length of the school track once. The walls, floor, and ceiling were concrete, cracked, and covered with slime. Brown water dripped from the ceiling at regular intervals, and he did his best to avoid being splashed.

He noted the lack of rats. Rodents avoided areas that yielded no food, but he didn't think that was a plausible explanation. Perhaps there were none because they were easy prey for the cannibals.

His eyes registered faint light ahead. It reminded him of standing on a subway platform in New York City, gazing through a dark tunnel at the next platform. His hand tightened on the meat cleaver.

"Get down!" Jim said.

The three of them hit the salt pile, seeking cover. Another metal spear slammed the steel behind them, producing a thundering echo, and fell onto the salt. Keeping his head low, Paul picked it up.

"They're trying to kill us," Brian said, almost squealing.

"They're throwing blind," Jim said. "There's no way they can see through this snow any better than we can."

"This is just like the one I used at Tommy's house."

Jim examined the point on the end. "They used a grinder for this."

"What are we going to do now?" Brian said. "They've got us pinned down."

Jim made a sucking sound and spat. "They've got spears. We've got real weapons." He slung his rifle from his shoulder. "They've got to be between us and the fence, which means they don't have any cover." He snaked up the salt pile.

"Be careful," Paul said.

"They won't see me until I start shooting." Jim set his left shoulder on the salt, supporting the rifle, and aimed with his right. He peered through the scope out of habit, then fired the rifle. With the gunshot still echoing, he pulled back the bolt, ejecting a shell, and fired again.

A spear rocketed into the salt beside him. He fired twice more, then slid down for cover and put in a fresh magazine. "I saw sparks. I think there's a car out there, upside down. They're hiding behind that."

"I don't believe this," Brian said.

"We didn't come out here because we *didn't* believe these things are out here," Paul said.

Jim crawled to the far end of the truck. This time he stood and fired twice over the salt. Then he ducked and returned to Paul and Brian. "I think I got one of them."

They heard a clanging sound above them.

"Was that another spear?" Brian said.

"No," Jim said. "They're climbing up there from the road. There must be more of them. They've got us surrounded."

Dan snapped awake. A few feet away, Helen stood putting her robe on over her nightgown. Tommy stood near the fireplace.

"What's going on?" Dan said.

"Tommy heard something in the kitchen."

Trapper got on all fours and looked at him.

"He wasn't the only one," Dan said, sitting up on the cot.

Piper sat up on the sofa bed. "What is it, Mom?"

"Wake your brother."

Rising, Dan reached for the rifle leaning against the wall.

BLACKcreek

"Did you hear that?" Korbel said.

"No, what?" Gigi said.

"It sounded like gunfire."

Korbel threw off his blankets, took Gigi's phone, and exited the kitchen. Gigi followed him a moment later. The living room was cold. He unlocked the front door and swung it open. They stood in the doorway, listening as snow blew around them. Two shots rang out in the distance.

"Sounds like a firefight right down Ninety-fifth," he said.

"That's where the snowplow hit us."

"Maybe the cavalry's arrived. Or maybe it's looters." He stepped back, closed the door, and locked it. "I think I'll keep my gun warm."

Crouching low, Ken took his thumb off the keychain flashlight and duck-walked to the end of the tunnel. Three metal steps before a low wall led onto a metal grate landing, and he hid behind the wall. Thirty feet beyond the landing, a dozen figures huddled around the fire in a square brick grill located in the center of a circular chamber twenty feet in diameter and two stories high. He recognized Grandma and Grandpa, Broken Nose and Crooked Jaw, the older girl and the little girl. He counted two other women and four boys with long hair. All of them wore furs. They sat cross-legged, gnawing cooked meat from long bones. Ken did not need much imagination to determine the contents of the grill. A catwalk covered with furs circled the chamber, providing a makeshift second floor, and clotheslines covered with furs crisscrossed dormant pipes in the ceiling. Lanterns hung at two levels, dispersing an equal amount of light.

Where was Marcus? Ken's stomach tightened.

Grandma rose. She used a knife to skewer more meat from the grill and set it on her plate.

"Nt t'mch," Grandpa said. "Y'knw sh dn't t'yt."

"Y'tll hr tht," Grandma said. She stabbed another piece of meat and shuffled toward Ken, who ducked lower than the landing. Metal squeaked against metal, then crashed, a high-pitched shriek. A metal trapdoor of some kind.

"Cm nd gt't," Grandma said.

Ken heard the meat splash into liquid below, then Grandma returned to the chamber, her footsteps clanging. Ken raised his head high enough to peer over the landing. Grandma rejoined the party, and from the right side, Crazy Eyes, the female who had brought Marcus into the tunnel, emerged from an area Ken could not see; there must have been side rooms or halls in the abandoned industrial basement. She still held Marcus in her arms.

Ken's chest swelled. His son was alive!

Paul drew the .22 from his coat pocket.

"I want a gun," Brian said.

Jim looked at him.

"I want to live."

Several footsteps echoed overhead. Holding the rifle in one hand, Jim raised his coat and took out the .38. He flipped the safety with his thumb and handed the revolver to the teenager.

"Squeeze the trigger; don't pull it. You'll have a better chance of hitting something. Don't shoot yourself or either of us by mistake."

Brian weighed the gun in his hand.

Jim shifted the rifle into his other hand, reached into his left pocket, and took out a box of ammunition, which he also handed to Brian.

They stared above them, waiting. The wind howled. Snow swirled.

Three figures armed with spears dropped from above onto the salt.

Helen grabbed a flashlight and walked into the kitchen, followed by Dan with his rifle. She shone the flashlight around the kitchen, then moved into the middle of the room. Dan moved behind her to check the back door. Piper and the boys crowded the doorway.

"Everyone hold still," Helen said.

Everyone froze, and she concentrated on listening. A scratching sound rose to fill the kitchen. A *chewing* sound.

Helen moved the flashlight beam over the oven, then the refrigerator.

"It's just that rat again," she said.

Moving into the kitchen, Evan pointed. "It's coming from under the sink."

Heads turned to the cabinets below the sink. One of the doors bounced open an inch and closed again. Helen flinched and Piper yelped.

"That's one big rat," Dan said.

Aiming the flashlight at the opposite wall, Helen snatched a broom. She crept toward the cabinets.

"Be careful, Mom," Evan said.

Helen rotated the broom like a baton, then slid its wooden handle through the pull on the door of the first cabinet. Silence fell on the kitchen. As the end of the broomstick reached the pull on the second cabinet, the door flew open and a dark shape the size of a cocker spaniel leapt out. Helen jumped back and Piper screamed. The animal bounded past Helen. At first she thought it *was* a cocker spaniel, with its long ears and lack of a discernible tail. Then the creature leapt and sank its long front teeth into the wrist of Evan's arm, which he had raised in a defensive gesture. Evan screamed and so did Tommy, and Evan fell onto the floor with the three-foot-long rabbit on his chest.

"Get back!" Dan said. Squeezing past Piper, he ran into the dining room and aimed his rifle over his stump.

Evan screamed at the top of his lungs.

"Don't shoot," Helen said. "It's too dark!"

Trapper leapt forward and locked his jaws over the nape of the rabbit's neck and shook his head. The rabbit relinquished its hold on Evan to snap its jaws at the blood-hound's side. Trapper tore a chunk of flesh and fur from the rabbit, freeing it to attack him. Piper grabbed Evan and pulled him away from the fight.

Trapper snarled as the rabbit knocked him onto his back, his short legs kicking to defend himself. Dan crouched beside them, braced the barrel of the rifle over his stump, and fired at point-blank range. The impact knocked the rabbit back, and it rolled across the floor and came up crouching in the far corner. The rabbit pinned its ratty-looking ears back and let loose a deep hiss. It had bald patches on its body, revealing orange tumors on its skin, and its eyes were bright pink. Dan had to lay the rifle across his knee, barrel pointed at the carpet, to chamber the next round. The rabbit leapt even as Dan swung the rifle into position. He fired a round into the beast's chest, flipping it in midair like a jaguar. It fell to the floor with a loud thump.

Evan continued to scream. Helen ran to his side and inspected his bloody arm. The rabbit had taken a chunk out of his forearm.

"You'll be fine," she said. "We just need to get you bandaged up."

"Will I need rabies shots?"

Helen looked at the dead rabbit, which bled all over the floor. "I don't know. But at least we have its body, so they can check it for rabies."

Dan circled the rabbit. "In all my years, I've never seen anything like that."

"I have," Tommy said.

Standing with his back to the rear picture window, Dan

set his rifle on his toe. "I think I'll start the generator and then put this thing on ice."

The window shattered behind him and a metal spear erupted from his chest.

In the darkness at the end of the tunnel, Ken peeled off his coat, which he feared would make too much noise. Removing the two long knives from the pockets, he slid one into each of the back pockets of his slacks, shoving the blades through the fabric. His navy blue sweatshirt featured the colorful emblem of the Buffalo Sabres, so he took it off, reversed it, and pulled it back on. Then he waited. He knew he could not wait too long, though: at least five men had gone hunting, and he had no idea when they would return with fresh kills.

The cannibals took turns belching. Grandpa stood and stretched. Adjusting the furs on his waist, he turned and shuffled away, vanishing into the same area where he'd seen Crazy Eyes. A bathroom, Ken supposed.

Marcus cried. Crazy Eyes separated her furs, revealing a skinny, wrinkled breast covered with sores. She raised Marcus to it and forced his mouth around her elongated nipple. Ken closed his left hand into a fist. His first priority was to rescue his son, but he hoped he had the opportunity to kill the woman. He felt certain she had done the same to Jenny, or Jenny would have been here.

Then why hadn't they brought Jenny's corpse back?

The woman had come alone, with Marcus. Perhaps the men had gone back for Jenny.

His chest rose and fell.

Marcus turned his head away from the woman's nipple and cried, and she forced it back again. Then she cried out; he must have bitten her. Ken smiled.

Grandma handed Crazy Eyes a baby bottle filled with brown water. Crazy Eyes took the bottle and pushed it into Marcus's mouth, and he drank it. Ken's temples throbbed with fury.

The cannibals settled down onto the furs around the fire, Crazy Eyes nestling with Marcus. Grandpa came back and surveyed the figures. Except for Grandma, the women lay in protective fetal positions. Grandpa lay next to Broken Nose. Ken hoped their full bellies would put them to sleep soon.

Paul, Jim, and Brian stood to confront the three mutants who had just landed at the top of the salt pile. Each of the deformed men gripped a metal spear in his fur-covered hands. Jim aimed his rifle at the mutant in the middle and fired a round into his chest. The mutant grunted, twisted away, and disappeared over the crest of the salt.

While Jim pulled back the bolt on the rifle, Paul gripped the .22 in both hands and squeezed the trigger twice, the gunfire echoing within the steel sides of the truck. At least one of the rounds struck the mutant nearest him, but that didn't stop the man from raising the spear over his head with one arm, ready to throw it. A third round caused him to stagger, drop the spear, and totter backward.

Brian aimed the .38 at the final mutant. The weapon shook in his hand, either from fear or the intense cold, and when the teenager fired, the mutant smiled through his translucent whiskers. Brian fired again, and the mutant drew his spear-throwing arm back. Jim fired his rifle and the mutant toppled. Brian's hand continued to shake.

"Get it together," Jim said.

A spear drilled through Jim's left thigh.

Dan's mouth opened, his eyes rolled in their sockets, and he fell facedown on the floor, over the carcass of the rabbit. Fissures in the window radiated from the round hole the spear had made in the window. Piper screamed, and Trapper went on a tirade of barks.

Helen shoved the flashlight into Tommy's hands. "Everyone get upstairs, now!"

She ran to the window and closed the drapes. When she turned around, the kids were already running to the stairs. Trapper remained, barking. Crouching, she picked up Dan's rifle. She glanced at the spear, sticking into the air, and pulled it out of Dan's back.

"You too, Trapper."

She ran to the stairs with one weapon in each hand. The flames in the fireplace lit the stairs enough for her to see them. Trapper continued to bark in the dining room.

"Trapper, come!"

The dog looked at her.

"Come!"

He ran to her, then followed her upstairs, where she saw the beam from the flashlight bouncing on the hallway ceiling. Turning at the top of the stairs, she squinted into the flashlight coming from Evan's bedroom.

"Not in there," she said. "The window overlooks the flat roof. They can get in through there. Get into our room—it faces the street."

Piper, Evan, and Tommy hurried out of the bedroom and into the one next to it. Helen followed and tossed the spear onto the bed, then rushed into the bathroom. Trapper followed her.

"What are you doing?" Piper said.

Helen returned with a plastic bucket containing a first-aid kit and a roll of toilet paper, the dog at her heels. She set the bucket on the bed, then closed the door and pushed in the lock. She laid the rifle on the bed and crossed the darkened room. "Tommy, shine that over here."

Tommy aimed the flashlight at the armoire standing against the wall.

"Piper, give me a hand."

Piper joined her, and the two of them pushed the armoire against the door. Helen picked up the spear and leaned it against the armoire, then picked up the rifle and examined it.

"Piper, open that first-aid kit. Disinfect that bite on your brother's arm and bandage it."

Piper moved closer to Evan. "Sit on the bed, squirt."

Evan sat down, and Piper took the first-aid kit out of the bucket and opened it.

"You should sit too, Tommy."

Tommy sat beside Evan. Trapper paced at his feet. "What if we have to go to the bathroom?"

Piper selected a bottle of disinfectant. "What do you think this bucket's for?"

Helen sat on the chair against the wall, between the two windows facing the street, and rested the rifle across her lap. She wished Paul would come home.

Jim screamed and fell to his knees, half the spear sticking out through his thigh and the back of the leg. Blood spotted the salt. He did not let go of the rifle. Over the crest of the salt, half a dozen screaming voices rose on the wind: war cries.

Paul and Brian backed against the steel, and Jim pulled back the bolt on his rifle.

The enemy stormed over the salt pile.

Snores rose from the piles of filthy fur around the cauldron.

Ken eased himself over the edge of the landing. The cold metal of the grate pressed against his flesh. He was careful to keep the grate silent as he moved along it. Clutching the cleaver in his right hand, he wormed to his left, moving one foot, pulling his body forward, moving the other foot, pulling again. Rancid moisture rose from below. When he had crawled half the distance to the chamber, he looked down through the grate and saw light dancing on liquid an indeterminate distance below. When he resumed crawling, his belt buckle scraped the grate, producing a sharp scratching sound that echoed. Wincing, he froze. None of the cannibals stirred.

He resumed crawling again—until a high-pitched wail from below ricocheted off the ceiling and the walls around him. His heart slammed in his chest as the cannibals woke and sat up, except for Grandpa, who stood. Feeling exposed, Ken pressed himself against the grate. The wailing below grew louder, and Grandpa looked straight at him.

TWENTY

The silhouettes of the mutants climbed onto the top of the salt pile. Paul shifted to his left, gaining distance from Jim, who remained on his knees. He wanted to lessen the odds that a wild throw might result in one of them being struck by another spear. But Brian moved closer to Jim. Paul waited until the mutants were close enough to see through the snow to open fire. One leapt into the air with a snarl. Paul squeezed the trigger, hitting his attacker at point-blank range, then dodged the body as it struck the steel behind him and fell at his feet. He estimated he had ten shots left before he would need to reload.

At the same time, Jim raised his rifle, took aim, and fired. His target fell backward. Jim slid back his bolt. Brian fired one shot, then another. A silhouette faded into the snow.

"I got one!"

More shapes formed within the snow. Paul and Jim fired at the same time. The snow claimed two mutants, and two more took their place. Paul fired, but Jim's rifle clicked.

"I'm out," Jim said. He fell forward and supported himself on one hand.

Brian fired two more rounds, taking down one mutant.

The next time he squeezed the trigger, the gun clicked.

Feeling the burden of protecting all three of them, Paul shifted to his right and dropped to one knee. Two of the mutants climbed over the crest. He fired at one and struck him in the shoulder. The second hurled his spear, which struck the steel six inches from Paul's head. Paul fired twice at him and he slumped over the salt. The other pushed off the snow, turning away to flee, and Paul shot him in the back. The mutant fell from view. No more attackers appeared.

"Mom, something's wrong with Tommy," Evan said as Piper finished bandaging his arm.

Helen set the rifle down and ran over to Tommy, who sat trembling, his eyes fixed on the door. "Tommy? Are you okay?"

He continued to shake and stare ahead, so she moved between him and the door.

"Tommy?"

The boy swallowed, his face lit from underneath by the flashlight in his hands. "They killed Mr. Bartkowitz . . ."

She caressed his cheek. "Yes, they did. But he died keeping us safe. Now we have to take care of ourselves. Do you understand that?"

He nodded.

"Good." She hugged him.

Then a weight crashed against the other side of the

door, causing all four of them to jump and Trapper to bark.

Grandpa hobbled forward, and Ken leapt to his feet. Grandpa stopped and looked at the meat cleaver in Ken's hand. A smile spread across his pocked face, revealing crooked teeth between gaps. A rumbling laugh escaped from his lips as he drew a bone-handled knife from beneath his furs and moved forward.

Ken spread his legs apart and bent his knees, then reached behind him and drew one of the knives from his back pocket. Grandpa stopped again and drew a second knife. He lumbered forward. Ken waited for him to get closer, then circled him, reasoning that the more they moved, the more trouble Grandpa would experience on his disfigured feet.

Grandpa squinted with one eye and followed Ken's movement. He feinted with one blade, then the other. Ken ducked and weaved. If he could take down the alpha male of the tribe, he would have less trouble getting Marcus away from the females.

Grandpa lunged with a knife and Ken jumped back to avoid the blade. Grandpa continued his momentum, swinging the other blade. Ken ducked below the powerful arm and swung the cleaver in a downward arc behind him, striking Grandpa's calf. Grandpa's knee buckled and he went down on it with a loud grunt but popped right back up. Ken suspected the cleaver had not even penetrated the hide Grandpa wore for pants.

Grandpa faced him, then closed one nostril with his thumb and blew green snot out the other nostril. He charged at Ken, swinging both blades at him from a multitude of angles. Ken stutter-stepped backward, too intimidated to parry the blows. He knew that if his back struck a wall he was finished, so instead he planted one foot and swung the meat cleaver over his head with all his strength. The rectangular blade cleared the knives and bit into the top of Grandpa's skull. Grandpa squeezed his eyes tight and screamed. Ken leapt forward, shifted the knife into his right hand, and drove it into Grandpa's belly, twisting it. Grandpa sank to his knees, and Ken jerked the blade out of his belly and buried it in one side of the man's throat. Grandpa clawed at the knife and Ken jumped back, giving him room to fall facedown on the metal grate.

Panting, Ken faced the chamber. The women and children stood before him, bones and knives clutched in their hands. The wailing from below returned, filled with anguish. Ken drew the remaining knife from his back pocket, and the women and children charged at him, their pink eyes and shiny blades glinting. Grandma got in the first blow, driving a knife deep into Ken's chest, below his left collar. One child bit his thigh, another his calf. Screaming, he dropped his knife, which clattered on the grate. Crooked Jaw stabbed him, then Broken Nose. The last thing he saw before he went down was Crazy Eyes holding his son.

BLACKcreek

Paul scrambled up the salt pile. Between the gusts of wind, he glimpsed bodies lying in the snow, the wind beginning to bury them. A hand seized his wrist and he cried out. A mutant who lay bleeding in the salt a few feet away leered at him, then opened his mouth, revealing his four rows of teeth. Then his head slumped. Paul freed his hand and slid back down the salt.

"I don't think there are any more," he said.

"Good thing," Jim said, wincing.

"What are we going to do?" Brian said.

"The first thing we're going to do is reload," Paul said.

Grimacing, Jim managed a chuckle.

Paul ejected the magazine from the .22, then took another from his pocket and slapped it into place. Then he took Jim's rifle. Jim took two cartridges out of his coat pocket and gave them to him. Paul put a fresh cartridge into the rifle, which he slung over his shoulder.

Brian took off his gloves and figured out how to pop the cylinder on the revolver. He shook the shells out and loaded six fresh bullets. "We have to get Mr. Makowski out of here."

Paul looked Jim over. "Agreed, but we're not going to do it with that rod sticking through his leg."

"This is a lot worse than an arrow," Jim said. "You aren't breaking it in half."

"No, I'm not."

"Did you think to bring any booze?"

Paul shook his head.

Jim looked at Brian. "I don't suppose you smoke weed?"

"No, sir."

"Then let's get this over with."

Paul and Brian helped the tall man stand, and he groaned.

"At least it missed the bone," Paul said.

"Thank heaven for anatomical favors."

Paul examined both ends of the spear, then moved behind Jim. "I guess we'll follow the tried-and-true procedure. Brace yourself."

Brian wrapped his arms around the old man. "Squeeze me as hard as you want."

Jim locked his hands behind the teenager's shoulders. "I'll try not to break your back."

"Step on his foot," Paul said.

When Brian had done so, Paul planted one foot against Jim's heel and crouched forward. "Ready?"

"Count to three," Jim said.

"One . . ."

Paul seized the rod with both hands and lunged forward. Arching his back, Jim screamed as the rod slid through his leg. Paul fell to his side and pulled the rod the rest of the way out. Jim continued to scream. Brian held him upright. Tossing the bloody spear into the salt, Paul jumped up and helped Brian support his neighbor. Tears streamed down Jim's face.

Paul took off his gloves, unbuckled his belt, and pulled it free of his belt loops. Kneeling, he wrapped the belt around Jim's leg, above the bleeding wound. Then he removed a pocket knife and pulled out the corkscrew, which he used to create a new hole in the leather.

"Resourceful of you," Jim said in a weak voice.

"I was a Boy Scout." Paul secured the belt and stood facing Brian. "Go get your snowmobile."

"Alone? There could be more of these things out there."

"Both of you go," Jim said. "I'll be okay. Just leave my rifle."

"I'm afraid if we set you down, you won't be able to get up again."

"That's on you."

"Get behind the bed, all of you," Helen said as the weight continued to smash against the other side of the door. "Piper, take that spear."

Evan and Tommy scrambled behind the bed, and Piper joined them with the metal spear. Trapper barked and howled.

Helen picked up the rifle. "Keep that light on the door."

Tommy trained the flashlight on the armoire and the door. Wood splintered, then snapped. Something pulled a strip of the panel out, then pushed the armoire back one foot. An arm covered in fur reached in. Helen raised the rifle to her shoulder and took aim. The hand popped the lock. She resisted the urge to run over and shoot it point-blank. The arm disappeared, then the door opened and the armoire slid back. A figure shuffled into the light, and pink-ish-white eyes glared above a hawkish nose. Helen drew in a breath and squeezed the trigger. The deafening gunshot drove the figure back, and a body collapsed in the hallway.

Paul and Brian drove their snowmobiles around the snow-plow and parked side by side just short of the salt spill. They climbed off their machines and waded through the snow. Fresh snow already blanketed the corpses of the mutants like shrouds. They scaled the salt and raised their hands at the top, then slid down. Jim sat at the bottom of the pile with his back against the steel bottom of the truck, his rifle gripped in his hands. The salt around his leg had turned deep red. Paul took the rifle from him and slung it over his shoulder, then grabbed one wrist with both hands. Brian grabbed the other wrist and they pulled Jim screaming to his feet.

"I'll never even make it up this pile," Jim said.

"It's lower at the end," Paul said.

They led him toward the end of the truck near the cab.

"I'm not going back yet," Paul said.

"The devil you say?" Jim said.

"We came out here for a reason. I'm finding that baby. This attack only proves our theory."

"You're crazy—it's too dangerous."

Paul and Brian supported Jim, who hopped on his right foot and dragged his left, one hand clawing his rifle.

"I don't think so," Paul said. "How many of these goons could there be? None came to help after we finished them off."

They descended the salt, and the wind pounded them.

"You want me to ride all the way back to your house alone in this?" Brian said.

"No," Paul said. "Jim could lose too much blood. Just take him back to Colvin and start knocking on doors. I'll come looking for you after I've checked out the rest of the area."

They loaded Jim onto the seat of Brian's snowmobile and he moaned.

"Good luck." Jim held out his rifle.

"Thanks. You too." Paul slung the rifle's strap over his shoulder.

Brian climbed onto his snowmobile and started the engine. The snowmobile climbed the slope of snow and rumbled away, vanishing into the whiteout.

Paul got on his snowmobile, started its engine, and followed. Leaning right, he circled the plow. When he reached 95th Street, he leaned left.

Piper rose from behind the bed first, then Evan and Tommy. She held the spear in both hands. Helen held onto the rifle.

"Did you get him?" Evan said.

"Yes."

Helen crept to the door and stared at the still body on the floor. She set her hand on the doorknob. "I think we'll stay up here for n—"

A twisted, lumpy face appeared in the open doorway, and a second mutant clad in fur forced the door open. Helen and the kids screamed. Staggering back, Helen raised the rifle again. The mutant shoved the door the rest of the way open. Taking aim, Helen squeezed the trigger. The weapon issued a hollow click.

Hobbling on club feet, the mutant charged at Helen with a hunting knife. Helen pulled back the bolt on the rifle. The mutant seized her throat with his free hand and forced her back. They tumbled against the blinds over the window and kept going. The window shattered and both of them fell through it, disappearing into the snow-filled night.

Following the GPS, Paul leaned left and turned onto Frontier Avenue, which ran parallel to Colvin on the far side of the containment field. As he passed 100th Street, where he knew the fence surrounding the containment area rose from the snow, a figure appeared in the glare of his headlight. He came to a sudden stop, rocking forward.

A white deer stood before him, its eyes glowing pink in the headlight. He remembered Jenny had commented about seeing an albino deer. The animal turned its head and sprinted away. Paul gave the machine gas and started forward once more. When the GPS showed he had reached 101st Street, he leaned left again, heading back toward Colvin.

He slowed down, relying on his memory to tell him where his destination lay. The cinder-block house rose from the snow on his right like a gravestone. The snow completely covered the four-foot-high fence that protected the property, and Paul rode toward the small one-story house. The snow on the ground reached the sills of broken windows, which revealed rotting plywood behind them. A metal sign on what remained visible of the door read, THIS PROPERTY HAS BEEN CONDEMNED.

Wind and snow embraced Helen the instant she went out the window, the wooden blinds protecting her from the broken glass. The shocked expression of the mutant filled her vision. Tumors covered his face, and she saw up the crevices that served as his nostrils. The bedroom window shrank in slow motion, obscured by snowfall, and she braced herself for the inevitable impact. She thought of her children upstairs and Tommy and Paul, wherever he had gone . . .

Then she slammed into the snow, which served as a cushion, and sank more than two feet into it. The impact of the mutant landing on top of her hurt more than her landing, and the rifle's barrel struck him across his chest. She heard his knife slice into the snow. The fiend punched her face, which startled her more than it hurt, and pushed off her, groping in the snow for his lost weapon.

Korbel straightened up in the kitchen chair when the doorbell rang.

"Are you expecting company?" Gigi said.

"Maybe it's another stranded cop." Standing, he took

his pistol from the stovetop. Its grip warmed his fingers.

Gigi took out her phone and stood as well. They went through the house, and she held the phone over her head, providing illumination. The house was freezing now. Standing at the front door, he peered through the peephole and saw nothing. Still holding the phone, Gigi drew her Glock from its holster. Korbel unlocked the door and opened it, leaving the chain lock in place.

A white man wearing a helmet with a glowing headlight stood on Korbel's stoop, snow up to his hips. Behind him, a snowmobile idled with its headlight on. A tall man sat slumped forward on the snowmobile's seat.

"Please help us," the man said. He had a youthful voice. "My friend's hurt, and no one else will open their door."

"What happened to him?" Korbel said.

"Someone threw a spear into his leg."

"Were you involved in all that shooting just now?"

"We were attacked over on 95th Street."

"Attacked by who?"

"I honestly don't know. Looters? Please, mister. It's cold out here and we're in trouble."

The man removed his helmet and Korbel studied the teenager's features.

"Maybe I don't want you bringing your trouble into my house."

"My friend's bleeding. Just help me fix him up and we'll be on our way if you don't want us to stay."

Korbel closed the door, removed the chain, and opened it again. "Bring him inside."

Evan and Piper crowded together at the broken window, with Tommy behind them and the wind in their faces. Tommy swept the front yard with the flashlight, which illuminated the falling snow in its beam. Below, the mutant sank into snow up to his thighs as he pulled his knife free. Helen tried to scramble away from him backward but only succeeded in digging herself deeper into the snow.

"Mom's alive," Evan said. "Throw the spear!"

Leaning forward, Piper raised the spear. "I might hit Mom . . ."

"Throw it!"

The snow and wind numbed Helen's body. She tried to get up, but her movements only entrenched her. The mutant waded toward her, waving his knife hand. Seeing her fate, she prayed for the safety of her children.

"Y'klld m'brthr, y'fckng btch!"

Using both hands, she packed a snowball and hurled it at her hunter. It struck his face and he stopped to wipe away the snow. She packed another snowball, and as she cocked her arm to throw it, a metal shaft emerged through the mutant's belly.

The spear! One of the kids had thrown it from the window.

The mutant groaned in confusion, looked at the spear, grabbed it with both hands, then fell face-forward into the snow. The other end of the spear protruded from his back. Helen looked up in the direction of the window but saw nothing.

The light from three different phones bounced around the living room walls as Korbel led the way into the kitchen. Brian supported Jim, and Gigi brought up the rear. Brian set Jim in a chair, and Gigi wrapped a blanket around him.

"You'd better sit down too," Gigi said.

Brian collapsed in the other chair and Gigi wrapped the blanket around him.

"Thank you," he said.

"I'll see what I've got in the way of bandages," Korbel said to Jim. "You may have to settle for towels."

Gigi looked from Jim to Brian.

"I'm a cop," she said. "Start talking."

Straddling the snowmobile, Paul raised its seat and removed a small crowbar from the storage compartment. He slid the crowbar through a loop on his snowsuit, then climbed on top of the seat. With his hands pressed against the concrete wall, Paul kicked in the plywood behind the broken window. He cleared the remaining shards of dirty glass, then climbed inside, his headlight illuminating the rotting interior. Any furniture had long ago been removed, and graffiti covered the walls. Somehow, kids had managed to get in at one time or another. With the wind howling behind him, he moved forward. A sharp, hollow rattling sound caused him to drop into a fighting crouch, and the headlight pinpointed a dusty beer can he had kicked.

He took the rifle from his shoulder and prowled the house with it held in both hands. A tattered mattress lay on the floor in one of the two bedrooms. He moved his head-lamp over cigarette butts and syringes on the floor. Black mold covered the bathroom walls and ceiling. Like the wallpaper, the linoleum in the kitchen peeled. The light located a wooden door—leading to the basement, he assumed. He crossed the floor, which buckled beneath his weight. For a moment he feared he would fall straight through it, but it held. He turned the doorknob. It had been locked from the other side, and there was no keyhole. He slung the rifle over his shoulder and slid the crowbar from its loop. He wedged the crowbar between the door and its frame, then pushed on the bar with both hands. Wood splintered and the door flew open.

A wooden staircase descended into darkness that swallowed the beam from his headlamp. Paul returned the crowbar to its loop, drew the pistol from his pocket, and descended the creaking steps. The smell of rotting wood filled his nostrils, and he tested each step before setting his weight upon it. Damp darkness clung to him like a living thing.

Helen rolled over and crawled through the snow to the garage. The icy snow cut her fingers and scraped her knees through her nightgown. The garage door opened before she reached it and the kids stood there. Tears rolled down Evan's cheeks. Piper held the flashlight now and Tommy held the rifle. Helen tried to stand, but she collapsed into the snow sloping into the garage as Paul had. Evan helped her to her feet, which ached from cold.

"Are you okay, Mom?"

She hugged him. "Yes."

"Piper threw the spear."

She looked at her daughter through tears. "Thank you, honey."

"Mom, do you know how to turn on this generator?" Piper said.

Helen looked at the machine. "I have no idea."

Piper pulled the overhead door down.

The narrow basement was only half as long as the house. Rust on the floor outlined where the washing machine, dryer, water tank, and furnace had once been. Mold grew on the walls, and multicolored mineral deposits formed a rough texture where they met the floor. A pool of black goo had hardened into tar over the drain in the middle of the floor. Dark, rounded shapes filled each corner from floor to ceiling: giant hornets' nests, like the one he and Evan had seen on the side of their house. A filthy tarp hung on the far wall. Swallowing, Paul moved toward it and tore it down, revealing a perfect square in the concrete, three and a half feet by three and a half feet. An underground crawl space stretched into the darkness beyond the wall.

Leaning forward, Paul aimed the headlamp around the crawl space. Gas lines and rusty pipes ran along the ceiling, shrouded with cobwebs. His heart beat faster, and his fingers twitched. He knew he had found the entrance— or at least *one* entrance—to the mutants' lair.

Sliding the pistol back into his pocket and the crowbar into the loop, he pulled on his gloves and climbed through the opening.

They entered the living room through the side door, and Helen went straight into the dining room, where Dan and the rabbit lay dead on the floor. Behind the drapes, the hole in the picture window remained the same size; the mutants had not broken through it. Snow blew through the back door into the kitchen. Hurrying over to it, she tried to close it, but too much snow blocked it.

"Get pots and pans and help me get rid of this snow," she said.

Piper touched her shoulder. "Mom, we'll do this. You're all wet. Go sit by the fire and warm up."

"We don't know if there are any more of those things out there. We're not splitting up. We're staying together."

"I'm not putting down this rifle," Tommy said.

Helen looked at him. Even though the rifle had become useless, she saw it made him feel better. "That's fine, Tommy."

Evan had already scooped up a load of snow with a spaghetti pot.

"Dump the snow into the sink until that's full," Helen said.

Paul dragged himself forward through the crawl space, dirt clinging to his damp snowsuit. The ground had been worn smooth by the passage of other bodies. He turned his head from side to side, sweeping the darkness with the light on his helmet. His left hand met a wooden edge. Grabbing the edge with both hands, he pulled himself forward and gazed down a square shaft two and a half feet wide and perhaps a dozen feet deep. Mismatched wood comprised the walls, and makeshift ladder rungs ran the height of the shaft. Rotating his body, he swung his legs over the edge and descended into the darkness.

TWENTY-ONE

Helen closed the back door and locked it. Wind blew through a smashed pane in its window, so she found a box and had Evan and Piper tape the cardboard to the door frame. With Tommy guarding her, she went into the living room, took the blanket Dan had used on the cot, and threw it over his corpse and the dead rabbit. She used duct tape to cover the hole in the window.

"All right," she said. "We're going back upstairs to cover that broken window and so I can change my clothes."

Upstairs, she gazed at the dead mutant.

"Help me get him to the window."

Piper and Evan helped her drag the corpse to the window, lift him, and throw him out to the yard below. None of them looked to see where the body landed. Then they pushed the armoire against the broken window. Helen went into the bathroom and got a towel, then returned to the bedroom and entered the walk-in closet. Closing the door, she left the kids alone while she changed her clothes.

When he had neared the bottom of the shaft, Paul slung the rifle from his shoulder and dropped it to the dirt floor. He turned in a half circle, sweeping the darkness, and found himself standing in a square room with a wooden frame build around dirt walls. The room was empty, except for a single door made from uneven planks. He opened the door and entered the next room, which was not a room at all: he stood in a concrete sewer tunnel. Someone had knocked a hole in the side of the tunnel and built the door over it. An unlit lantern hung on the wall beside the door, and three others rested on the bloodstained floor, where bodies must have been dragged. The ledge upon which he stood overlooked a trench at least two and a half feet deep. Easing himself into the trench, he followed the dark blood trails.

They made camp around the fireplace. Helen heated up some canned soups, and they ate. She looked at the clock on the wall. Almost four hours had passed since Paul, Jim, and Brian had left.

"Do you think they're okay, Mom?" Piper said.

"Yes," Helen said. "I'm sure of it."

"But it's been so long."

"Get some sleep, honey." She looked at the boys. "All of you."

Tommy shook his head.

"Okay, Tommy. You keep watch with me."

Piper and Evan crawled into the sleeping bags on the floor, and Helen put more wood on the fire.

BLACKcreek

Carrying the rifle, Paul took his time traveling through the sewer so his footsteps would not echo. He needed the element of surprise on his side. Two tables came into view, surrounded by buckets. Four ropes tied into nooses hung from pulleys mounted on the ceiling. More ropes hung from wooden boards bolted into the wall. The beam from his headlamp illuminated bloodstains everywhere. He examined several knives lying on shelves beneath the table. Blood covered them as well, some of it recent. He stood and resumed his journey.

Piper and Evan slept side by side. Helen hadn't seen them do that for years. Tommy sat next to the fireplace with his back against the wall. His eyelids wilted, drooped, closed. Helen closed her own eyes. All of the children had been through so much, but at least Tommy knew his mother was safe. Helen and her kids had no idea what had happened to Paul, Jim, and Brian. Rising, she stretched. Tommy's eyes shot open, and she smiled at him. Then he closed them again. She wanted to take the rifle from his hands, but she feared upsetting him. She circled the unoccupied sofa bed and pulled back one drape to check the weather. She could not tell if the snow continued to fall, because the wind blew in several directions at once. Trapper growled behind her.

Helen turned to the dog. Tommy had opened his eyes. Trapper's lips had pulled back, baring his teeth and showing his gums.

"What is it, boy?"

The dog faced her direction. She turned back to the window just as it exploded and a figure holding a metal spear smashed into her.

When he saw light ahead, Paul switched off the light on his helmet, but he maintained the same purposeful pace, grateful for the dirt that covered the front of his snowsuit. A chamber came into view at the end of the tunnel, two stories high with a fire roaring in a permanent grill. Two bodies hung upside-down from ropes, a bucket beneath each of them. Both men were naked. One looked forty years old and had a long beard, a body covered with sores and lesions, and clubbed feet. The other was Ken. Dead. Inside a dresser drawer perched on an old television console, a baby cried: Marcus.

Figures clad in fur moved around the hanging bodies. Cutting them. Flaying them.

Reaching the end of the tunnel, Paul climbed a short ladder onto a metal grate landing. Thirty feet away, the women did not notice him. He switched on his headlamp and raised the rifle to his shoulder.

"Stop what you're doing, now."

The women jerked their heads in his direction, fear on their disfigured faces. Around the chamber, sleeping children woke.

"I've come for that baby. Give him to me."

One of the women ran for the wooden drawer where Marcus cried. Paul guessed she was the one who had taken him—who had murdered Jenny. He squeezed the trigger and the gunshot echoed around the chamber. The woman went down with a strangled cry and did not get up. Paul chambered another round in the rifle and re-aimed it.

"I'm not here to take chances. All of you back up."

The oldest woman moved backward until she could move no farther, and the other females and children copied her. Paul hoped he could take Marcus without any additional violence, but he would take whatever action was necessary and feel no remorse.

"Tk th'chld nd'g," the oldest woman said with spittle flying from her cracked lips.

"I intend to." Paul moved forward, his footsteps echoing on the metal grate. Then he stepped on one of the furs laid on the floor before the grill, and his foot pushed straight down and he tumbled into empty space.

Helen heard Piper scream as she fell back onto the sofa bed. Shards of broken glass rained around her as the mutant loomed over her. She seized his spear with both hands, and the mutant tried to pull it from her. Patches of hair covered his tumor-laden head, and when he roared at her she saw all four rows of teeth in his mouth. She pulled the spear toward her, and when he pulled it back she let it go. His momentum carried him backward, and she hoped he would fall out the window, but he landed on the back of the sofa. Standing, he raised the spear over his head with both hands, ready to drive it straight down at her. She could not believe she had endured so much, only to find herself at the wrong end of a spear again. Trapper barked and Piper and Evan squealed.

A rifle shot split the air, and the mutant's eyes widened. The bolt of a rifle slid into place, and another shot rang out. This time, the mutant toppled backward through the window. Scrambling off the bed, Helen saw Tommy lower the rifle and pull the bolt back.

"You have to chamber the bullet," he said.

Exhaling, she looked at the broken window. "We've got a lot of work to do."

With the fur blanket pressing against his hands, Paul had no idea how far he fell, or what would break his fall—or his bones. He struck something thick but liquefied, like mud. As the gooey substance covered him, he recalled the underground system had once been a sewer line. But this substance was warm.

His hands and feet felt solid ground, like the bottom of a swimming pool, and he pushed himself upright, emerging from the slop, which poured off him in chunks. Several inches of thicker goo was settled at the concrete bottom, and he slipped and landed on his butt when he tried to stand. Dim orange light illuminated the slick surface, and he stood a second time, the substance reaching his hips. He wiped the light on his helmet clean and rubbed his fingers together. The substance felt like jelled chicken fat clinging to a roasting pan.

The light shone on the oily substance, tinged orange and yellow. He stood in a tank of some kind, maybe twelve feet in diameter. Tipping his head back, he saw the women and children standing on the grate fifteen feet above, peering down at him. The women held spears, the children knives and bones. He pressed his hands against the slimy wall. He was easy pickings, and even if he survived somehow, there was no way out.

The fur rug undulated before him like an octopus, and he reached into the substance, found the rifle, and pulled it out. He doubted it would fire. Aiming it at the mutants above, he squeezed the trigger. Nothing happened. The mutants laughed at his useless weapon.

The oil around him moved. He turned in a circle, his movements slowed by the thickness of the goo. Something was in there with him. Something *alive*.

Clutching the barrel of the rifle like a club, he backed up.

A figure rose from the oil.

The woman appeared old and fat, and her belly spread out, forming the pool of oil: she was part of it, and it was part of her. Her head held a mass of hair that melded into the slickness of her enormous breasts, which were formless.

When she raised her flabby arms, oil poured off them. Even her eyes were orange laced with yellow.

"Trn'ff tht dmnd lght," she said, her gargling voice echoing around him.

Like Paul, she was a teacher. Whatever had happened to her, her children had picked up her speech, and their children had learned it from them.

"Like hell I will," Paul said.

Laughter echoed from above.

The woman sank into the pool, vanishing. Paul knew there was no room for a person her size beneath the surface; she had simply dispersed her mass. As he moved through the oil, he understood he moved through *her*.

She re-formed behind him, and he tried to run but his boots lacked traction. He turned to face her, and as she bellowed, the stench of cooking grease overwhelmed him. She had been down here all these years, mutating, her fat mixing with toxic chemicals and her own waste. He raised his rifle and brought its butt down on her head, which separated without blood or crunching bones. When he pulled the gun free, it left a deep gash where her brain should have been, a crevice separating her eyes. The woman flailed her arms, and Paul beat at them with the rifle. She caught the barrel, jerked it away from him, and tossed it aside.

Paul reached into his pocket and took out the .22. He had no reason to believe it would work any better than the rifle, but when he pulled the trigger the barrel discharged a thundering roar. The round tore into one of the woman's breasts, but the hole closed almost as soon as it had formed.

He fired again. And again.

The woman unleashed a shuddering scream and bore down on him as if pulled along a giant track beneath the surface. Paul wanted to dive into the foul oil to escape her, but he didn't want to risk damaging the pistol, so he gripped it in both hands, aimed it at her chest, and opened fire. The gunfire pocked her skin as if she were made of melted wax, and her scream grew louder. He moved out of the way, and she slammed into the wall. Her head re-formed, her eyes emerging in what should have been the back of her skull. He aimed the gun at her head and fired one shot after another, each one deafening, until the gun would fire no more.

She moved toward him, quick but halting, and he pistol-whipped the lump between her shoulders, which seemed to have a greater effect than the bullets, each blow producing a soggy splat. A gunshot rang out, and for a moment he believed he had somehow discharged the gun again. Afraid to look up, he heard two different guns firing, neither one of them the same make that he brandished. Screams followed.

A spear fell from above and sliced into the oil, and the woman's body quivered. Remembering the crowbar at his side, he shoved the .22 back into his pocket and pulled the tool free. His heart pounded as he wailed on the misshapen body with the curved end of the crowbar, creating furrows and trenches. Using his left hand, he squeezed one of the flabby arms to keep the body from fleeing, and his fingers squished through fat. Red appeared within the yellow and orange: blood rising from the core of the monstrosity. The body stopped moving, and Paul found himself whacking a slab of fat, which sank below the surface. Gasping for breath, he staggered back, waiting for the creature to rise again. It didn't, and above him the gunfire had ceased.

"Hello!" He cupped his hands around his mouth. "Hello!"

Two shadows fell over the grate above, then two pairs of boots. A man and a woman, both black, looked down at him.

"Mr. Goodman?" the woman said.

He felt tears on his cheeks. "Yes!"

"Just a minute." She walked away.

"Wait! Is the baby okay?"

"The baby's fine," the man said. "That's a hell of a predicament you've got yourself in."

"How did you find me?"

"My name's Korbel Sloan. Your friends came to my house and told us where to look for you. We didn't believe them at first, but we took their snowmobile to that overturned snowplow and found those bodies in the snow. Ugly motherfuckers."

When the woman returned, she held a coil of rope. She threw one end down, and the noose swung over his head. He did not have to ask where she had gotten it. He raised his arms and grabbed the noose, and they pulled him out of the oil.

"Damn, you're heavy," the woman said.

"It's this shit that's all over me."

They hoisted him higher.

"What happened to the . . . people up there?"

Korbel looked around. "Don't worry about them."

Paul closed his eyes and tightened his grip on the noose.

"Hurry—my hands are slippery."

"Almost there," the woman said.

Korbel grabbed Paul's collar and pulled. "Damn, you are slippery. This isn't going to be easy."

Kneeling on the grate and wincing with effort, they pulled Paul onto the metal. He rolled onto his back and saw the deer hides hanging above. Panting, he sat up and they helped him to his feet. As he moved around the grill, he avoided looking at Ken's naked corpse. The bodies of five women lay scattered around the floor.

"What about the children?"

"Is that what they were?" the woman said. "They ran through that tunnel." She pointed at the mouth of another sewer line.

Paul moved to the drawer on top of the TV console and gazed at Marcus, nestled on a fur blanket. He had been washed and wore a fresh jumper. "Hi, little guy."

The baby burbled.

"You followed me through that crawl space?"

Korbel nodded. "Good thing you left your snowmobile where we could see it."

The woman lifted Marcus out of the drawer. "I'm Officer Brown, by the way. Don't let these clothes fool you; they belong to him."

Paul looked her over. "Thanks for coming to my rescue."

"That's my job. Let's get this poor guy out of here."

TWENTY-TWO

February 14

After she had dragged Dan's corpse and the carcass of the rabbit into the garage, Helen played with the generator and got it running. Then she went back into the house and opened four cans of soup, which she poured into one spaghetti pot. The wind continued to howl and blow snow, but the return of even a slight bit of sunlight filled her with cautious optimism.

"Mom!" Piper called out from the living room, her voice filled with excitement.

Helen's heart beat faster, and she ran into the living room, where she had folded the sofa bed into the sofa, past the mattress from upstairs that she'd laid against the broken window, to the foyer. The foyer door was open, and the front door too, and all three kids stood at the storm door. Trapper wagged his tail as Helen joined them. Through the plastic pane of the storm door, she saw two powerful headlights moving through the snow out front.

Paul felt panic as he steered the snowmobile into his driveway. Visibility had increased enough that he could see the front picture window and his upstairs bedroom window had been shattered. Then he saw the frozen, bloody figure splayed out in the snow outside the picture window. But the garage door was open and Jim's generator roared. As he approached the garage, Helen emerged from the side door, followed by Piper, Evan, and Tommy. They stood with excitement visible on their faces.

He slowed to a stop as close to the garage as possible, then hopped off the snowmobile. Gigi handed him Marcus, wrapped in a coat, and he staggered forward, leaving her on her own. Behind her, Brian helped Jim dismount. Helen took Marcus from Paul's hands as he half fell into the garage.

"You poor thing," Helen said to the baby.

"Is everyone all right?" Paul said. Then he saw the shapes beneath the blankets on the floor.

Helen hugged Marcus to her. "They got Dan. You were right about everything."

"I know."

Gigi and Brian helped Jim into the garage. Piper ran over to them and embraced Brian.

"What about Ken and Henri?" Helen said, trepidation in her voice.

Paul shook his head, and Helen glanced at Gigi.

"This is Gigi Brown," he said.

"Officer Brown," Gigi said.

"She helped save my life."

"Thank you," Helen said.

Jim stared at the blanketed bodies.

"I'm sorry, Jim," Helen said. "He saved Evan's life."

Jim bowed his head. "That poor dumb Polack."

Paul looked at Evan and held out his arm. Evan came over to him and hugged him. Paul kissed Helen, who made a disgusted face.

"What have you got all over you?" she said.

"I'll explain later. Let's get inside."

They set Jim on the sofa, after pulling it closer to the fireplace, with his injured leg stretched before him. Trapper sat on the floor beside him, and he scratched the dog's head.

"I guess you'll be coming home with me soon," he said.

Paul looked at the mattress covering the picture window. "You're all going to Jim's house, with the generator."

Helen shook her head. "I fought for this place. *We* fought for it. I'm not leaving."

He smiled. "You fought for family. For friends and neighbors."

"I boiled coffee," Helen said. "Do you want some?"

"Hell, yes."

"Gigi?"

"Yes, please. But we have to get going soon."

Helen raised one eyebrow at Paul. "You're leaving again?"

"We left a friend back at his house in Black Creek Village," Paul said. "It doesn't seem right to deny him our hospitality after he helped save my life. First we're going to check on the retirement community and make sure the people there are okay. At some point, we have to get Gigi to a police station. There will be a lot of questions, and we have a lot to show them."

"There are bodies under the snow all over our front yard," Helen said.

"All the more reason for us to relocate to Jim's."

"After we report what happened, the police will come here next," Gigi said. "They'll want to speak to all of you, and we have to get Jim to a hospital."

"Did you get them all?" Helen said in a serious tone.

Gigi shook her head. "Some kids got away."

Helen turned to Paul. "Are you going to tell the police everything?"

"Not everything. They wouldn't believe me. I'm not sure I believe it myself."

"We've all been through a war," Gigi said.

Helen turned to her children. "Piper, Evan—get over here and hug your father."

Piper and Evan joined them.

"You guys too."

Brian and Tommy made their way over to the group.

Piper hugged Paul. "I'm glad you're okay, Daddy. I was worried about you."

Paul kissed her forehead. "I was worried about you too."

"We handled it," Evan said.

"I'm proud of you," Paul said.

Standing before the fireplace, the Goodmans held each other, surrounded by friends and neighbors.

"It's going to be days before things get back to normal," Helen said.

"Weeks," Paul said.

But they knew things could never be the same for Teacher's Island and Black Creek Village.

MEDALLION

For more information
about other great titles from
Medallion, visit

medallionpress.com

Read On Vacation

Medallion Press has created
Read on Vacation for e-book
lovers who read on the go.

See more at:
medallionmediagroup.com/readonvacation

CRIXEO™

WHERE LIFE AND ART INTERSECT.

A digital playground for the
inspired and creative mind.

crixeo.com